Praise for

THE EXCHANGE OF PRINCESSES

"The strength of this novel, sprinkled with authentic quotes, rests on a story that history itself furnished."
— *Le Monde des livres*

"To take history seriously only to grasp its ironic tragedy, this is great art... With delicious detail Chantal Thomas explores the hidden indignities of a century that exploited childhood even as it was inventing it, a delight of the form that is now wholly her own."
— *Le Figaro*

"The exchange of these princesses is straight out of a Cold War spy novel, taking place on an island in the middle of a river that serves as the border between the two kingdoms. But none of these young protagonists will play the adults' game and the princesses will end up going home. Chantal Thomas excels at humanizing history and exposing what is at stake (or 'revealing its relevance'). How do these children, sold in such a way by their parents, feel? Will they love or hate each other? These are the universal, timeless questions that this 'historical' novel plays with, and which render it strikingly contemporary."
— *Vogue* (France)

"We love [*The Exchange of Princesses*] because, as always with Chantal Thomas, winner of the 2002 Prix Femina for *Farewell, My Queen*, her stories dance on volcanoes. In her, the mighty of our world finish by bumping their noses against the whims of fate...A must-read if you still shy away from historical novels. That will change."
— *Le Parisien*

"Delicious like childhood and cruel like life." — *Télérama*

"Chantal Thomas made history a pungent, political, and intimate epic, told by a narrator whose empathy does not detract from the satirical irony."

— *Le Magazine littéraire*

"[With this] little-known episode in history, Chantal Thomas writes a superb novel about violence against women and children, [showcasing] marriages as absurd as they are forced."
— *Phosphore*

"Impressive." — *La Vie*

"A fascinating novel." — *L'Express* (France)

"Through her voice—sensitive, alive, contemporary, sometimes raw—[Thomas] manages to recreate how these sacrificed children lived, felt, feared, hoped, and suffered."
— *Point de Vue* (France)

"[Thomas] mixes fact and fiction to create her own novelistic space of a time that is at once free and cruel... What Thomas details here, in this story of lives in gilded cages, is the birth—or rejection of—desire in children who do not have the words to articulate it because they, too, are locked up in the absurdity of etiquette and formal rituals that have been imposed on them."
—*La Croix*

"Chantal Thomas, a scholar brought up on Sade and Casanova, has clearly chosen, in her past few books, to hone in on dying aristocracies—not out of snobbery, but because what she has to say about our 'beautiful present' is reflected through, in her mind, the traditions of the past."
—*Le Point*

"With the verve and delicacy for which she is known, Chantal Thomas reaffirms in these intense, feverish, and sensual pages her eye for detail and the painting of a scene, and her ability to turn a phrase that snaps like a riding crop."
—*Lire*

"Chantal Thomas [is a] philosopher who brings historical erudition, pediatric science, bright tales of the heart, and breathtaking stories to the art of the novel and to theater."
—*Le Nouvel observateur*

"To these sacrificed childhoods, these bruised fates, this history disdained by historians, Chantal Thomas's beautiful novel grants a late and dazzling revenge."
—*Sud Ouest*

"A beautiful saga." —*Madame Figaro*

"Thanks to Chantal Thomas for having crafted such a joyful book out of such sad fates."
—*Libération, Supplément livres*

"As with *Farewell, My Queen* (winner of the 2002 Prix Femina) and *Le Testament d'Olympe* (2010), [Thomas] avoids the pitfalls of the historical novel by combining historical documents—letters, excerpts from Saint-Simon's Memoirs—with fiction."
—*Le Temps, Samedi culturel*

"With elegance and subtlety, Chantal Thomas pursues sensitive evocations of eighteenth-century France."
—*Le Journal du dimanche*

"While very classic, her writing still surprises, distilling irony in each sentence like a poison... Like Saint-Simon revised and edited by Sade."
—*Les Inrockuptibles*

THE EXCHANGE OF PRINCESSES

The
EXCHANGE
of
PRINCESSES

Chantal Thomas

TRANSLATED FROM THE FRENCH BY
JOHN CULLEN

WITH A FOREWORD BY
MARTHA SAXTON

OTHER PRESS
NEW YORK

Copyright © Éditions du Seuil, 2013
First published in French as *L'échange des princesses*
by Éditions du Seuil, Paris, in 2013.

Epigraph copyright © Éditions Stock, 2010

Translation copyright © John Cullen, 2014

This work, published as part of a program providing publication assistance,
received financial support from the French Ministry of Foreign Affairs, the
Cultural Services of the French Embassy in the United States, and FACE
Foundation (French American Cultural Exchange).

Foreword copyright © Martha Saxton, 2015

Production Editor: Yvonne E. Cárdenas
Text Designer: Julie Fry
This book was set in Perpetua with Poetica and Trajan by
Alpha Design & Composition of Pittsfield, NH

10 8 6 4 2 1 3 5 7 9

Library of Congress Cataloging-in-Publication Data

Thomas, Chantal, 1945–
[Echange des princesses. English]
The exchange of princesses / by Chantal Thomas ; translated from
the French by John Cullen ; foreword by Martha Saxton.
pages cm
ISBN 978-1-59051-702-4 (paperback) — ISBN 978-1-59051-703-1 (ebook)
1. Orléans, Philippe, duc d', 1674–1723—Fiction.   2. Arranged marriage—
Fiction.   3. France—History—Regency, 1715–1723—Fiction.
I. Cullen, John, 1942- translator.   II. Title.
PQ2680.H493E2413 2015
843'.914—dc23
2014043505

Publisher's Note:
This is a work of historical fiction based on factual events. Characters and
incidents in this story are in part the product of the author's imagination or are
used fictitiously.

For Alfredo Arias

in memory of his show Les Noces de l'Enfant Roi

And something told me, and tells me still,
that disregarded stories, one day or another,
will have their revenge.

—ERIK ORSENNA, *L'Entreprise des Indes*

FOREWORD

In 1721 Philip D'Orléans, regent of France, devised and set in motion a masterstroke of *Kinderpolitik*: two marriages of four royal children ranging in age from three to fourteen. Philip was hoping to ensure peace between Spain and France and lengthen his control over his eleven-year-old nephew, Louis XV, king of France. To this end, he promised his neglected, bleak, and turbulent daughter, Louise, aged twelve, to the unprepossessing Luis of Asturias, aged fourteen and heir to the throne of Spain. At the same time, he engaged his mournful nephew to Mariana Victoria— infanta of Spain, half-sister of Luis—a plucky three year old who would make her betrothal journey to France accompanied by a trunk of beloved dolls. Chantal Thomas's ability to inhabit these children's hearts reveals the emotional chaos their guardians' routine betrayals and manipulations inflicted on them. All the young royals probably would have been well advised to choose dolls as the primary recipients of their affections.

At the time that Philip was orchestrating these nuptials, a movement was underway that would revolutionize ideas about child raising. Beginning in the eighteenth century and gathering momentum in the next, childhood increasingly came to represent to parents a time in which they should protect and cherish the innocence of their children before the cares and duties of maturity set in. They were to encourage their childish sympathies and intelligence. Affectionate child rearing led to parents beginning to permit their offspring to choose their spouses based on mutual attraction and respect rather than on matters of property and fortune.

The Spanish monarchs and the regent's faction at court were oblivious to this developing trend and joyfully anticipated the prospect of the double marriage. The adult puppeteers wrote congratulatory letters to one another in their various charges' names, expressing pious sentiments of devotion and hope in glorious marital and national futures. The ventriloquized children, meanwhile, complied and either tried to silence their feelings of confusion, dread, and sadness, or acted them out.

The ruthless utilization of royal children over the centuries is hardly news, but Thomas splices together the assaults on these children's feelings and desires with surreal depictions of the extravagant clothing and luxurious entertainments that accompanied them, bringing the velvet-clad abuse to life and rendering the emotional wreckage that ensued powerfully touching. It was decreed, for example, that the boy king, who has lost his mother, father, grandfather, and great-grandfather, would have to sacrifice his *Maman Ventadour*, who had taken care of him since infancy. She was to travel to Spain to accompany the tiny infanta to Paris. When they arrived, the infanta, now coddled by Madame de Ventadour, fell worshipfully at the feet of her graceful intended spouse and would pass her years of engagement trotting around after him hoping in vain to elicit a flicker of affection. For his part, Louis was seized the moment he met his betrothed by furious, inexpressible jealousy over her possession of *la Ventadour*. Meanwhile, the Spanish ambassador in Paris celebrated the future union of the thumb-sucking girl and her shut-down fiancé by building an artificial rock in the center of the Seine (in front of Mariana's windows) and placing on it a columned temple, decorated with paintings of Roman gods and goddesses. Lighted boats circled the island, bearing musicians playing their instruments. The event culminated in a joust between gondoliers and a conflagration that took the temple down and ignited a lengthy display of fireworks.

In Spain, Louise, whose only education has consisted of going to the theater now and then with her father, Philip, has begun to digest the facts that her future husband's sole interest is hunting and that her in-laws are grimly devout. Her arrival is marked by an auto-da-fé, in which the grand inquisitor presides over the torture and burning at the stake of numerous yellow-clad heretics, including, Prince Luis informs his bride-to-be, eleven women.

The rhetoric surrounding the French and the American revolutions accelerated the change toward protecting children and nurturing their abilities and—at least for boys— autonomy. Thomas's novel provides a frightening portrait of what preceded "the invention of childhood." She shows us children as actors in a game they often barely understood, costumed in silk, satin, and jewels, in an international play about naked power. It is little wonder that Louise — of whose hapless body so much was expected — expressed her misery and contempt for her abusers by rejecting the fine clothing designed to adorn and appease her and, eventually, by tearing off every piece of her clothing altogether to escape from the tableau vivant that imprisoned her. Thomas documents with wit and skill the others' fates, less dramatic, but arguably more painful.

Martha Saxton, Professor
History and *Sexuality, Women's and Gender Studies*
Amherst College

❧ I ❧
An Excellent Idea

PARIS, SUMMER 1721

In the Regent's Bath

"No hangover can stand in the way of a good idea," says Philip d'Orléans to himself, inhaling the strong fragrances of his bath and closing his eyes. Were he to open them, his field of vision would be obstructed by his large, pale paunch, afloat in the hot water; and although the sight of that beached animal's belly of his, that soft demijohn distended by nights of debauch and gluttony, wouldn't completely spoil his delight in his good idea, it would certainly diminish it. "My children are big and fat," declares the Princess Palatine, his mother, who herself is not thin. As the thought of his mother is always agreeable, his corpulence becomes a matter of complete indifference to him. But should he recall the words she's always happy to add — "Big fat people don't live any longer than anyone else" — he'd feel a frightful pang of sadness. Two years ago, his adored eldest daughter, the Duchess de Berry, died in a horrifying physical state, her obesity augmented by — or so it was said — the early stages of a pregnancy. The speed at which she'd burned out her young existence, her thirst for pleasure and extinction, the delirium of theatricality and self-destruction in which he had so loved to join her — all that had left her incapable of engendering anything but her own death.

He knows he shouldn't dwell on the Duchess de Berry. He mustn't think about her in these evil hours, these leaden, alcoholic hours. Stick to the present, and to whatever fosters belief in a future... Yes, it's a good idea, he repeats to himself, plunging his head underwater. He's found the solution to two vexing problems: one centers on the political need to neutralize Spain and prevent a new war, and the second results from his secret, crafty desire to put off as long as possible the time when little King Louis XV might beget a dauphin of France. It won't be tomorrow, since the boy's only eleven years old and won't come of age until his thirteenth birthday, and even then... But the best course is to address the matter now. If the king has a son when he dies, then that son will naturally inherit the crown; but if the king dies without a male heir, then... then... perforce... the crown would belong to him, to Philip d'Orléans, regent of France, nephew of the late King Louis XIV, who throughout his reign took pains to keep his brother's son well away from the government, to treat him like a good-for-nothing, and all the more rigorously because the Sun King was aware of the young man's capabilities. Except in Louis XIV's service, intelligence was no asset at the court of Versailles.

By a smooth transition, this reflection leads the regent back to his admirable idea. The bathwater's cooling down, but he doesn't care, he's happy with his plans for the future.

He's a man who's scrupulous and careful in accomplishing his mission, though things aren't easy, what with the suspicions of poisoning that weigh on him, suspicions incessantly revived by the old court party; but should the occasion authorize him to ascend to the throne in all legality, he can very well see himself as king. Philip I? That title's already taken; there was a Capetian Philip I. He fought doggedly against William the Conqueror and got himself excommunicated for repudiating his wife, Bertha of Holland, who had been chosen for political reasons...as if there were any others, the regent thinks, as if there were any such thing as marrying for love, at least as far as he was concerned...and this point, though not so painful as the death of his daughter, still rankles him. Philip II, then? Why not? Philip II, called "the Debauched." A naive but irresistible vision; power, once tasted, is difficult to give up. It's no use to be clear-sighted, to know that the more power you acquire the less you count personally, since you're nothing but a pawn on the chessboard of the ambitious who are working away feverishly below you. No, you hold on, you postpone as long as possible the moment when you must step outside the circle of light and away from the hum of praise and compliments—the moment when you're going to find yourself alone in the dark, hunted out of the world, stricken from the ranks of the living. Philip II—wouldn't that complicate relations with the current king of Spain, Philip V? Yes, quite a bit, and not only because the king of Spain's named Philip too; he would also be in the running for the French throne if Louis XV were to disappear. Of course, Philip II is a title that has been taken before: there was Philip II of Spain, called Philip the Prudent, the gloomy builder of El Escorial, an arch-pious, slow-moving bureaucrat. From the Prudent to the Debauched, a long story...

The regent's daydreams slowly dissolve in the mists of his bathroom. A single question remains: How will Philip V react to this excellent idea of his? The regent strokes himself vaguely. He starts to doze off in his bath. Two chambermaids take hold of him, one on either side. They lean over and pull him up by his armpits. Their breasts jiggle in the steamy air. The regent smiles, blissfully happy.

But perhaps he's not giving so much thought to his hang-over as he is to Cardinal Dubois...Dubois, a man who not only has never stood in the way of good ideas but is positively bursting with them, especially in matters of diplomacy. And the regent's good idea, the excellent idea he's congratulating himself for, might have been suggested to him by the cardi-nal, his former tutor, the doer of his dirty work, a creature who plumbs the depths of degradation and scales the peaks of distinction.

Working with his customary speed and effectiveness, the cardinal sees to it that the king of Spain, Philip V, the for-mer Duke of Anjou and a grandson of Louis XIV, is apprised of the main points of the idea/solution, which will assure a complete reconciliation and a solid alliance between the two kingdoms. And Philip V, under the influence of the French ambassador in Madrid, M. de Maulévrier, vigor-ously supported by the king's confessor, Father Daubenton, a Jesuit who can manipulate the king's will almost as well as the queen, gets enthusiastic about the project. As a rule,

Philip V is not given to easy enthusiasms. With his demeanor of an old man worn out before his time, his buckling knees, his pigeon toes, his pallor, the dark circles that enlarge his eyes, he doesn't give the impression of someone who expects very much from the future. And in fact he's got no earthly expectations whatsoever. All his hopes lie in heaven, not in the world. But when he reads the letters from Paris, the thick black cloud customarily hanging over him evaporates. He rereads the letter and then has it read to him by his wife, Elisabeth Farnese. When he writes his reply to the regent, he doesn't feel he's responding to the proposition; he has the impression that he's its source. And he would appear to find the idea breathtaking. So perfect a plan seems to have been conceived not by a human mind, but by Providence.

The Duke de Saint-Simon, Ambassador Extraordinary

In his memoirs, Saint-Simon describes for posterity the "*conversation curieuse*," the interview in which Philip d'Orléans, the companion of his childhood, apprises the duke of the brilliant idea. The two men are almost exact contemporaries. The regent is forty-seven, Saint-Simon forty-six. The passing years, war wounds, and nocturnal excesses have left their mark on the regent. His brick-red complexion designates him as a serious candidate for a stroke. The brilliance of his presence, dimmed by his weak eyesight and the stress he operates under, shines through only intermittently. Saint-Simon, decidedly shorter than the regent and just as imposingly bewigged, looks much younger, and because of his regular life, the heat of his imagination, his passion for analysis, and the fact that he brings the entire weight of his existence to bear on every instant, he is formidably present. Profoundly different though the two men are, they're united by the duration and sincerity of their friendship and by the pleasures of intelligence, the excitement that comes with quick wit and unspoken understanding. Nevertheless, Saint-Simon seldom departs satisfied from his conversations with the regent. The scene the two of them play out is always repeated. Saint-Simon, brimming with initiatives and impatient for them to be realized, harasses the regent, who suffers the assault with lowered head and contrite face. It's not that the duke bores him. Certainly not! Nor that the regent disapproves of the duke. Not in the slightest! On the contrary! But—and here's the cause of his distress—the regent doesn't have the courage to go the way of reason, which is namely, in Saint-Simon's view, his own way. The regent stoops, hunkers down, grows annoyed at himself, but does not act according to reason. He makes the wrong decision every time. And why? Because he's weak, because he's already been taken in by Dubois, and because for all the duke's acuteness, his interventions come too late.

This conversation, however, goes differently. The regent's in excellent humor, proud of his news, proud of the secret he wants to confide to his friend. Saint-Simon has grievances: he's never been invited to any of the Palais-Royal dinners given in the pink-and-gold dining room, cushioned like a jewelry casket (no matter that the mere thought of those orgies repels him, especially the fact that His Highness the Duke d'Orléans, a grandson of France, acts as the chef), and his opinions are rarely heeded in the Regency Council—without counting the thousand daily wounds he suffers from barbarians who don't respect the rules of etiquette and the permanent scandal caused by the arrogance of Louis XIV's bastards, who are in ascendance everywhere. But Saint-Simon is so flattered and touched by his friend's demonstration of confidence in him that he forgets all complaints. He takes pleasure in recalling the scene:

> Early in June, I went to work with His Highness the Duke d'Orléans and found him alone, walking up and down his grand apartment. As soon as he saw me, he said, "Ah, there you are," and taking me by the hand continued, "I cannot leave you in ignorance of the thing I desire and prize above all others, which will give you as much joy as it gives me; but I must ask you to keep it utterly secret." Then he began to laugh and added, "If M. de Cambrai [Cardinal Dubois, archbishop of Cambrai] knew I had told you, he would never forgive me." Thereupon he informed me of the accord which he had reached with the King and Queen of Spain, of the arrangements by which our young King and the Infanta of Spain were to be wed as soon as the girl came of age, and of the agreed marriage between the Prince of Asturias and Mlle de Chartres [Saint-Simon's error; he means another of the regent's daughters, Mlle de Montpensier]. If my joy was great, my astonishment surpassed it.

Perhaps Saint-Simon finds the difference in rank between the betrothed parties surprising, but he's especially flabbergasted by the spectacular nature of the reversal by which the son of the king of Spain—upon whom, two years previously, the regent declared war — has become his future son-in-law.

Upon learning of these impending marriages between France and Spain, between the French Bourbons and the Spanish Bourbons, this creation of alliances between the continent's two most powerful kingdoms, uniting two branches of a single family — in other words, the realization of Europe's worst fears — Saint-Simon's immediate reaction is to advise keeping the matter a deep secret, so as not to infuriate the other countries. For once, the Duke d'Orléans can give him a guilt-free response: "You are right, of course, but that is impossible, because the Spanish desire to announce the declarations of marriage at once, and they wish to send the Infanta here as soon as the proposal is made and the marriage contract signed." Curious haste, Saint-Simon points out, given the ages of the four young persons involved. Their betrothals are admittedly premature. The Prince of Asturias is fourteen years of age, the regent's daughter twelve. Louis XV, born February 15, 1710, is but eleven. And as for Mariana Victoria, the infanta of Spain, her date of birth was March 31, 1718. Louis XV's future wife, the future queen of France, is not yet four years old!

Saint-Simon doesn't find the ages of the betrothed parties surprising, in fact doesn't give them a single thought, and in this he resembles the authors of the agreement. What stuns him is the audacious stroke of marrying a daughter of the House of Orléans to a son of Philip V, a man veritably steeped in hatred for that family and for the regent in particular. A little later in the interview, having recovered from his amazement, Saint-Simon thinks about drawing some personal advantage from the project. He asks the regent to appoint him to bring the marriage contract to the court of Madrid for signing. In the same breath, he proposes to bring along his two sons, Jacques-Louis, Vidame de Chartres, and Armand-Jean, in order to obtain for them and himself the title of grandee of Spain. Saint-Simon desires grandeur. The regent smiles. For if the Duke de Saint-Simon is *pas grand* — that is, not tall — his elder son, Jacques-Louis, is even shorter than his father. His nickname is "the Basset."

The regent accepts. Saint-Simon, therefore, will be the "ambassador extraordinary" for a far from ordinary marriage.

Saying Yes with a Bad Grace

In the beginning of August, a messenger from Philip V arrives at the Palais-Royal, the regent's Parisian residence, with dispatches confirming that "His Catholic Majesty, in order to give His Royal Highness indubitable proofs of H.C.M.'s friendship, affection, and desire to maintain immutably good terms with the King, with his own family, and with H.R.H. the Regent, requests his daughter H.R.H. Mlle de Montpensier's hand in marriage to H.R.H. the Prince of Asturias, and proposes at the same time the marriage of the Infanta of Spain, H.C.M.'s only daughter, to the King."

Among those close to the Duke d'Orléans, joy is total. That the king of Spain should be offering his son, the Prince of Asturias, the successor to the Spanish throne, in marriage to one of the regent's daughters is indeed pretty incredible. But this is the necessary condition for the marriage of the infanta to Louis XV. The marriage of Mlle de Montpensier, born of the terribly discordant union between the Duke d'Orléans and Mlle de Blois, bastard daughter of Louis XIV and his mistress Mme de Montespan, is part of the deal. The young girl's father informs her in passing of her betrothal. Louise Élisabeth d'Orléans, known as Mlle de Montpensier, is a barely domesticated child, having been raised in a state of sumptuous neglect. She was removed from the convent at the age of five and like her sisters has been more or less forgotten ever since. Their mother has no interest in her numerous and useless female progeny. Their father's idea of educating them is to take them to the theater from time to time. Perhaps Mlle de Montpensier rebels against her father. If so, the offense, like everything she says and does from now on, will be charged to her bad character. An ugly child when she was little, she's grown much prettier but hasn't become any more sociable. She's silent, hobbled by a sort of chronic ill will, by a solitariness that turns people away from her. In response to the latest twist in her fate, she tries on a Spanish dress and, thus arrayed, walks around the palace. She shows herself to the Princess Palatine, her grandmother, who writes: "It's amazing how Spanish she seems — she's very serious, almost never laughs, talks very little. She came to see me a few days ago wearing a Spanish dress; it suited her much better than French clothes do." Does this mean that her whole Spanish existence is going to suit her better than her life in France? Her grandmother jokingly calls her "the Spanish fly." Louise

Élisabeth doesn't much like joking, and she's not certain it's a well-intentioned joke anyway.

Luis, Prince of Asturias, son of Philip V and his deceased first wife Maria Luisa of Savoy, is two years older than his proposed fiancée and thus better able to speak his mind; nevertheless, his acceptance is gained with as little difficulty as hers. Philip V summons the boy. His marriage is announced to him as a settled matter. The possibility that he might have an opinion about it is excluded a priori. In all haste, a portrait of Mlle de Montpensier is brought from Paris and given to the prince. As he shares his father's sexual disposition, he wears himself out masturbating over the image of his future bride. Semen spatters the fiancée's face — her lovely eyes, full lips, strong nose. The portrait is removed from Prince Luis's chamber.

On the other hand, there is one person whose opinion is indispensable: Louis XV. The fact that he's only eleven in no way authorizes his subjects to disregard his views. It should be an easy matter to coerce acquiescence from a boy of his age, but the regent's not certain of success. And without Louis XV's consent, the entire scheme will collapse. Broaching the subject of marriage to the young king, a nervous, melancholic, suspicious child, is not a prospect the regent relishes. The king dreads surprises, from which he expects only catastrophes. When he was still very little, he fell ill and cried out to his Maman Ventadour, "I'm dead"; later, having experienced his first ejaculation, he will be convinced he's unwell and consult his valet de chambre. Since he has spent much the greater part of his young life in an orphan's solitude, his early childhood darkened by the succession of deaths in his family and by the malevolent rumors they nourished, mistrust is his first reaction. This tendency is only enhanced by the fear he constantly reads in the eyes of his entourage, prominent among them his elderly tutor, Marshal de Villeroy: the fear that he too, the boy-king, will perish. Marshal de Villeroy never leaves his side, day or night. He sleeps beside his bed and permits nobody but himself to offer him a handkerchief. He monitors the slightest gesture made by the king or to the king at table, carries the key to the butter dish destined for the king's use, and would in no circumstances, not even under torture, agree to resign his post.

As a child of five, Louis XV was brought to his great-grandfather Louis XIV's deathbed, kissed his august ancestor, and heard him predict, "Little one, you are going to be a great king…"; now the boy uses that memory as a charm capable of making the Grim Reaper delay his scything. Brutally sudden death frightens the young king. When it's transmuted into a religious rite, he pays it homage without difficulty and even, deep down, loves it. Raised to be a Most Christian sovereign, he accepts the daily duty of attending at least one Mass as a natural occurrence, like opening his eyes in the morning and receiving the first courtiers admitted to his *petit lever*, his rising ceremony. But more often than not, because of the solemnities attached to the continually recurring feast days and the mourning that's so much a part of his family history, other religious services are added to his daily routine. His life is punctuated by requiems, Masses for the dead. His birthday falls between the anniversaries of his father's and mother's deaths on the twelfth and eighteenth of February. On April 14, he attends the Requiem Mass for the grand dauphin, his grandfather; on July 30, the date of his great-grandmother Maria Theresa of Spain's death, he attends the requiem for her; and on September 1, the one for Louis XIV, who died on that date in 1715. Death thus embalmed, thus inscribed in the squares of the sacred calendar and in a schedule of ceremonies whose details (bows, genuflections, benedictions, psalms, canticles, prayers) he's quite mastered, no longer has anything in common with catastrophe. This child, everyone says admiringly, was born for ceremonies. In them he displays a diligence and a staying power exceptional for his age. He's compared to Louis XIV, every minute of whose reign had to belong to some form of ritual. Etiquette is a Mass; the boy has instinctively understood that.

But Louis XV's history is all his own, and he preserves it as the only way of maintaining contact with his family: from Te Deum to Te Deum, he's reminded that his parents, grandparents, and great-grandparents really existed, and that between the Paradise where they reside and the court of France over which he reigns, the passage is constant.

After postponing his task several times over the course of more than a month, the regent chooses a day when the Regency Council is meeting, so that if Louis XV's answer is yes, as anticipated, the regent will be able to make the announcement to the members of the council. On the morning of September 14, after dithering for a few moments in the anteroom, he enters the king's chamber in the Tuileries Palace. To give himself courage and to make a stronger impression on his young sovereign, the regent has brought along Cardinal Dubois, M. le Duc (Henri de Bourbon-Condé, who supervises Louis XV's education), Marshal de Villeroy, and the Bishop of Fréjus. Saint-Simon, along with other courtiers but even more impatient than they because more directly concerned, is waiting outside. Unable to hold out any longer, they leave the anteroom and penetrate into the royal apartments: "The King's back," Saint-Simon writes,

> was turned toward the door through which we had just entered; the Duke d'Orléans, redder than usual, stood opposite us, and M. le Duc was next to him, both of them with long faces; Cardinal Dubois and Marshal Villeroy flanked them; and the Bishop of Fréjus was standing very close to the King and a little to one side, so that I could see his profile and what appeared to be his embarrassed expression. We remained as we had been when we entered, behind the King, and I behind everyone else. I craned my neck in an effort to see him from the side and very quickly drew my head back, for I saw his flushed face, and his eyes, at least the one that I could see, were full of tears.

A little later, the regent hurriedly confides to Saint-Simon that upon hearing the news of his marriage, the king burst out weeping, and that they—the regent, M. le Duc, and the Bishop of Fréjus—"had been hard put to extract a yes from him, and then afterward had met with the same reluctance on his part to go to the Regency Council." These are men used to overcoming opposition. Princes, diplomats, army generals, they surround the boy. They trot out their repertoire of bows and bombastic formulas, and they're sure they can talk him into yielding. The balance of power is too unequal. However, in spite of his eleven years, he's the king, and they're his subjects; consequently, there remains the tiny but real possibility that His Majesty will say no, or that His Majesty will react as he is already wont to do, by taking refuge in silence, by retreating into a sulk from which there is no appeal and thus mutely stating his refusal. His tutor, even though he opposes the project, insists: "Come, my master, the thing must be done with a good grace." The boy-king murmurs a distraught yes, a yes with a bad grace. Yes to the marriage and yes to the announcement of the marriage in the present session of the Regency Council. The circle of powerful men breathes a collective sigh of relief. The boy resumes weeping. And not with just one eye, but with both, and with all his heart. Barely recovered, he appears before the Regency Council, where people remark his swollen eyes. When the regent asks him if he "thinks it well" that the regent announce the marriage to the council, the boy nods. "There we are then, Sire, your marriage is approved and passed, and a great and fortunate business settled," says the Duke d'Orléans.

After the council, the king takes refuge in his chamber. He curls up in an armchair and sobs. For all that, Marshal de Villeroy doesn't leave him, but like the Duke de Saint-Simon a little while ago, Villeroy feels embarrassed at the sight of his king in tears. He feels as though he were committing a sacrilege. And like the duke, he averts his eyes. He stares at a point in the room. He remains so for a long time, upright and unmoving, frozen by the sound of choked sobs.

At the same time, Cardinal Dubois is in his cabinet, congratulating himself on Louis XV's acceptance. He immediately dictates, in the name of the weeping little boy, the following letter to Philip V:

> I cannot sufficiently express to Your Majesty the great joy and gratitude with which I accept a proposal that heralds all I could most wish. The delight it brings me is increased by the knowledge that it corresponds so well to the sentiments of the King my great-grandfather, whose examples and goals shall always be the rule of my conduct. Knowledge of his virtues and respect for his memory constitute the most considerable part of the education which I receive; and filled with him as I am, it seems to me that I see him ordaining this union, which further strengthens the ties of blood by which we are already so closely bound. The tender feelings of friendship and consideration which I owe you as my uncle will be only augmented by those which will be your due as my father-in-law. I will regard the Infanta of Spain as a princess destined to form the happiness of my life, and I shall count myself happy to be able to contribute to hers, and it is by that attention that I promise to demonstrate to Your Majesty the sincere gratitude that I feel toward you.
>
> Louis

The exultant cardinal adds a personal note for Elisabeth Farnese:

> The Infanta will be adored in France. She will be brought up as His Catholic Majesty has been; and so obliged are we to the Queen of Spain for her sacrifice of the charming Princess who is the object of her predilection that she will be a Queen in France before her daughter, and with her.

He puts down his pen, congratulates himself again, and sends for his mistress. After a brief interlude, he goes back to work. As in every commercial exchange, transport presents a fundamental problem. In the case of the princesses, who fall into the category of fragile merchandise, the situation is worrisome. The main road from Paris to Spain, the road used by the post, has an insufficient number of suitable accommodations and, being paved only in part, is impracticable for ordinary coaches. There's not enough time to repair it. Stones will be used to fill the deepest holes, and all along the route, officials will be careful to station workers provided with horses to assist the travelers and their teams. To get them out of difficult predicaments, horses, oxen, and mules will be kept in reserve.

We must imagine the princesses, with their beautiful dresses and their curled hair, their music boxes and their dolls, their decks of cards and their sets of jacks, being regularly pulled out of muddy ditches by workers who complain without stint as they toil. Since they speak in dialect, they don't mince their words regarding this nuisance of a job, this goddamn princess transit (or in other, more carefully chosen words, those of a colleague of an official named de Tourny in Bordeaux, "This accursed labor for the passing princesses!"). The workers catch pneumonia, slide with their animals in mud, get run over by coach wheels, while the little princesses find amusement in so chaotic a journey and stare in amazement at the filthy faces of all those poor devils lined up there to keep them safe.

Cardinal Dubois imagines nothing of this. His is a political mind. He who desires the end desires the means. His direction and planning proceed on a much higher plane than the bodies they may affect—and all the more so since the bodies in question belong to little girls! And therefore, in the darkest hours of the night, he dips his pen in the inkwell again and continues: as to the honors that are to be paid to the principals when the exchanges take place, Mlle de Montpensier must be treated as a daughter of France and the future queen of Spain, and the infanta as the queen of France. Finally, he concludes, M. Desgranges, the master of ceremonies, is in possession of "all orders and instructions necessary to arrange what must be done."

Yes, a brilliant idea, an idea faultless in its symmetry.

MADRID, SEPTEMBER 1721

"Me, I'm queen of France" (Mariana Victoria)

A messenger leaves the Palais-Royal, gallops day and night, and on September 21 arrives in Madrid, groggy from the heat and the superhuman effort of his journey. He gets down off his horse and staggers. His dispatches, snatched from his hands, contain the news that both propositions of marriage have been accepted, namely the proposed union between the Prince of Asturias and Mlle de Montpensier, and especially the one "which is to be effected between the most high, most mighty prince Louis XV, by the grace of God King of France, and the most high, most mighty princess Doña Mariana Victoria, Infanta of Spain..." Philip V and Elisabeth Farnese weep tears of joy. They read and reread the lovely written portrait of Mlle de Montpensier, concocted with impunity by Dubois:

> All Mlle. de Montpensier's inclinations are to the good, to honor, to dignity, to piety, and it seems that she was born to

live with Their Catholic Majesties; so much so that one cannot but recognize that the same Providence which formed this princess inspired in the Catholic King the design of choosing her for the rank destined to be hers.

The king and queen of Spain delay the official announcement to the court and the people until the arrival of the king of France's ambassador extraordinary, the Duke de Saint-Simon.

However, one person, inasmuch as she is the future queen of France, remains to be informed: the infanta, the "most high, most mighty Doña Mariana Victoria." Normally, their tutors and governesses bring *los Infantes* to the queen every morning while she is at her toilette. They are also entitled to a second interview of five to ten minutes' duration at the end of the afternoon, when the king and queen return from the hunt. But today, the infanta's governess, the Duchess de Montellano, fetches the child shortly after she awakens and escorts her alone to the Hall of Mirrors, which is adjacent to the royal chamber. Mariana Victoria had to drop Carmen-Doll on the spot. She came close to breaking her nose! Having to leave her playmate devastates the little girl. She keeps turning back to look at Carmen-Doll and insists that her favorite must be taken care of in her absence. To be summoned alone, and so early...The child wonders whether she's done something stupid, whether she might have to do penance. It must have been a serious error, a whipping's the best she can hope for! She bows so fast that she doesn't give herself time to examine her parents' faces to see if they look stern. She's still at their feet when she hears a voice muffled by emotion pronounce these historic words: "I do not wish you to learn from anyone other than myself, my well-beloved daughter, that you are Queen of France. I believe I cannot place you more advantageously than in that royal house and in so lovely a kingdom. I think you shall be happy. As for me, so complete is my joy at seeing this great affair concluded that I cannot express it to you, loving you as I do with more affection than you could possibly imagine. Go and tell your brothers the good news, and kiss them tenderly for me. I kiss you too, with all my heart," he concludes, without making the slightest gesture.

Is the infanta immediately informed that she's going to live in France in order to receive a French education? Almost certainly not. It's a secondary matter. Mariana Victoria doesn't understand her father's little speech very well. She does grasp, however, that he's not cross, and that he's taking a new interest in her. Usually so stingy with his words, he speaks to her, to her alone and to nobody else. She's his *well-beloved daughter.* And when she dares to raise her head and fix her eyes on her parents, she's shocked to see on their faces an expression completely new to her! They're holding hands, her mother as always on her father's left, and their countenances are radiant with respect. This confuses their well-beloved daughter, their only daughter, their Mariannina, Her Majesty the Queen of France. She makes another bow, backs up, is gathered into the Duchess de Montellano's arms. Her father and mother are still close to each other, conversing in their customary hushed voices. Once her feet are back on the floor, Mariana Victoria is eager to return to her favorite doll. But Señora de Montellano leads her in another direction. She whispers to the child, "As His Majesty your father told you, you are to announce the good news to your brothers." And so Mariana Victoria, who is tiny, blond, and pale, a small vision of light in her ample morning dress, takes a few steps into the salon where Don Carlos, age five, is in the middle of a violin lesson under the direction of the Venetian master Giacomo Facco. The boy stops playing, ready to make fun of her. In her shrill little voice, and with her very clear enunciation, she says to him, "Me, I'm queen of France," and then dashes away, leaving Don Carlos to his surprise. She goes into the room where the youngest infante, Don Felipe, barely a year old, is sleeping. She leans over his bed and shouts into his ears: "The queen of France!"

"*All* your brothers," the governess clarifies.

Influenced by her mother, Mariana Victoria considers only her mother's sons as her real brothers. Her half-brothers, the sons of Maria Luisa of Savoy, Philip V's first wife, receive a cold upbringing and are relegated as much as possible to the status of foreigners. Their endless sorrow at having lost a universally adored mother is rendered yet more painful by Elisabeth Farnese's meanness toward them.

On her way to her half-brothers' apartments, Mariana Victoria has the impression that the day has reversed itself and that she's walking into the night. Narrow corridors. Closed doors. No sound. Besides, Don Luis's door doesn't open. She's told that the prince has gone out. As for Don Fernando, eight years old, the stepson most harshly treated by his stepmother, he rises from his little desk, where a candle is burning in the middle of the morning, and salutes smartly. Don Fernando is still in mourning, not just for his late mother, but also for the recent death of his elder brother by one year, his dear Don Felipe. Philip V also suffers from this loss, but he forces himself to suffer in silence. Don Felipe, son of Maria Luisa, is dead, but Don Felipe, son of Elisabeth Farnese, is alive.

Back in her room, Mariana Victoria finds Carmen-Doll turbaned with bandages and lethargic, but with a crown on her head. She cradles the doll, consoles her, plays with her crown. Carmen-Doll comes around, recovers. She moves her red lips, and now she's the one who sings for the infanta. She sings the child's three names, Maria-Anna-Victoria. "Victoria" stands out joyously.

PARIS, AUTUMN 1721

Festivities on the Horizon

Louis XV roams through the rooms in the Tuileries Palace, which has remained practically unchanged since his great-grandfather Louis XIV abandoned it for Versailles. The boy-king pets his cats, gazes at the park, fishes in his pond, participates in a miniature hunt organized just for him, plays war games by himself. He tries to avoid the thought of his proposed marriage. His chance to dream about his future has been taken away. It's been decided for him. But why wouldn't he love the infanta of Spain? Why not, after all? He could begin by loving her as a little sister or cousin (she is in fact his first cousin; their paternal grandfather was Louis, the grand dauphin, eldest son of Louis XIV; the pope, thank God, has signed the dispensation for consanguinity) and after years and years — nine years, to be precise — love her as his wife. He could also, just as easily, remain uninterested in the whole business. A marriage? How important can it be? That's the attitude expressed by his best friend, the

Duke de Boufflers, who's recently been married. "And so I presently have a wife, but it will be a long time before I can sleep with her," he told the king with an air of detachment. As for the king, he sees only the shame of having a baby for a wife. He sulks. He speaks to no one except the woman he calls Maman Ventadour, his governess, from whose care he was removed at the age of seven, when he "passed to the men." Nonetheless, he dines with her in her apartments once a week, and she continues to be his *maman*. With her as with everyone, he's most often silent, but in his turmoil he confides to her the reason for his chagrin. Mme de Ventadour, instead of reacting with her usual affection, seems unsympathetic and ill at ease. After the boy leaves her, he's seized by a feeling of intense loneliness and his suppressed anger gnaws at him. When the Duke of Osuna, the ambassador extraordinary of the king of Spain, has a private audience with Louis XV, the boy neither smiles nor speaks. A pastel portrait of the infanta is held up for him to see; he averts his eyes. Louis XV takes no pleasure in looking at girls, whether big or little, whether in pictures or in the flesh. And least of all this girl, with whom he is pledged to live together until the end of his days.

For reasons of policy, the regent doesn't want the two marriages to be made public at the same time. The king's is announced first, and then Mlle de Montpensier's, even though the actual order is the reverse. The regent's enemies are enraged. The Parisians make jokes. There are festivities on the horizon, a bright clearing in harsh weather. But the great event that autumn, for Paris and for all of France, is the arrest of Cartouche. The Spanish marriages are a matter for negotiation between the two royal courts and don't really concern the people, while Cartouche's incredible audacity, the army of outlaws he's raised, the shadowy power undermining official authority — all that indeed concerns the people, and inflames them. They follow Cartouche's exploits closely. Through him, the French take their revenge for their humiliated lives. However, when he's arrested, they express their satisfaction. Publicly, in the name of virtue, in all good conscience, they desire the death of their hero. In private, they continue to tell one another tales of his high deeds, to dream of his escape, to be certain that his men are going to pick up where he left off and that his fearsome army hasn't stopped fighting. It's always festive to see someone punished, and Cartouche, given his stature, will surely receive exceptional treatment — for he's an exceptional man. The common people aren't the only ones fascinated by him. Writers and great ladies visit him in his cell in the Conciergerie. Cartouche, his legs weighed down by chains (he calls them his "garters"), laughs at everything, sings obscene songs at the top of his voice, and teaches them to his guards. As thoroughly as his feats of brigandage, his cheerfulness amazes all. The festivities attendant upon the Spanish marriages — what can they offer compared to the thrill to be provided by the public execution of such a criminal? On the one hand, child's play; on the other, bloodshed.

Child's play...the Parisians have it right. These marriages are child's play, but organized by adults. Will the children be able to breathe life into them and animate them with their imaginations? Do these particular children even have a childhood that can be saved? And for that matter, who in this period can lay claim to a childhood? Certainly not the children of the common people, put to work as soon as they can stand up straight! But how about these royal children? Apart from the luxury in which they grow up, will it be granted them to enjoy a carefree time before they must take up the worries and responsibilities of adulthood? A time for playing, for devoting all their energies to exploring the world and its sensations? At present, like miniature, brightly painted marionettes, they concentrate all their efforts on correctly executing their assigned moves. For them, the festivities begin in the form of religious ceremonies that follow one another in close succession. In Paris, Mlle de Montpensier is baptized; shortly thereafter, in the church of the royal abbey of Val-de-Grâce, she is confirmed at the hands of Cardinal de Noailles, archbishop of Paris; then, a few days before her marriage, her confessor, the parish priest of the church of Saint-Eustache, gives her her first communion. Confirmation, first communion, matrimony; the sacraments are dispensed at emergency speed. In Madrid, the infanta is also baptized. Will the sequence be the same for her — confirmation, first communion, matrimony? No; Mariana Victoria is deemed too immature for confirmation and communion. She will skip directly to matrimony. The young bride-to-be, just baptized and adorable in her white lace, shivers under the drops of holy water.

The day before the marriage contract between Mlle de Montpensier and the Prince of Asturias is to be signed, King Louis, accompanied by the Count de Clermont and the Marshal de Villeroy, goes hunting at the Château de la Muette. The hunt and the male entourage make him merry. The air smells of mushrooms and damp wood. He feels like laughing, like riding on, plunging haphazardly through fields and forests.

The two contracts are signed on November 16. Madame, the Princess Palatine (whose unhappy marriage to Monsieur, Louis XIV's brother and the regent's father, began on that very day fifty years before), stands proxy for the little infanta, while the Duke of Osuna, ambassador extraordinary of Spain, represents Don Luis. The king doesn't hide his displeasure, but a sad face has never been an obstacle to the smooth progress of a ceremony. As for Mlle de Montpensier, however terrible her bad humor is and whatever secret horror awaits her, the ceremonial is sufficiently brilliant to drown out any false note that may come from so small a person. In the evening, King Louis leads her out to open the ball. Do they know there was once a notion of marrying them to each other? And a marriage between the king and her little sister, Philippine Élisabeth, Mlle de Beaujolais, seven years old, was considered as well. But such machinations are beyond the dance partners. They aren't informed of any plans concerning themselves. Besides, these particular plans aren't serious. They're just false rumors designed to anger the king of Spain and intensify his desire that his own daughter, and not a daughter of the despised House of Orléans, become queen of France. The rumors were bait, which Philip V has swallowed. The king and his cousin dance without exchanging a word. From time to time Mlle de Montpensier's somber face glows bizarrely. A masked crowd hedges them round. The masks are impatient for the fete to begin, for the moment when they can *really* start having fun—that is, the moment the marrying children clear the floor.

The regent rejoices in the success of his plans. He participates in the ball triumphantly, a conquering hero, at least during the first few hours. At a certain point, however, a bout of nausea compels him to leave the room, and he spends the night retching and vomiting.

That evening, after the signing of the marriage contracts, after the ball, and after dutifully accompanying his cousin, the future queen of Spain—who turns out to be as little delighted with her destiny as he is with his own—the king attends a performance of Lully's *Phaëton* at the Palais-Royal. It's his first opera. Confronted with the magnificent sets, the vivid costumes, the bright, sumptuous lighting, the shock of the voices, he's seized with a kind of exhilaration that by the last act has dwindled into total dejection. The revelation that strikes him is the opposite of rapture. He discovers the limitless boredom music brings him. Through *Phaëton*, he glimpses the innumerable operas, like so many trials, that he'll be obliged to endure. He crosses his arms and falls asleep with his cheek against the gold thread of his formal coat.

No Goodbye

Two days later, amid general indifference, Louise Élisabeth sets off for Spain. Her mother hardly looks at her.

Her grandmother, the Princess Palatine, comments on her departure: "One cannot say that Mlle. de Montpensier is ugly, but she is surely the most unpleasant child alive, in her way of eating, of drinking, of speaking. She makes a person lose all patience, and so I shed no tears, and neither did she, when we bade each other farewell." The king wishes her a good journey to Madrid and returns to the Tuileries. The regent, following the laws of etiquette, accompanies his daughter as far as Bourg-la-Reine, about six miles to the south. Mlle de Montpensier shares her coach with her father and her brother, who will soon leave her; with her governess, the horrible Mme de Cheverny, all covered with red blotches and disfigured by scurvy, who will leave her at the border; and with the Duchess de Ventadour, the infanta's future governess, who won't be crossing into Spain either.

Mme de Ventadour is, without doubt, the best disposed person in this business, but given her devotion to her king, her present assignment both flatters and troubles her. He kissed her coldly this morning and thus spoiled her leave-taking a little, but at bottom she's calm. She knows she's in no danger of experiencing with the infanta the transports of maternal love she experienced with the little king. And besides, isn't he an orphan? Whereas the infanta is no such thing. She has a mother indeed, a mother who won't let herself be overlooked; moreover, the duchess thinks with tears in her eyes, could there be a handsomer boy in the world than her king? There's no chance that the infanta will put him in the shade. The still beautiful "Maman Ventadour," feeling stronger and younger, settles into the coach and abandons herself to the vanities of appearance. She's been named *maîtresse du voyage*, mistress of the journey. She's traveling in grand style, escorted by eighty splendidly dressed body-guards. But they look drab next to the 150 guards, led by the Prince de Rohan-Soubise, who bring up the rear of the march.

Mlle de Montpensier is frowning. She mutters that her corset's too tight, that it's beastly cold in the coach. Her father remains calm, but underneath the kind facade his impatience is perceptible. He wants to have done with this farewell farce. And yet Mlle de Montpensier's behavior seems quite acceptable if he thinks about the crises and sui-cide threats of her sister, Mlle de Valois, married one year earlier. More than threats; she was prepared to do anything to avoid joining her husband, the Duke of Modena. She pur-posely visited the convent at Chelles, on the pretext of see-ing her sister the abbess, but in reality because she knew the place was afflicted by an epidemic. "Don't go there," she was told, "or you run the risk of catching smallpox." "That's what I'm looking for," she replied. But all she caught there was the measles, which at least gained her a little time. She stopped eating and wept incessantly. On the day of her proxy mar-riage, people noticed her swollen face, her dejection. She cried so much she couldn't articulate a single word.

Fortunately, Mlle de Valois is now in Modena; other-wise, she would be capable of communicating her rebellious spirit to her sister. Not that Mlle de Montpensier is docile, but she's still ignorant of desire, and she doesn't know that its imperatives have nothing to do with politics. Of this fact Mlle de Valois is well aware. The Duke de Richelieu was her first master in debauchery. The Duke de Richelieu, that popinjay, that pervert, that relentless destroyer of the peace of families and states, that plague, that brilliant shit-stirrer...the word "brilliant" is an exaggeration, the regent thinks, correcting himself, but "plague" is thoroughly accurate. His daughter Charlotte Aglaé—Mlle de Valois—is in Modena, but she's trying to return to France. She writes one letter after another, complaining about her in-laws and, most recently, demanding the annulment of her marriage on the grounds of impotence. Her father-in-law has had a wall built between her apartments and those of his other daughters-in-law. But she doesn't give in...She's not especially beautiful, the Duchess of Modena, with her ugly teeth and her big nose, already ruined by tobacco, but she has character and a taste for combat...More than mere threats of suicide? The regent remembers her "accident," which took place shortly before her departure. Mlle de Valois launched her horse at a gallop through a small doorway. She didn't duck and struck her head with such force that she was thrown backward onto the animal's croup.

Mlle de Montpensier says she's too hot, opens her window, sticks her head out. The rain destroys her coiffure and trickles down her neck.

The regent feels great relief when they reach Bourg-la-Reine. He kisses his daughter, pinches her cheek amiably, and jumps out of the coach.

SPAIN, WINTER 1721

The Duke de Saint-Simon's Three Bows

The Spanish capital breathes an air of expectation and excitement. For the past three months, rumors about a marriage between the infanta Mariana Victoria and the king of France, and also about other royal unions, have been spreading. On the streets, in the marketplaces, in the taverns and the churches, people discuss, hope, assume. To know the truth, it would be necessary to penetrate the Royal Alcázar, an immense white-stone building with narrow windows and a jumble of rooms, to reach the interior of the palace, and to gain access to the royal chamber. It's there that the king, in spite of his antipathy for this dwelling place, spends most of his life, at the queen's side, *glued to her*. The people detest the Italian woman and continue to love Philip V's first wife, the adorable and courageous Maria Luisa of Savoy, *la Savoyarde*, *la Savoyana*. Still today, when the king and queen move about Madrid, at the passage of their coach the crowd cries out, "*Viva la Savoyana!*" Elisabeth Farnese is wounded by such outbursts, but not gravely. She has lived through a child-hood and an adolescence in which affection had no place. Her father died when she was very young. Her mother, a haughty, vindictive woman determined to break her daughter's char-acter, succeeded in making it hardly different from her own. Her contact with Elisabeth was rare, and she relegated the girl—practically a prisoner, unknown at court—to attic rooms high up in the enormous ducal palace in Parma. Elisa-beth's only visitors were teachers, priests, and, when needed, physicians. This system, far from making the young girl more yielding, hardened her. She chose to dedicate herself to her studies, and should a marriage possibility present itself, she resolved to realize it come what may. Love didn't enter into her daydreams. Besides, she wasn't a dreamer. In her rela-tionship with the king of Spain, she soon understood that she must employ all the resources of her personality and her body, not to try to eliminate the ghost of Maria Luisa of Savoy, but to set a screen around it, to block its apparitions. She doesn't deviate from her plan. The king's attached to her. Excessively so, and she could wish for some intervals of independence, but since that's impossible, she does all she can to augment the king's need of her, to ensure that their union becomes still closer, clammy, unbreathable—a knot of embraces. The king and queen form a single, indivisible entity.

The brocade curtains, adorned with mother-of-pearl, silver, and gold, are drawn, both those on the windows and those around the canopy bed. Philip V and Elisabeth Farnese seem to be agitated by contrary feelings. Sometimes they smile and savor in anticipation the happy event of their daughter's marriage; sometimes they interpret the delay in the ambassador extraordinary's arrival as a bad omen. The king tends toward pessimism, but his wife reassures him. They say their prayers. The monarch is brought his morning beverage, which serves as his breakfast: a white, hot liquid, a mixture of bouillon, milk, wine, egg yolks, cloves, and cinnamon. The queen takes up her tapestry, which she keeps within reach on a little table. On the days when the king works with his minister of state, the Marquis de Grimaldo, she follows the conversation closely. Without laying aside her needle and thread, she participates and makes decisions. In fact, she takes a more active interest than the king, who's silent and morose most of the time and manifestly tormented when there are political matters to be dealt with. There's no difference between the way he talks to his minister of state and the way he grinds out his prayers.

When the queen's in bed, she's never busy with her tapestry for long. The generally gloomy and dull king undergoes a change when the desire to make love comes over him. At those times, he displays great ardor and vehemence. He flings himself upon her. His amorous temperament is gossip material for servants and courtiers. When the queen refuses him, it's said that the result is bedlam and tumult in the royal bedchamber. The king shouts and threatens. The queen shouts and complains. She calls for help, weeps. It seems unlikely that anyone would come running…When she finally yields, the king's pleasure is even more intense, and he gives her whatever she desires.

But today, under the winter sun of this limpid morning, as she considers the miracle of the new rapprochement with the kingdom of France, she has no reason to refuse the king. She puts down her tapestry and caresses him. "How handsome you are," she murmurs to the ugly face leaning over her. Whereupon, without interrupting his thrusting, the king grunts, "But why hasn't the Duke de Saint-Simon arrived yet? Didn't he leave a month ago, or am I wrong?"

Philip V's calculations are correct. His lust hasn't clouded his judgment. The ambassador extraordinary has fallen well behind schedule. To begin with, the diabolical Cardinal Dubois, by assiduously multiplying the obstacles that Saint-Simon had to overcome before his departure, caused the duke to make his travel arrangements on short notice, which obviously cost a great deal more. The same Dubois imposed on him a ruinously expensive retinue and military accompaniment. Then, during the French portion of his journey, a combination of bad weather and an abundance of receptions considerably slows Saint-Simon's progress. And after that, when they finally reach the border, the French company is most thoroughly searched. Since the plague is still raging in Marseille, they have to open each parcel. Every person coming into Spain from France represents a risk of contagion. The Duke de Saint-Simon, suspected of bringing the plague in his baggage! It's too much! He gets indignant, he rants and raves, but he's forced to comply. And to round out the sum of his cares, in Burgos the elder of his two sons falls ill, a victim of smallpox, the scourge that kills people by the thousands, especially children. Saint-Simon has to leave the young man behind. He also leaves his other traveling companions: his younger son; his brother the Abbé de Saint-Simon; various friends, including the Count de Lorges and the Count de Céreste; and several servants, who are going to follow in coaches while he, Saint-Simon, aware of the royal couple's impatience, continues on horseback. Worried about his sick son, stressed by the great number of messages with which the king and queen of Spain steadily bombard him, he urges on his horse.

At the end of the month of November, in the middle of the night, Saint-Simon enters Madrid. He's gone practically without sleep since leaving Burgos. His Excellency the ambassador's body is in bad shape, and likewise his morale.

He has but a poor understanding of Spanish. It's a tongue he dislikes, a brutal, loud tongue whose sounds remind him of sneezes. A language that suits the lice-infested people who speak it. And as if their spoken language weren't enough, the Spaniards sing, too, and their bizarre, indefinable songs get directly on his nerves. Wherever he stopped, in the most remote hamlet, out in the countryside — and the windswept expanses of Castille have nothing in common with the pleasant copses of *la douce France* — in places one would believe uninhabited, a song, often accompanied by a guitar, would arise, a piercing, maddening song. Most of the time, he couldn't see the singer, but at some point the awful lament would always start up, usually out of nowhere. It sounded like something halfway between the mewing of a cat and the cries of a hysteric. And to top everything, the singers would express their torments amid exhalations of olive oil! It was enough to make you puke! Were Saint-Simon to classify, in ascending order of repulsiveness, all the annoying things he's encountered on this trip, he would have to put olive oil at the top: an emetic that makes an already crude cuisine impossible to swallow. On the night when he first sets foot in the capital of Spain, which is even more dimly lit than Paris, the Duke de Saint-Simon is feeling queasy. And as he follows his guides, who are happy to have arrived and therefore cry out more vociferously than usual in their ignoble lingo, his morale bottoms out.

Above everything else, the Duke de Saint-Simon believes in hierarchy, in the sacred rituals of etiquette. He's fastidious about questions of honor and courtesy. His journey to Spain, with its dirt roads, its arid plains swept by icy winds, its sporadic groups of dirty, sunburned peasants and ragged beggars, seems to him like a trip to another planet. The discrepant combination of poverty, superstition, and the desire to sing is beyond his understanding. He'd certainly like the title of grandee of Spain for himself and his sons, but if the older one has to die of smallpox in Burgos and the younger one, like himself, is afflicted with a liver disease brought on by too much rancid olive oil and nervous disorders caused by musical intolerance, then wouldn't that title — so sweet to murmur to himself, so awesome to imagine amplified into echoes from hall to hall and palace to palace — wouldn't that title be too dearly bought?

Nay, says Saint-Simon when he's finally in the apartment prepared for him, sitting before a blazing fire at a table on which he spreads out the precious documents entrusted to his charge: a portrait of King Louis XV and a copy of the marriage contract, written in Spanish. The French version, which he has incessantly requested from the infernal Dubois, has yet to come into his hands. He tenses up at the thought of it. To relax, he steps over to the window and verifies the presence of the royal coach that has been placed at his disposition at any hour of the day or night. There at least is something that corresponds to his idea of respectability, and it leads him, now that he's starting to feel better, to ponder a thorny question: At what time will he be able to present himself to the king and queen? *As soon as possible*, they've stressed in their innumerable messages. But what does "as soon as possible" mean to a king and queen of Spain? If he were in Versailles, he'd present himself without hesitation at the *petit lever*, but what to do here, where Their Majesties shut themselves up in private, where they sometimes, according to rumor, even go back to bed in the course of the day?

What Saint-Simon has learned about the way Philip V and his wife lead their lives alarms him. Their schedule, he's been told, is as follows. They are awakened at eight; they remain in bed together, say their prayers together, get up, get dressed, and go to Mass together. After the Mass, they play billiards for a while and then read some devotional work together. Then they dine, and after dinner they play piquet or some other card game or chess, take a walk, or go hunting (an only moderately risky activity, given that the sovereigns sit in a coppice shaped like a theater box and from there, without budging an inch, fire on the animals peasant beaters drive in their direction). They return to the palace to read together, deal with political matters together, do good works together. Then they have supper together, pray together, and return to their bed. When they walk, they walk exactly side by side. If by chance they are disunited, because there are other people present and the queen, caught up in a conversation, drops off the pace, the king stops and waits for her. Only at the moment when she gets out of bed and puts on her shoes — and when she goes to confession — is the queen separated from the king; but in the latter case, if she stays too long whispering with her confessor, the king comes looking for her. It goes without saying that their *chaises percées*, their commodes, touch each other, and that in no case, not even when one of them is ill or during the queen's lyings-in, does the king sleep in a separate bed. Saint-Simon finds all this disquieting. The only reassuring element, the fact that the royal couple, a sort of two-headed monster, both speak French, doesn't suffice to dispel his apprehension.

Saint-Simon picks up his wig. In his ignorance of the proper etiquette, how can he know the right time for him to make his appearance before the sovereigns? Why not hasten to wait upon them right away? But then, should he appear in full court costume, with all his decorations, or in simple court costume? And here, with this last question, His Excellency the ambassador extraordinary condemns himself to a night of insomnia. By the dirty light of dawn, filled with incertitude, he decides on eight-thirty in the morning and full court costume.

And suppose it's a terrible blunder, suppose an untimely arrival discredits him forever? Saint-Simon has to admit that the full court costume, with its stiffness, its heavy fabric and brocade and embroidery, doesn't make his move any easier. He has trouble making himself understood and gets dropped off at a secondary entrance. A side entrance for suppliers, thinks the horrified French envoy. Down ugly brown corridors, marred with scratches and here and there showing the stains of water damage, the ambassador extraordinary advances. Sick corridors, he's thinking, just at the moment when nausea overcomes him, seizing him before he can even name its origin, as intense as in the worst of all the inns that punctuated his journey. As incredible as it may seem, the royal palace, the Alcázar, stinks of olive oil. Behind the doors of rooms where vile fried foods are sizzling, he can hear voices jabbering away in Spanish. "Good God, where am I?" groans Saint-Simon. He turns back, takes other corridors, encounters servants who, as soon as he addresses them in French, spit on the floor and run away; he passes through antechambers as attractive as storage rooms. All the same, they offer him the opportunity to sit down and recover himself a little. The odor has almost disappeared. He's breathing better and would be ready to press on again—ready to be the man for whom his splendid ceremonial outfit was made—if he didn't have the feeling of eyes on him. Saint-Simon peers in their direction and discovers a group of dwarfs, richly arrayed, their hair down to their feet. Creatures who have no sort of consideration for a duke and peer of France. They shake their big faces at him and make gestures whose mocking intent pierces him through and through. A little more and he'll collapse!

But suddenly, in one of those reversals of fortune in which a desperate man can no longer believe, the introducer of ambassadors stands before him. He speaks to Saint-Simon in French, exudes a fragrance of mimosa, and explains to him, with many apologies for having missed him when he left his coach, that he wandered by mistake into the *Casa española*, the Spanish House, but that his lucky star eventually led him into the French House, the *Casa francesa*. These are two enemy worlds, locked in a war that has lasted since Philip V's reign began and is not confined to a virulent culinary struggle between proponents of a cuisine based on olive oil and those of a cuisine based on butter. The introducer could go on, but they've arrived. As if by magic, Saint-Simon's in the royal chamber. Their Majesties, still abed but in a decent posture, give him a warm welcome. The king's wearing a nightcap and a white satin jacket; the queen's lace nightdress has a very low neckline. They both receive him joyously.

A little later on this same day, in their official capacity — that is, out of bed and seated before a larger audience — the king and queen treat Saint-Simon with the same goodwill. And as for him, luck's on his side: he performs his three bows impeccably. Before the sovereigns depart, he has time to return to the threshold of the Hall of Mirrors, a sumptuous but long and narrow room (the king and queen enter and exit at the opposite end), to greet one by one the ladies lined up with their backs to the wall — and to do so without undue haste. Before he goes, he has a private conversation with Philip V. And finally the queen, as a sign of special favor, shows Saint-Simon the infante Don Carlos. The child is made to walk and turn around for the duke. Don Carlos does very well. He's neither crooked nor lame — no more than is his half-brother, Don Fernando. And the infanta, the future queen of France? Her Serene Highness Mariana Victoria is sound asleep.

Her slumber is all smile and contentment, the sleep of perfect trust, of complete innocence; she sleeps the sleep of an angel, her bed rests on a cloud.

Doña Maria Nieves, the infanta's beloved "cradle-rocker" since her earliest infancy, imparts a gentle swing to that bed as she sways the child to the rhythm of Paradise.

The Palace Ladies' Perfume

On the following day, the day the marriage contracts are to be signed, Saint-Simon, still radiant from his success, readies himself with extreme care; as he cannot fall short of yesterday, he once again dons his full court costume.

Mariana Victoria is awakened and awakened well. Perched on a little platform encrusted with precious stones, she holds herself very straight in her crinoline dress. She is, in fact, a beautiful child, though really small, pale, fragile-looking. But she has lively blue eyes, an inclination to imperiousness, and a way of handling her fan to which there is no reply. The private music that sings her victory song hasn't left her. She receives His Excellency the ambassador extraordinary with the natural hauteur that will soon enchant the French. Saint-Simon bows. He deems the infanta "charming, with a little air of reasonableness and not at all embarrassed." As for her, her eyes do not light on the ambassador.

Saint-Simon also sees Don Luis, Prince of Asturias, a thin but good-looking and elegant young man. He can barely stand to wait any longer for his fiancée. But Mariana Victoria is calm. She has grasped that she's going to become the queen of France—and besides, her brothers have started giving her precedence at every opportunity—but she doesn't exactly understand when that condition is to come about, or how.

That same evening, or perhaps another, and perhaps to help the infanta get a clearer idea of her destiny, she's shown a portrait of the infanta Maria Theresa of Spain, painted by Velázquez. "She was the daughter of Philip IV of Spain and Elisabeth of France," the child is told. "She married her first cousin Louis XIV, your great-grandfather. She became queen of France, just as you will become queen of France by your marriage to your first cousin, King Louis XV."

Mariana Victoria considers Maria Theresa. She examines the red cheeks, the potato nose, the swollen lower lip, the thick wire wig stuck with silver butterflies. *"Muy fea!"* (Very ugly!) the infanta proclaims, and covers her eyes. She's reprimanded. She must offer her apologies to her great-grandmother, the queen of France. She does as she's told, all the while ogling the painting next to the portrait of Maria Theresa. At first, she wants only to avoid looking at the ugly infanta any longer, but then she's captivated by what she discovers: a pretty blond infanta in a white moiré crinoline, posing beside her dwarf and observing her with a proud look. "The infanta Margarita," someone tells Mariana Victoria, making a slight bow toward the picture. "That's not true," the child proclaims. "That one there, that's me."

The signing of the contract takes place in the Great Hall. While the document is being read aloud, the infanta has a flash of understanding: she's going to marry the king of

France. Her mother holds the infanta's writing hand while she signs. Mariana Victoria concentrates on her task with all her might, leaning so far forward that her cheek and almost her lips graze the paper, like a first kiss to her little husband and great king.

Everyone's surprised by the bride-to-be's patience during the session; by contrast, her mother the queen asks aloud at one point, "Will this go on much longer?" When the infanta is offered the portrait of Louis XV surrounded by diamonds, she receives it like a reward. She asks if she can keep it. "Of course," she's told. "It belongs to you, it's your husband's portrait, he was happy to send it to you." When the Prince of Asturias hears these words, he's moved to protest. The portrait of *his* future spouse was taken away from him; he demands that it be returned. "No," is his stepmother Elisabeth's only reply. Perhaps he thinks of his own mother then, of his grief at having lost her, and feels with increased weight the unhappy burden of being so alone between this wily Italian woman and his melancholy father. Perhaps, not only because of sexual frustration but also out of a desperate innocence, he wants Mlle de Montpensier to be a companion that he can love.

"Where is she?" he asks. "Where is the princess on her journey?"

That evening, in an immense room sparkling with candlelight and shimmering with the reflections of gold and bronze and marble, the king and queen give a magnificent ball. They themselves remain at one end of the room, facing the entrance, with the infanta by their side. They're sitting on high gilt armchairs, behind which red velvet stools have been placed for important personages. Along one wall, other stools and cushions are occupied by the wives of the grandees of Spain and their eldest sons, while the girls are on the floor, on the carpets that cover the whole room. On the other side, facing the women and the young people, some courtiers are standing in front of the windows. In an adjoining room, wine flows in profusion and tables are laden with the most extravagant tiered cakes and pastries of all sorts. Everyone chats and laughs and exchanges courteous gestures as sensual as caresses. The general joy is like an undulating streamer that springs from the hands of the royal couple and their daughter. And it's at the instant when this ribbon touches Saint-Simon that he, who so far has been brilliant and valiant and practically possessed by his mission, starts to feel himself going down.

He's feverish and parched, but he doesn't have the strength to stand up and go into the next room, where wine is streaming in fountains, to have a drink. Nevertheless, he's happy; since the cause for celebration is the infanta's marriage, this party's in his honor as well. He therefore remains seated, perspiring, a little sick, but also satisfied. The king and queen dance. He admires them wholeheartedly and is considering taking his leave when he's spotted by an old acquaintance from Paris, a woman more than fifty years old, who — no, it's not possible! — who apparently has the perverse intention of making him dance. Panic! Saint-Simon hides behind a column; his persecutrix catches him out and drags him before the king and queen, and it's from Their Majesties themselves that he receives the *order* to dance. He tries to be excused on the grounds of his fatigue, his age, his utter incompetence in the matter of dancing, but in vain; his protests produce the opposite effect. The duke does as he's told. Minuets, contredanses, chaconnes—nothing is spared him. He feels as if he's going to die dancing. He has to be laid down, fanned, given a glass of wine to drink, and transported to his coach. The ball is indifferent to his fate and continues without him. The king, the queen, the Prince of Asturias, and all the court, young and old, dance until dawn.

The infanta is implored to be a good girl at the ball. She's a wife and a queen, yes, but too little to avoid being knocked about by other dancers. As is the case wherever she goes, she's accompanied by her governess, the Duchess de Montellano, who sits on a red velvet stool behind her and watches her. Despite the duchess's remonstrations, the infanta taps her feet to the rhythm so insistently that she's taken down from her high, golden-fringed armchair and authorized to dance with her brother Don Carlos. The entire ball stops to look at the brother and sister, so charming and joyful as they hop about in time to the music. While being escorted back to their rooms, they're able to admire the fires and illuminations burning in celebration all over Madrid. They slip behind the curtains and stand there holding hands with their noses pressed against the window. This is one of their games: hiding behind curtains, pressing their noses against the misted windowpanes, and making nose drawings on the glass.

On the evening in late November when she and her parents, accompanied by a grand cortege, make their way to the Royal Basilica of Our Lady of Atocha, Mariana Victoria is even prettier than the little girl in white in Velázquez's painting. Much prettier, in her gold and lilac crinoline. Not because of the crinoline, but because of her excitement at the sight of the huge, incredible gift she's been given: the city of Madrid, her city, celebrating in her honor. Rich cloths adorn the windows of the buildings the cortege passes, and upon the company's return from the basilica, the Plaza Mayor is all lit up. And for a change, the child doesn't hear the upsetting cries of *"Viva la Savoyana! Viva la Savoyana!"* The people greet the royal family with cheers and acclamations: *"Viva Mariana Victoria! Viva la reina de Francia!"*

The infanta has a passion for the ladies of the palace. They wear dresses as multicolored as parrot feathers and make even more noise than parrots do. Seated on carpets with their legs folded under them and their skirts spread out around them, they kiss the infanta, passing her from one to the other. The little girl, intoxicated by being whirled about, caresses the ladies, inhales them, clings to one's necklace, keeps another's flower, sucks a piece of chocolate. The ladies smell of amber and oranges. The infanta is suffused by their perfumes, by their warmth. She's fond of heady scents, smacking kisses, full-throated songs. That evening, they kiss and hug her harder than usual, take her hands and make her jump along with them in their dances. Mariana Victoria shouts with fear and pleasure. She continually wants to start over again. The ladies of the palace are like her, always ready to start over again. And later in the night, when they're told that the party's over, that they have to let the infanta leave, a leaden weight comes down on their gathering. They fall silent, stretch out on their carpets, light candles. Waving their fans, they bid her farewell. The infanta sees them disappear in a blaze.

To Lerma, Slowly

The departure for France takes place twice. First the infanta leaves Madrid for Lerma. Her parents make regular sojourns in the palace near the Alarzón River built by the Duke of Lerma, the favorite of Philip III, and she has often traveled there, though never with so much baggage and so numerous an entourage; however, she doesn't differentiate between what belongs to the royal retinue and what to her own. The departure seems precipitous to her. She's not allowed to bid farewell to Don Fernando, who's in bed with measles, or to Don Carlos, who's showing early symptoms of the same disease.

The impressive cortege makes its first stop at Alcalá de Henares, which lies only a short distance from Madrid. Thus the pace of the infanta's journey has been set: incredibly slow, little more than a standstill. To go from Madrid to Lerma, the court will take fifteen days — fifteen days to cover around fifty leagues, which averages out to less than three and a half leagues (around nine miles) per day — enough time for the twenty-five-year-old Marquise de Crèvecoeur, one of the queen's most beautiful maids of honor, to die.

Mariana Victoria is a particularly beloved little girl, always the center of attention. This makes her dance about, but sometimes, for no apparent reason, she starts to cry and buries her face in Maria Nieves's bosom.

In Lerma, the court adopts a somewhat livelier rhythm — but barely, for the king is suffering a crisis of melancholia, and neither the constant presence of Elisabeth Farnese nor the singing of the castrato Valeriano Pellegrini suffices to lift him out of his personal abyss. Aware that something serious is afoot, the infanta refuses to be separated from Maria Nieves for a second. This dark-haired, pink-skinned, radiantly healthy young woman represents for the child a distillation of her obscure memories as a contented nursling while simultaneously embodying in a single person Mariana Victoria's multiple, supple, warm, glowing, and much-loved palace ladies.

The portrait of Louis XV, sparkling in its diamond frame, joins the images before which Mariana Victoria says her prayers. She prays to it fervently and starts to live in its sight. Her parents lavish all sorts of considerations upon her. Everywhere she goes, her brother the Prince of Asturias takes great care to step aside so that she can precede him. M. de Popoli, the prince's tutor, gives him back the portrait of Mlle de Montpensier, which shows her fair complexion, her black hair, her almond-shaped eyes, her unsmiling lips. She's an attractive girl. If she were a flower, she'd be a periwinkle, the prince says to himself, slipping his hand inside his underclothes. He's exercising his willpower. He doesn't masturbate until after he's said his prayers. He often talks about his fiancée with his brother and even with his stepmother. He asks again, "Where is Mlle de Montpensier? Where is the princess on her journey?"

BAZAS, DECEMBER 22, 1721

Distraught Missive

The princess herself couldn't say. She's been traveling for a month and has but the dimmest idea of her current location. Ensconced in the eight-horse carriage she seldom leaves, Louise Élisabeth plays cards, quarrels with her governess, flies into absurd rages, spends entire days sulking, obtains permission to take walks in the rain, catches cold, and pretends there's nothing wrong — up to a certain point, namely while traversing the Blaye region near Bordeaux. In the "Naval Palace," specially built for her arrival, the little girl looks quite pale and shaky, despite the calm surface of the water.

And so Mlle de Montpensier is in the Bordelais. A land of vineyards and gently rolling hills. Low skies, the beige waters of the Garonne River, the white stone and red roof tiles of the middle-class houses — these would fill her view, if she would only raise her eyes from the black interior of her coach, which swallows her up. She's too young and too chaotic to make sulking a way of life, but she gives herself over without resistance to her dark moods, as though guided by a compass of despair. When stormy weather rendered it impossible to sail from Italy to Spain and Elisabeth Farnese had to make an overland journey of three months to get from Parma to Madrid, she employed the time in preparing for war, in refining her plan to conquer the king her husband and seize the reins of power. In stark contrast, Louise Élisabeth, utterly insensible to the grand destiny supposedly awaiting her, is a catastrophe incarnate. A raging catastrophe.

To satisfy the demands of the Spanish sovereigns, her parents-in-law, the pauses in her journey are continually abbreviated. The stages get longer and longer. The royal honor guard capers about. The troops in the Prince de Rohan-Soubise's little army do not cease to cut a fine figure. The prince himself is magnificent. He and his dashing cavaliers take delight in their speed and in the fine Graves and Sauterne wines. But for her, for Mlle de Montpensier, who has become the Princess of Asturias and will later be the queen of Spain, for this totally bewildered twelve-year-old girl whose family has rid itself of her as of an unloved stranger, the headlong journey is an ordeal.

Dashing isn't her style, and now, after so many grueling days, she feels frankly awful. She's been extracted from the general malaise she's accustomed to—the hatred that binds her parents, the unique personality disorder for which each of her sisters is remarkable, the odious boy who is her brother, the scenes of drunkenness, gluttony, and lechery that form the kaleidoscope of her short memory—her natural atmosphere, in other words. And instead of feeling

better, she's lost. In Bordeaux she isn't allowed to go out-
doors because of the risk of smallpox. In Bazas, where she's
just arrived, she's the one who doesn't feel like going out.
The vineyards have been succeeded by the Landes forest, a
sort of wilderness into which no one ventures lightheart-
edly. Moreover, she's about to fall ill. She's ill already. She
suffers from earache, she has difficulty swallowing. She shivers as she tries to write a note to her father. With an effort,
she forms big, ugly letters that resemble a series of more or
less crooked sticks:

> Basace, December 22, please alow me, my dear papa, to have
> the honnor to wish you a happy new yeer in advanse and take
> my leeve of you again and ashure you, no words being able to
> express my deep gratitude for all you have done for me, that
> I shall show it thrugh all my life by my good conduct and my
> efforts to please you. I shall also strive to do justise to the
> royal house, wich I esteem beyond meashure. M. de la Bilar-
> derie kept me from burning...

Louise Élisabeth's fingers are covered with ink; she
wipes them on her dress and rings for someone to change
her. She's made some lucky escapes, no doubt about that.
In Chinay, the house she was staying in caught fire, and
she was barely rescued in time. The next day, in Brioux, it
was her wardrobe that went up in flames. And then, while
traversing a forest, the troops of her cortege turned out to
have been infiltrated by members of Cartouche's army. A
band of brigands made off with a quantity of silver plate and
three trunks filled with rich gifts for the Spanish. The girl

wonders how many more inconveniences are in store for her. She's already had some intuition of one inconvenience — and a horrid inconvenience at that, she says to herself, swallowing painfully — namely the face and form of Don Luis. Aagh! Aagh! Is she going to have to lie down naked next to him and let herself be touched? Is he going to be equally naked next to her? And suddenly the expression *nu comme un ver*, naked as a worm, crosses her mind and fills her with revulsion.

BEHIND THE WALL OF DOLLS,

DECEMBER 1721

The Uprooting

Of all this—the fires, the thieves, the promised young bride's illnesses—no one in the Spanish prince's entourage is remotely aware. The only kind of news that's propagated (with difficulty, considering the times) is positive. What Don Luis knows, essentially, is that Mlle de Montpensier is getting closer to him, as is the blessed day of their marriage. The prince is moved. He contemplates the portrait once again. If he looks closely, he can see that the young girl's lips are smiling slightly...Don Luis is mad for hunting, and he has no doubt that his future wife shares his passion. He has secretly ordered the best gunsmith in Spain to make two hunting guns as gifts for Louise Élisabeth.

The great event, however, is the departure of the queen of France for "her" country. The Masses, the concerts, the balls, the Duke of Lerma's extravagant hospitality all delight Mariana Victoria when she's in the moment, but after she goes to bed, she can't sleep. She weeps and cries out. She hears footsteps in the darkness. By way of preparing her for her new life, her mother speaks to her only in French—in a charming, bookish French made musical by her Italian accent. Excited and anxious as the child is, she has to make an effort to understand. She answers in Spanish, the language that's the most foreign of all to her mother's ears.

When it comes time to say goodbye, the little girl is brought to her parents. Her mother wipes away a few tears, her father fingers his rosary. They each impart counsel that the child must not on any account forget. This is no simple matter in the case of Elisabeth Farnese's recommendations, whose subject is none other than forgetting, but forgetting of a partial kind. The queen says to the girl, "Become entirely French, my daughter, forget your Spanish years. All the same, never forget your parents, or your brothers, or what your grand establishment in the most beautiful of kingdoms owes to our generosity." She holds her daughter's hands. Mariana Victoria would like to withdraw those hands from her mother's viselike grip. She'd also like her mother's eyes to look upon her more gently. They force her to lower her own, even though she feels it would be best if she could manage to look her mother in the face. But she doesn't dare. She's trembling too hard, she's too disconcerted. "Don't forget to forget." The queen repeats her recommendation in French and Italian. Mariana Victoria, seated sideways on the Duchess de Montellano's lap, feels herself slipping off. She very much wants this conversation—this seriousness, this emotion—to end. Under her extensive array of protective medals, her little heart is wildly pounding. Now it's her father's turn. Unlike the queen, he speaks with lowered eyes, but that fact in no way authorizes the child to raise her own and look at him. "Your marriage with the House of France is a great joy to me," he whispers with an air of dismay. At this point the infanta would really like to slide to the floor and be comforted. The king explains to her, or to an invisible confessor, that this marital union will atone for the great crime of the thirteen-year-long War of Succession, a crime for which he, Philip V, born Duke d'Anjou, is responsible before the Lord. The king falls to his knees and prays to be forgiven for his sins. The queen, the Duchess de Montellano (holding the infanta, who has gone completely limp), the grand inquisitor, a group of courtiers, a bevy of priests and nuns, and a few dwarfs immersed in the shadows imitate the royal gesture. Mariana Victoria has an urge to take refuge among the dwarfs in the dark corner, but she doesn't have time to act. She is set on her feet and directed without further delay toward the Unknown. The king and queen give their daughter a ceremonious escort, not taking leave of her until they reach the foot of the stairs. There the royal parents are overcome by sadness and, as they will later declare, near fainting. Together.

What's the urgency that compels these parents, in the dead of winter, to dispatch a little girl they claim to cherish on a journey that could well kill her? Isn't her marriage nothing but a mirage, toward which they must rush headlong before it vanishes away? Mariana Victoria herself has already vanished from her parents' field of vision. And whether she dies or arrives at her destination, they won't see her again. They've said goodbye to a child who from now on, in their eyes, will be dead, except as she may be viewed in some more or less faithful portraits.

When Will We Get There?

Along the way, amid the cold and the jolting, the infanta constructs a wall between herself and the landscape, a wall of dolls placed vertically one on top of another and firmly intertwined. In the two parental recommendations she's received — to become *entirely* French and to atone for her father's sins — there's nothing specific about the duration of her journey. She's going away, that's for sure, but for how long, and where?

At Christmas Mass in the little village where the cortege makes a halt, the Infanta's chair is placed so close to the Nativity scene that the pressure of the crowd filling the modest church causes her to end up on the straw. Had the ass not blocked her progress, she would have gone farther. Back in the coach the following day, she opens the gifts the peasants brought her. Those that are appropriate — dolls and marionettes of various kinds — she inserts into the wall. She calls for handkerchiefs and shawls to fill the holes.

She doesn't cry too much and doesn't complain. All the same, for no apparent reason, she occasionally lets out a piercing scream.

Every morning she wakes up in a different room. She who, in the Alcázar or the Buen Retiro Palace, used to take so much pleasure in nestling in her bed and jingling the little bells suspended beside her (to protect herself from the threat of scary thunderstorms) and playing with the moon and stars that hung from a little arch above her head, she who would never fall asleep without putting Carmen-Doll to bed first, with her long brown hair spread out on a pink lace pillow identical to her own but smaller — she doesn't recognize a thing. She clutches Carmen-Doll to her chest and speaks to her until they doze off.

The infanta is terrified of black pigs. She thinks they carry the evil eye. The villages she passes through are filled with such pigs, enormous, stinking, blocking the road. The farther her journey takes her, the more black pigs there are. Pigs and priests and old women. And young ones too, whom she glimpses inside houses as dark as the pigs. The infanta travels hidden behind her wall of dolls. If she's unfortunate enough to catch sight of the outside world, she immediately covers her eyes with her hands. The outside world is too ugly.

When she grows weary of hiding her eyes, she asks to be blindfolded. And it amuses her to keep her blindfold on during the halts. Maria Nieves guides her. In the end, playing at being blind distracts her for a good part of her journey.

The infanta has a toothache. She forbids herself to cry. She's the person through whom the crime of a long, murderous war is going to be expiated. She offers up all her sufferings to God. He will take them into account and pour out their beneficial effects upon the soul of the guilty king. She doesn't cry; she lays her toothache as an offering upon the altar of her father's remorse.

She listens to the sound of the rain beating down on the roof of the coach. You're going far, far away, the sound of the rain tells her. Far from the ladies of the palace and the good smells and the kisses. She asks questions. About her parents, her brothers, her dogs. By way of a reply, she's given a bonbon. The infanta deafens her entourage with her cries. She has fits of rage. And then there's the water that filters in through the coach doors, there's the jolting, the mud, the cold, the fear of catching a disease. Being part of the infanta's retinue is a privilege; it's not a pleasure. Only Maria Nieves finds the jaunt delightful. She takes the child in her arms and has answers to all her questions.

"When will we get there?"

"One fine day."

"Where are we going?"

"We're going to France, your kingdom. But first we're going to Pheasant Island."

"Oh! An island where pheasants live? Do they know I'm coming? Are they waiting for me?"

"Of course. They've got a surprise ready for you."

Maria Nieves and Mme de Montellano, seeing in the pheasants the way to serenity, tell the child all manner of outlandish stories about them. The result goes contrary to their hopes. When it comes to the pheasants, the infanta is insatiable.

The roads don't get any better. In the long line of vehicles, there are carriages that get stuck in mud, tumble into ditches, break an axle. Whenever such an accident occurs, the whole cortege comes to a standstill, a golden opportunity for the black pigs.

The roads disappear, the horizon shows no way out, but over the course of one night — miraculously — the rain changes to snow. The morning sun dazzles. The trees are weighed down with whiteness. Everything black has fled. The infanta opens her eyes wide. She digs out an opening in the wall of dolls. In a hamlet somewhere at the foot of the mountains, the peasants, to mark the extraordinary honor of her coming, present her with ice sculptures made especially for the occasion: they depict the village chapel with its crown of birds, the cluster of pathetic hovels, the flocks of sheep, the poultry, the baker's oven. The infanta leans over the chapel, warms a bird in her hand. She begins to laugh again.

The snow comes down more and more thickly. The roads ascend, very steeply. One morning she's brought out, all wrapped up in an eiderdown embroidered with flowers. She amuses herself by picking and offering them, one by one, to her cradle-rocker and lullaby singer, the gentle Maria. Maria Nieves: Mary Snows. "Maria Nieves, you bring the snows," whispers the infanta.

On another day, she's placed not in her coach but in a sedan chair. There are no more roads. Only steep paths cut into sheer rock.

The empty coaches are brought along, sometimes on mules, sometimes by men on foot. Mme de Montellano is on a litter. She panics. Sweat soaks through her gloves and wets her rosary. Maria Nieves, who has become the goatherds' friend, charts the course.

The infanta's bearers are overjoyed with so light a burden. They could run up the mountainside. She feels their youth and the pleasure she's giving them, and, all pink in her eiderdown, she applauds the precipices.

Charlotte and Pasca

The little king is interested in geography. He loves to look at the large, multicolored map of the infanta's journey. He learns the names of Spanish towns and rivers and mountains. Although he retains them without difficulty, he fails to recognize them when the Spanish ambassador, the Duke of Osuna, reads him an article from the *Gazette*; the ambassador pronounces all the *u*'s in the Spanish way, not the French, and makes all the *r*'s sound like stones rolling along the bottom of a swift-moving stream. Besides, the king soon stops listening. He combs his two Angora cats, Charlotte and Pasca, while the ambassador addresses empty space:

Lerma, December 26, 1721. At noon on the 14th of this month, the Infanta of Spain, having taken her leave of the King, the Queen, and the Prince of Asturias, got into her coach and set out for France. At her side was the Duchess de Montellano, Camarera Mayor. The Infanta's Master of the Horse, the Marquis de Castel-Rodrigo, Prince Pio, and several other Lords who are going to meet Her were in the third coach and in the following coaches. Two hundred Body-guards rode on the flanks and to the rear of the Infanta's coach. She spent that same night in Cogollos, the night of the 15th in Gamonal, and the 16th in Quintanapalla, where she sojourned until the 19th in order to celebrate there the anniversary of the birth of the King, who that day entered upon his thirty-ninth year. Having been informed that smallpox was prevalent in several places along the route, the Marquis de Santa Cruz, High Steward to the Queen, charged with supervising the Infanta's journey, will assure that the said Princess passes only through districts where there is nothing to fear from bad air. News has reached us that Mademoiselle de Montpensier is approaching the frontier, and Their Majesties and the Prince of Asturias, who await her arrival here, spend their afternoons enjoying the delights of the chase in the countryside around the Town. On the 19th, the King's birthday, all was festivity at the Court, and that evening the Prince of Asturias gave a ball that went on until three o'clock in the morning.

Louis XV puts tiny lace bonnets on Charlotte's and Pasca's pretty heads. His little cats are perfect company for him. Why this huge fuss about transporting an infanta?

BAYONNE, JANUARY 1722

Engagement Guns

Mlle de Montpensier is received by the dowager queen of Spain, Maria Anna of Neuburg, second wife of Charles II, the country's last Habsburg ruler, known as *El Hechizado*, "the Bewitched." Louise Élisabeth is quite pale, her eyes watery, her hair unwashed. A cold sore on one corner of her lips deforms her mouth. The dowager queen has the girl sit across from her *in a large chair like her own*. An amazing honor, and a supreme mark of courtesy. The onlookers cannot stop commenting upon it. Louise Élisabeth should be flattered. But she merely wonders how she'll be able to swallow a few mouthfuls of hot chocolate without fainting.

The girl's eyes shift from the exiled old lady, a mass of resentment, to the enormous cup that has been filled with the thick concoction and placed before her. She finds chocolate disgusting. She doesn't like the old lady. She sees in her a woman of another kind. The old kind. Dowager queen. A creature, she believes, without the slightest relationship to herself or to her destiny. She endures the woman's dismal company.

Afterward, she returns to her apartments. The two hunting guns are brought to her, gifts from the Prince of Asturias. Magnificent, finely worked objects, works of art, and of course excellent firearms as well.

"They're for me? Really?" The princess loathes hunting and hasn't the smallest interest in firearms. She spends part of the night making crepes with her ladies.

The dowager queen, who declares herself delighted with their conversation, comes to see the girl in person, bearing gifts. For Louise Élisabeth: a ring, a case, a watch, and a snuffbox of gold and diamonds with a miniature portrait of Doña Maria de Neuburg. For the prince: a sword, a diamond-studded cane, and another cane made of porcelain embellished with gold, but with no ribbon, so that the princess herself can choose the color. All these gifts will be packed up, together with the engagement guns.

PHEASANT ISLAND,
JANUARY 9, 1722

"When will we get there? And what about the pheasants, are they still far away? What's the surprise they have for me?"

The cortege has passed the Pyrenees. It's no longer snowing. For the last few leagues before they reach the stretch of the Bidasoa River that marks the borderline between Spain and France, the infanta and her retinue progress to the accompaniment of energetic dancing. She's been given a little tambourine decorated with ribbons of every color. She beats her instrument to the rhythm of the trumpets, drums, tambourines, viols, and flutes that play a wild music of welcome for her.

"When will we get there? And what about the pheasants?"

After all the jolting, the rain, the mud, the snow, the Pyrenees, the fits of rage, and the outbursts of contentment, the infanta's tambourine finishes off the ladies who are her companions.

When the cortege comes to a complete stop, they call for smelling salts and groan about their physical pains. The Basques accelerate the music and the dancing. "These are devils," the ladies murmur, signing themselves and feeling worse by the minute. The infanta runs toward the Bidasoa, holding her tambourine in her outstretched hands, brandishing it high in the air and repeating, "Bidasoa! Bidasoa!" a name she finds enchanting. The river, swollen with snowmelt, exhibits the violence of a mountain torrent. "And the pheasants?"

They're busy preparing the great ceremony of the exchange of princesses.

By evening, Mariana Victoria has sung so much and run so much and been feted so much that she nods off without having to be told a story. In her sleep, she keeps a firm hold on her tambourine. It jingles softly from time to time.

Not far away, on the other side of the river border, Mlle de Montpensier, having been prescribed a decoction to gargle with, throws it in the face of the chambermaid who brings it.

January 9 begins for both princesses in the darkness of early morning. As this wintry day dawns, they're roused from their beds and their dreams, dressed, coiffed, and made up. The infanta is cold and grumbles a little. Mlle de Montpensier is burning up with fever and suffering the tortures of a raging headache. They're brought, each from her side of the Bidasoa River, to Pheasant Island, which lies in midstream. An elegant pavilion has been put up in the very center of the island. Two wings of equal size, one on the French side and the other on the Spanish, join a central salon decorated with wall coverings and canvases painted especially for the occasion. Exquisite pieces of furniture, masterpieces of the art of woodworking, have been made in both Saint-Jean-de-Luz and Paris, or indeed borrowed from the furniture storehouse at the château of Versailles. Boat bridges provide access to this enchanted pavilion, whose sole function is to be passed through.

Large crowds have formed on both riverbanks.

A pause to freshen the princesses' makeup — four rouged crescents, one on each cold little cheek — and the exchange ceremony, directed by the Marquis de Santa Cruz for Spain and the Prince de Rohan-Soubise for France, is about to begin. The salon is divided by a central line symbolic of the border that the two princesses must cross. It's high noon; it's time.

The infanta, coming from Spain, and Mlle de Montpensier, coming from France, step onto the floating bridge simultaneously. Louise Élisabeth, pallid and weak in the knees. Mariana Victoria, on the alert: watching for pheasants.

They advance toward each other: the future queen of France, looking determined, accompanied by Mme de Montellano, not yet recovered from her terrors, and by Maria Nieves, simply adorned with a few silk flowers stuck in her hair; the future queen of Spain, looking ill, accompanied by the beaming Mme de Ventadour. Their feet sink into the plush carpet, embroidered with the arms of the Borbones of Spain and the Bourbons of France. This diverts the infanta, making her forget the question of the pheasants. And so she amicably approaches Mlle de Montpensier, who tries hard to put up a good front.

They've reached the borderline.

They embrace affectionately.

They're about to cross the line; the thoroughly Spanish princess will find herself in France and the thoroughly French princess in Spain, uprooted from their origins, separated from their servants and their ladies-in-waiting, cut off from everything that could bind them again to their parents. Their past is a foreign country. The Prince de Rohan-Soubise and the Marquis de Santa Cruz unroll their pompous speeches. The two princesses have been instructed to smile upon each other and upon their parallel destinies: the French princess is going to marry Don Luis, heir to the throne of Spain; the Spanish princess is going to marry King Louis of France. Could a more perfect symmetry be imagined? Mlle de Montpensier bids farewell to the House of France, and the infanta is taken away from the House of Spain. The ritual progresses as flawlessly in reality as it did on paper. But at the moment when she's separated from Maria Nieves, the infanta bursts into howls of protest, goes into spasms, loses her breath. She writhes on the floor, right on the borderline. She catches her breath a little and starts howling again.

The attendees consider, without daring to touch, this bundle of rage and despair. The infanta's going to die. It's within her capabilities. And so, forced to choose between the death of the infanta and a breach of protocol, the directors of the ceremony, although viscerally invested in maintaining the ritual intact, resign themselves to saving the infanta, or in other words to giving in to her.

The infanta will keep Maria Nieves with her. She will set foot in France, she will cross the line, hand in hand with her sweet cradle-rocker and lullaby singer, the magnificent

young brunette nursemaid whose flower-bedecked hair has
come undone in all the agitation. What the infanta wants,
she wants badly, observes Mme de Ventadour. Meanwhile,
the audience can't take their eyes off the nursemaid.

Several gold-fluted columns, standing at intervals, decorate the salon. The infanta and Maria advance a very little
way into the carpet territory of France before coming to a
stop before one of the columns. Fat tears are still trickling
down the infanta's face, but she's beaming with joy.

Complete silence descends upon the salon. With a single,
uniform movement, the entire company makes a deep bow.

The little girl expresses her thanks as she has seen her
mother do, with a benevolence that in no way diminishes
the distance between the queen and her subjects, and then
she introduces her indispensable companion: Maria Nieves.
"Marie Neige," the child translates for the benefit of the
French, who are melting with desire.

The ritual is reestablished, symmetry has regained its
rightful place: the exchanged princesses turn toward each
other with a final gesture of farewell.

Then the infanta resolutely sets out across the French half
of the carpet territory, and Louise Élisabeth does the same
across the Spanish half of the carpet territory.

They cross the boat bridges in opposite directions. The
weather has turned fine. Providence receives thanks. The
exchanged princesses gleam in the sunlight. Standing on
opposite banks in the chilly air coming off the swift-flowing
river, their subjects acclaim them. People stretch out their
hands to touch the princesses' garments, as if to touch holy
relics.

❧ II ❧
First Steps on Foreign Soil

LERMA-MADRID,
JANUARY–FEBRUARY 1722

The Princess of Asturias Belches Thrice

Mlle de Montpensier's people are returning to Paris. Her cortege will form up again, just as before, except now the infanta will occupy her place. Mlle de Montpensier herself sets out at the head of what was the infanta's cortege. The French princess is surrounded exclusively by Spanish courtiers, men-at-arms, and servants. The fact that her entourage — her world — is leaving her elicits only a weak reaction from Louise Élisabeth. The inside of her throat is an open wound, her temples throb. She lies across her carriage seat; her only nourishment is orange quarters. Her entourage could add some supplementary stops to her journey and thus make the rest of it easier for her. Instead they do the opposite: in the name of haste, even planned stops are skipped. She covers in ten days the distance that the infanta traversed in thirty-five.

The areas where smallpox is raging have spread. It would be prudent to skirt them, as was done in the infanta's case.

Out of the question! Since the princess is already sick, one may as well plunge right into the epidemic. What difference does it make if such a proceeding risks the lives of those in her cortege? And in any case, there's no tricking the will of God.

If the journey to the border was exhausting, the return trip has more than its share of nightmares. "Such a tiresome inconvenience!" the ladies-in-waiting exclaim as they cross the Pyrenees again, their feet wrapped in blanket rags, like the poorest of the poor. Fortunately, these roads of adversity will not extend beyond the ducal palace at Lerma, where the festivities, balls, hunts, and high Masses have not ceased since the infanta's departure.

At her own departure, Mlle de Montpensier was rather pretty; she's much less pretty when she arrives. She's got a rash on her face, over the last several miles she's been vomiting continually, and her lips produce neither a word nor a smile. Prince Luis doesn't seem to notice that anything's amiss. He greets her joyfully, as do the king and the queen. Only Saint-Simon, still a little weak from his recent bout of smallpox but as keen as ever in his judgment, perceives the gravity of the situation. Louise Élisabeth is depressed beyond endurance and bent on destruction: so what if she's sent back to Paris? She can only be better off there! Her meeting with her betrothed has confirmed her apprehensions. The Prince of Asturias has the same effect on her as a bat. His thin, spindly body, his long, ashen face, his invisible lips, his gray eyes — she doesn't like anything about him. And a baby bat, to boot, because the worst surprise in a collection of bad surprises is that Don Luis is quite short.

Mlle de Montpensier is offered sweet Malaga wine, almond cakes, baskets of fruit pastes made from quinces and candied angelica stems, stuffed pancakes, cream concoctions sweeter than sugar. She has but one desire: to be left in peace. She says no to the sweets and no to the festivities. The king and queen pull faces and turn away. Don Luis contemplates his promised bride with tears in his eyes.

Saint-Simon is aware of the danger: Louise Élisabeth is capable of continuing to refuse for a long time, a very long time. "This nasty brat's a demon of negativity," Saint-Simon says to himself as he orders a hot, lemon-flavored drink for her. The royal wedding and its aftermath are of capital importance. The ambassador extraordinary thinks it his duty to intervene, and he intervenes in a categorical manner, according to a concept of staging and direction that derives from his experience at the court of Versailles. So that the marriage may be considered a fait accompli, so that the union may be considered definitive, the young married couple is enjoined to get into a regal four-poster bed together immediately after the religious ceremony and to lie there, propped up on pillows and holding hands, while the court, the entire court, passes in front of them. Grandly attired, the courtiers, with measured steps, file past the conjugal bed of the future king of Spain and his wife. The Princess of Asturias, bulging-eyed and trembling from head to foot, watches this parade of mummies. One after another, the courtiers—the men, in accordance with the custom of the country, are all dressed in black—make a reverence in front of the royal bed; their procession resembles nothing so much as a ceremony of condolences.

After the last witnesses have passed, the prince wishes to take advantage of the situation; his tutor, the Duke de Popoli, removes his bride from his hands just as he once removed her portrait and obliges the prince to rise from the bed. The boy can't hold back his tears. The voice of his father, who has never postponed sexual gratification for more than a quarter of an hour, sternly reminds him that the marriage is not to be consummated until 1723. He must therefore restrain himself for another year, and with a girl unlikely to inspire prenuptial liberties.

The *Gazette*, by contrast, describes much more harmonious proceedings:

> On the 20th day of this month, the Princess d'Orléans arrived at the Palace at around two o'clock in the afternoon. The King, the Queen, and the Prince of Asturias, who were dining at the time, left the table and went to meet the Princess at the gate of the Palace Court. Their Catholic Majesties escorted her to the apartment prepared for her, and after a few hours of repose, she was brought with the Prince of Asturias into a hall where an altar had been raised. There Cardinal Borgia, with the customary ceremonies, received their mutual promises and gave them the Nuptial Benediction. That evening there was a magnificent supper, and after the supper a ball. Four stools had been placed in the ballroom: one for the Papal Nuncio, another for the Duke de Saint-Simon, another for the Marquis de Maulévrier, and the last for the Vidame de Chartres, who is recovering from an illness. After the ball the Prince of Asturias was undressed at the door of the bedchamber in which the Princess was undressed in the presence of the Queen. When the Princess

was in the bed, the Queen escorted the Prince of Asturias
to her. The Duke de Popoli took up a position beside the bed
on the Prince's side, and the Duchess de Montellano on the
Princess's side. Then the bedchamber doors were opened and
the lords and ladies of the Court allowed to enter the room.

Louise Élisabeth is eventually escorted back to her apartment, not only sick but now also shocked; nonetheless,
the messages sent by the successively exchanged, married,
undressed, and exposed princess hew to the official line, at
least in their contents. Let's stay close to her while, fighting
her illness as well as the rules of orthography, she writes a
letter to her father:

> On the day befor yestarday, the king, the Quene and the
> prince came to see me, but I hadd not yet arrived here; on the
> followwing day I arrived and was married the same day, how-
> ever, there are still serremonies to do to-day. The King and
> the Queen treet me very well, as for the prince, you have all-
> reddy hurd enugh about him. I remane with very depe respect
> Your very homble and obedent dauter Louise Élisabeth.

Let's stay close to her out of a kindness she's not accustomed to, out of sympathy for her youth and for her solitude
as she enters the reign of disaster.

The next day there's a hunt and a grand ball. The princess
doesn't show herself. She refuses to appear at the ball given
in her honor. Her condition worsens. She has swollen gan-
glia. The Lerma–Madrid trip is a replay of her suffering on
the way from Bayonne to Lerma.

In Madrid she does as she did in Lerma: she goes to none of the balls given in her honor. She says no, no, and no. ¡No! She refuses, she opposes. She thrusts her head under the bedclothes. She barricades herself behind a wall of silence. The truth is that in addition to everything else she's as sick as a dog. Even if she wanted to, she wouldn't be able to budge from her bed. She will not show herself, she will not dance. The prince is frightfully disappointed. This refusal to attend a ball strikes him as a terrible thing. For reasons of etiquette, he's only ever danced with his stepmother, Elisabeth Farnese, the sole woman whose rank is comparable to his, and only his wife can free him from that fatal partner. The king and queen don't hide their vexation. They think about having the marriage annulled. It's been discovered that the Princess of Asturias has two very inflamed glands in her neck, her throat is swollen, her fever won't go down, her spots are multiplying. She's inherited her father's infected blood, her parents-in-law say. They have but one desire: to reject this damaged creature, this creature of Shame. Infected with a venereal disease. They've been deceived about the quality of the merchandise. Elisabeth Farnese calls her daughter-in-law "the Goiter Girl."

Saint-Simon thus has all the more reason to congratulate himself on his idea for the nuptial ceremony, on how it firmly sealed the marriage by a public exhibition of the young couple in bed together. He has succeeded in his embassy. The king and queen are pleased to pay attention to him, the prospect of his return to France lies before him, he looks forward to the benefits that will accrue to him from this mission. He expatiates at length upon the beauty of the event: the reunion of the two branches of the House of Bourbon, a subject that inspires him. But he himself ramifies in two directions. He's under no illusions as to the Princess of Asturias. That little girl—a mere twelve and a half years old but a daughter of France and, some day, the queen of Spain—gets on his nerves. She's a creature who exhibits nothing but "the sullen, dismal temperament of a dull and empty-headed child." He can't believe his ears when he hears her first remark on the customs of the Spanish court. One of the privileges of the grandees of Spain is that they may keep their hats on their heads in the presence of royalty. A grandee of Spain does not uncover himself. Who doesn't know such a thing as that? Yet, on the occasion of the Te Deum given to honor her arrival on Spanish soil, the Princess of Asturias asks the following question: "These gentlemen aren't taking off their hats—is it raining?" The shame! The embarrassment! But the "dull and empty-headed child" is capable of much, much worse!

Shortly before setting out on his return journey to France, Saint-Simon asks the princess to be so kind as to allow him to bid her farewell. He will transmit whatever messages she wishes to send to her parents. Louise Élisabeth receives him in a beautiful hall and in accordance with proper decorum. She's standing under a dais, with the ladies on one side of her and the grandees on the other. The red blotches on her morbidly swollen face are accentuated by a layer of makeup. For a headdress, she's chosen to wear a large diamond star with a feather sticking up out of it. She grants Saint-Simon leave to present his compliments. And he's off:

I made my three reverences and spoke my compliments. I then paused, but in vain, for she said not one word in reply. After some moments of silence, as I wished to give her matter for a response, I asked her what communications she had for the King, for the Infanta, for Madame, and for their Highnesses the Duke and Duchess d'Orléans. She looked at me and belched loudly in my face. The sound echoed around the room, and my surprise was so great that I remained speechless. A second belch, as noisy as the first, followed. At this I could no longer keep my countenance and lost all power of repressing my laughter. Turning around and casting my eyes to the right and the left, I saw that all had their hands over their mouths and that their shoulders were shaking. At last a third belch, even louder than the first two, threw all present into confusion, and put me to flight together with my suite, amid shouts of laughter all the more raucous for having broken through the restraints which everyone had striven to maintain. Spanish gravity was thoroughly disconcerted, all was disorder, no reverences, and everyone, fainting with laughter, escaped as best he could, while the Princess, for her part, remained serious. Those belches were the only answers she made me.

What further answer was needed? The princess, belching in his face, had resoundingly disgorged her marriage.

A EUPHORIC PASSAGE
THROUGH FRANCE,
JANUARY–FEBRUARY 1722

The queen of France, coddled by Marie Neige, idolized by Mme de Ventadour, and surrounded by her court of dolls, marionettes, and puppets, begins a triumphal journey. She's the queen-infanta, in fact, for fastidious labor to determine the proper protocol in her case has produced a booklet, *Report on the Question of Giving the Infanta the Title of "Dauphine,"* which stipulates that although the Spanish have referred to the infanta as "the queen of France," for the French she will be "the queen-infanta," a title that she inaugurates. In the optimism of the moment, nobody pays any attention to what seems to be only a nuance, especially since in France she'll continue to be given, most often, the title of queen—and it's indeed like a queen that she's treated at every stage of her journey.

Her tender age increases the people's enthusiasm. It's as though, impervious to the ridicule of history and its verdict of absurdity, they see nothing less than fabulous in the idea of having a child for a queen. Marie Anne Victoire, Mariana Victoria, Mariana, Mariannina, Mariannine dances comfortably through the collective delirium. Approval of her is unanimous. She seduces everybody along her route with the innate coquetry of little girls, that natural premonition of the workings of desire, and with the irresistible way she alone has of playing the queen for real. On the day after the exchange ceremony, the Prince de Rohan-Soubise is impressed: "The infanta is infinitely pretty and looks very regal and resolute." M. de Lambert, a noble of the House of France, admires: "Everything about her is lovable, including her sulks." But it's Mme de Ventadour who finds herself literally captivated by the charm and intelligence of the little queen consigned to her care: "She's filled with graciousness and kindness toward me...It is to be feared that she'll turn all our heads with admiration of her." The letters that Mme de Ventadour writes to the king and queen of Spain tirelessly develop the theme of her raptures. She loves the infanta so much she could eat her up with kisses and squeeze her breathless. If the duchess writes so often, it's as much to pour out her feelings as it is to give news. Her missives, filled with trivial anecdotes and innocent details of daily life, should be read in the light of her affection. How the infanta sleeps, how she eats, how she has "transports of joy that last the whole long way," how she cuts short a militia review to return to her puppet theater; nothing leaves Mme de Ventadour indifferent.

January 10, St-Jean-de-Luz
Our Queen slept marvelously well. We're all enchanted by her. Every now and then she asks for her nanny and sometimes cries, but that never lasts more than a moment. I have her nurse give her everything necessary for her to grow accustomed to her state. Which she will do quite soon. This

morning she kissed the King's portrait and yours, Madame, and ordered me to be sure to give you her compliments.

January 31, Bordeaux
I have nothing but good news to relate to Your Majesty concerning her dear little Queen. Last night she had a toothache again, but the reason she gives for it is charming: she hadn't eaten any jam in the previous three days. Otherwise, she sleeps soundly for nine consecutive hours, with unparalleled cheerfulness... There's no sort of delight that hasn't been imagined for her, and the city of Bordeaux has outdone itself in magnificence to welcome her. Every citizen wishes to see her, we are sometimes smothered, but we must let them have the satisfaction of seeing her because they make such an effort to do so. The King my master has sent word that he's afraid I love her more than him; nevertheless, he says, he's not cross... I do not doubt that the Princess of Asturias will succeed marvelously, as she has a great deal of wit, but I assure you, Madame, we French have not lost in the exchange.

...to reassure you of our little Queen's good health. She is bearing the journey marvelously well, everyone is delighted with her, sometimes she cries for Doña Louisa but then we bring her into the royal carriage, she gives her something to eat and is pleased to have me share this honor with Doña Louisa...

She will not wear even so much as a snood on her hair at night and does not like to be combed. I'm not curling it yet. In front, her poor hair has suffered from being on the road...

When I want her to drink something, there has to be a toast to the health of her papa the King and her *maman*.

She drinks to her parents' health, to that of the king of France, to her own. Her refrain is no longer "When will we get there?" Now it's "The king my husband, will he play with me?"

After Bordeaux (where she passed under a triumphal arch representing the Duchess de Ventadour depicted as Virtue and Marshal de Villeroy as Mentor), Mariana Victoria continues on through Blaye, Ville-Dieu, which she likes very much ("At first she said that we would like it there because it's the house of God, and then she ordered her chaplain to make the evening prayers long and the Mass longer than usual, and all this with the graces that are hers alone," notes Mme de Ventadour), Châtellerault, Tours-au-Château, Clermont, Montlhéry, Notre-Dame-de-Cléry, Orléans, Chartres…The roads are even more potholed and rutted than they were during Mlle de Montpensier's passage. "The Infanta continues on her journey in perfect health. Bad roads and the rigors of the season are causing her to make more frequent stops along her route than were planned," the *Gazette* informs its readers. Furthermore, the stages of the infanta's cortege must be different from Mlle de Montpensier's, because the latter's progress left so many outstanding debts! But Mariana Victoria rises above fatigue and wintry weather. A miracle, people say, surprised at her endurance. This "miracle" is rendered possible by the continual euphoria of her journey, by a golden halo that settles on her wherever she appears, on her blond hair, dry and limp from so much travel, on her pale forehead, on her vigorous little figure. The triumphal arches, the banners fluttering in the wind, the fanfares, the acclamations infuse her with incredible energy. She grows accustomed to her nomadic existence. She no longer feels lost at night; she's learned to re-create, every evening, a room made to her measure. She has reference points placed here and there in the immense spaces where she sleeps: some candles, a chair, an open parasol, pictures of her parents. Wherever she spends the night, she has the portrait of Louis XV hung over the head of her bed. Every evening, he's the last sight she sees. Carmen-Doll, insomniac, tense, with big red eyes as transparent as glass marbles, and Rita-Doll, round, chubby-cheeked, with a plaited wool wig, a doll you can trust, are posted as sentinels. Thus the infanta delimits spaces on the other side of which she's no longer at home. But on this side — and this is what interests her — everything's under her control. "My house," she says, after going down the corridors of her imagination and stepping over thresholds visible to her eyes alone. She invents as many nests for herself as there are pauses in her migration. Mme de Ventadour remains at her side, in the same room, and her cradle-rocker, the young, voluptuous, good-humored Marie Neige, is always within earshot. Mariana Victoria sleeps "with unparalleled cheerfulness," as her governess writes. And her waking is the same as her sleeping.

Whether in or out of bed, the infanta continues to feel the swaying of the coach in her body, a pitching and tossing that doesn't stop and keeps her slightly dizzy.

The "miracle" takes place because for the queen-infanta, the ardor of her people and the extraordinary festive radiance of her passage through France shine like a magnification of the ardent, unconditional affection her governess lavishes upon her. All along the way, Mme de Ventadour points out things to her young charge—the sky, a seagull, a few boats, a house, the road, some cows, a turkey, a mill, and so forth—and names them in French. She says her own name, Ventadour. The fascinated infanta repeats it. She hears it like the promise of a magical sojourn, endlessly open to the *vent d'amour*, the wind of love: "I will be good and obey Maman de Ventadour. She loves me very much, and I love her too, also I thank you for the pretty fans and the rosary. I am sending you some sachets. My health is very good."

The mean-spirited could point to a few hitches. In Bordeaux, the infanta's coach crashes into the large entrance gate of the city hall (a shock largely compensated for by a visit to Château-Trompette, the fireworks show over the Garonne River, the bonfires in all the streets, and the precious "Naval Palace" in miniature presented to her by the citizens of Bordeaux; there she also sees oysters for the first time and speaks to them because they're alive. But once the conversation has begun, swallowing one of them is out of the question!). In Chartres, she can't stop herself from crying out in horror at the ugliness of the bishop. But it's principally in Étampes, twenty miles or so from Paris, that things really do not go well. The event is recounted in a detailed report on the "passage of the Queen-Infanta." She is to stay at the Three Kings Inn, and the streets have been paved and covered with sand for her entrance. Desgranges, the master of ceremonies, halts the coach in which the infanta is riding with Mmes de Ventadour and de Soubise. The mayor, in the company of all the representatives of the bourgeoisie, some former aldermen, and officers, wearing their robes and coats and great white collars, declaims his speech:

> "Madame, He who holds the days of kings and queens in His hands today brings us the opportunity to assure you of our most humble respect and to bow in reverence before Your Majesty; at the same time, please allow us to say that the most remote centuries teach us that many persons of your rank destined to wear a crown at an age as tender as yours have made their people happy; we hope that you will do the same for us. I perceive that we tremble at the sight of a queen whose years are so little advanced, because we believe our happiness is still far removed from us; but reassure us, and let us be persuaded that the mere smile of a queen still in her cradle, so to speak, carried in her governess's arms, can exert more power over the mind of a king than the most courteous, the most energetic speeches. We beg Your Majesty to be so kind as to accept the present we offer You as the sole sign of our entire submission."

Whereupon the gentlemen of the town tendered their gift, which was a large wicker basket in the form of a litter covered with carpeting and gilt paper...in the middle of which was a cake pyramidal in shape and figuring four dolphins, and above it a crown with the arms of France and Spain painted in gold; around the base of the pyramid were cookies, different sorts of pies, fruit pastes, liquid jams, quince jelly, marzipan, sponge biscuits, sugarplums of various kinds, oranges, lemons, the most exquisite fruits of every type, divers liqueurs, and the whole in general worthy of being presented to a queen and well and symmetrically arranged in the litter, all of it sent from Paris. Gifts of trout, live pikes, and crayfish were also presented separately from the present.

The present was placed on the ground by order of the Infanta, who, after examining it carefully and finding it very beautiful, as did all the Court, grasped the crown and, wishing to take it in her arms, dropped it on the ground, where it broke into many pieces; and then she took the little banners that adorned the litter and gave them out, one by one, to several persons, saying that it was for the war.

Apart from making some false moves and trying some questionable initiatives, the infanta also has to suffer her share of colds, toothaches, and a series of exhausting ceremonies. But nothing very dramatic; her exhilarating trajectory absorbs all incidents. There are no more black pigs on the road, and at the end of it there's her king of diamonds, awaiting her arrival.

MADRID, FEBRUARY 1722

The Infected Blood of the Orléans Family

Louise Élisabeth is better. Her illness is harmless. The demands for her presence at balls, hunts, and suppers begin again. She continues to refuse everything. She says she likes to go to bed early and get up likewise, which puts her out of phase with the activities of the court and indeed of the country. At mealtimes, she systematically claims to have already eaten, and this is no lie, for she shares a family trait particularly striking and repugnant in her mother, namely that of eating anywhere and at any time, and of eating to make herself ill. Her older sister, the Duchess de Berry, was a champion in this field. They "guzzle" and "gobble," to use the terms employed by their grandmother, the Princess Palatine. That lady, always attentive to questions of proper dress and respect for traditional forms, recounts an incident involving the Duchess de Berry, who on the day after her marriage, at a supper given in her honor at Versailles, "guzzled" and "gobbled" such quantities of food and drink that she had to leave Louis XIV's table and run to vomit in the anteroom. Shortly afterward, still according to the Princess Palatine, her granddaughter was afflicted by a malady:

> The Duchess de Berry suddenly fainted away; we thought it an attack of apoplexy, but after the Duchess de Bourgogne sprinkled vinegar on her face, she regained consciousness and was immediately seized by violent bouts of vomiting. Nothing surprising about that: for two hours straight, while at the play, she had never stopped eating all manner of horrors — caramel peaches, glazed chestnuts, green currant candy, dried cherries with abundant lemon juice — and then at table she ate fish and drank the whole time...Today she's alert and she feels well again, but one day she will make herself quite sick with her gluttony.

It's a habit of gluttony that doesn't consist simply in overindulgence, but in stuffing herself because of a morbid need to regurgitate everything; in gobbling so much she could burst.

Now that people are reassured about Louise Élisabeth's health, they put up with her whims. She doesn't want to appear at table or at the ball — well, that's not serious. She's very distracted at Mass and doesn't have the best rapport with her confessor, who is however the most charitable of men — that's more serious, but still tolerable. On the essential point, the determination that *she doesn't have smallpox*, the king and queen are immensely relieved. And even more so the prince her husband, the boy-bat. Her in-laws' fear that she would contaminate their descendants with "infected blood" has been assuaged. Louise Élisabeth has practically never left her bed since she arrived at the Alcázar. Entrenched in the dark depths of an apartment she hasn't yet investigated in detail, she exploits her illness as long as possible to prevent her husband — and even more the king and queen — from paying her a visit. In order to make her attitude very clear, she instructs one of her physicians to inform her new family that she's not afraid they'll catch a smallpox rash from her, *she's afraid of catching a rash from them.* "Look at the state they've put me in," she says, lifting up her chemise and exposing her slender body, which is still covered with traces, still "reddened" here and there. The physician doesn't dare transmit the message. Like everyone else, he trembles before the imperious Elisabeth Farnese. But some well-intentioned persons convey the message in his stead. The ill will Elisabeth Farnese feels toward "the Goiter Girl" is redoubled.

Louise Élisabeth has made friends with some of the maidservants. They're the ones she rings for when nocturnal tasks need doing, after those crises during which she tosses her medicine vials and whatever else in her chamber displeases her out the window. This makes an infernal noise when the objects shatter on the paving stones of the courtyard; the people on the floor below hers shrink from the sound and go back to sleep. Instructions along the lines of "Make sure that's all right with the Princess of Asturias" are no longer questioned. The princess is convalescing, and her appetite's returning.

The king and queen, after a hunt in which they've killed an entire family of boars, parents and piglets, have part of the kill prepared for their daughter-in-law. Louise Élisabeth is sent some baby boar stew. Disgust—no longer, as formerly, swollen glands—prevents her from swallowing. The animals' dark blood won't go down her throat, but will soon go through the window. The prince has chosen to accompany the royal meal with a gift: a third hunting gun. He comes to offer it in person, and Louise Élisabeth thinks he's prepared to fire the weapon by way of obliging her to confess she's cured.

PARIS, MARCH 1722

"I love him with all my heart" (Mariana Victoria)

On Sunday, March 1, after a journey of more than two months, the infanta's cortege is arriving at its destination. Before they reach Paris, there's a planned overnight stay in the Château de Bercy, where the regent and his son the Duke de Chartres are waiting for her. It's a bad day, rainy and windy. Fat drops of watery mud spatter the windows of the coach. Inside, Mariana Victoria, wrapped up in a woolen shawl, is bawling. She's got a bad toothache, too bad for her to be able to play the heroine and give her father the gift of her suffering. The child is taken out of the coach and presented to the regent, who rejoices that she's made the trip safely. He doesn't so much as look at the weepy, struggling little thing. In any case, his sight is getting worse, a problem that renders reading difficult and makes him fearful of going blind. He bows in the direction of the wails and instructs his son to say a few words of welcome. The oaf pronounces two or three banalities about his complete accord with the paternal emotions hitherto expressed and with the unanimous joy of France upon seeing Her Majesty. He speaks of a medal engraved in honor of herself and the king and recites its Latin inscription. What in hell's the use of that, the boy thinks, he may as well recite it in Chinese, but all at once the little girl, whom a tooth cavity has been tormenting for days, no longer feels any pain. She grows calm, smiles, bursts out laughing. The Duke de Chartres, nineteen years of age, has been endowed with a peculiarly unstable voice, which features sudden leaps from deep tones to shrill pipings, from the high-pitched to the gravelly, as though a mature man, a chirping girl, a quavering oldster all coexisted in him. This isn't the normal voice break (for which he's too old); it's like someone divided into several persons. The disparate voices are triggered by a mechanism over which their host has no control. Gossip suggests that the cause of nature's joke on the duke can be explained by the boy's precocious familiarity with venereal diseases. The regent couldn't care less about an explanation. He has a musical ear, and his son's composite voice exasperates him. It makes him feel greater aversion toward the boy. Its effect on the little girl, by contrast, is magical. "Again!" she says, eager for the Duke de Chartres to keep talking to her with those voices that seem to jostle one another in him.

The Duke de Chartres would prefer to remain silent. Out of the question, replies Mme de Ventadour, firmly but respectfully. She's found a way of calming the infanta, as exploitable as her fascination for Los Trufaldines — the troupe of Italian comic actors whose lodgings were a few steps from the Alcázar in Madrid — and she's not going to let it pass. Supported by the regent, Mme de Ventadour arranges for the Duke de Chartres to sit at the infanta's bedside and say to her whatever comes into his head. "Again, again!" the infanta implores him. Her laughter echoes through the big house.

The following day, after kissing her king's portrait, the infanta goes to meet him. The interview takes place at Grand-Montrouge. She's wearing a silver and sea-green dress trimmed with fur and adorned with a collar and clusters of rubies. The king is there to welcome her at her carriage door. Someone opens it; she steps down. According to a contemporary report: "The Queen falls on her knees to greet the King, and the King himself kneels as he raises her up." Red as a cherry, the king says, "Madame, I am delighted that you have arrived in good health." The infanta rises to her feet. Louis XV's beauty takes her breath away. She's never seen anyone who compares with him. Even in her reveries while contemplating her fiancé's image, she's never been able to create a boy so perfect. She's suffused with love. And the feeling that pervades her is the very revelation of joy. She who has just left behind family and country puts herself entirely in the hands of this lord and king whom God has chosen for her. The little girl succumbs with great delight. The sight of the young king—his beautiful eyes, his elegance, his fluid movements—staggers her. An aura of perfection surrounds his first apparition, and that aura will reproduce itself, identically, at every one of her future meetings with Louis XV. He appears, and the ambient light gains in brilliance and warmth. Mariana Victoria feels a strange pang, a pang that merges with the most exalted happiness.

At the same moment—the moment when they see each other for the first time—a bolt, though not of the same passion, transpierces the king. Like his fiancée, he's touched to the quick. He takes her hand, raises her up, kneels down. He has often done this. At the age of twelve, he's already an artist in politeness and the refinements of courtesy. With his youth, and with a grace inherited from his mother, the bewitching Duchess of Burgundy, and developed daily by the Marshal de Villeroy, who will not rest until his charge walks, dances, eats, and rides horseback better than anyone in the kingdom, Louis XV is a combined incarnation of the child-king and courtly love. The infanta's enchantment is understandable. And it would be a fairy tale if the young monarch would succumb to the little girl's charm in like manner...Framed by the door of her carriage, the infanta looks too little to him, even minuscule, but that's not what he registers immediately; no, what strikes and wounds him in that first moment is that she appears before him clasped in Maman Ventadour's arms, plainly *adored* by the woman who, in his heart, occupies the place of his mother. In Maman Ventadour's very greeting he senses the new distance between her and him, he intuits the exclusive, fanatic, blind-to-everything-else way his former governess cares for her "Mariannine." The infanta is stricken with love for her king; the king is laid low by jealousy. As he dreaded, the duchess loves the little princess more than him. Death carried off his real mother, and now the infanta has robbed him of the woman who took his mother's place. He's orphaned again. He feels like crying, feels his face flushing while he pronounces words any automaton could

mouth in his stead: "Madame, I am delighted that you have
arrived in good health."

This welcoming formula may well sound flat, and in any
case banality is surely the order of the day. Since he cannot
choose to remain silent, the boy utters as neutral a sentence
as possible. But to the infanta's ears, saluting her arrival in
good health amounts to recognizing her worth. Arriving
alive is no mean feat, but arriving in good health to boot!
Blow the trumpets! Hail to victory! Let the king's music
sound! Standing next to Louis on one side and Mariana Victoria on the other, M. de Villeroy, the king's tutor, and Mme
de Ventadour, the infanta's governess, exchange a complicit
smile above their charges' heads. They are measuring the
success of their enterprise. M. de Villeroy, still vigorous
and quite the flirt, would like to congratulate Mme de Ventadour, who was once his mistress, more expressly, and to
do so with gestures that would recall their former affection.
After all, they say through their smiles, the little king and
the very little queen are our children.

Below them, the bride and groom are behaving like
windup toys. "Monsieur," "Madame," "Your Majesty." Such
good children, such good conduct. Prints, written reports,
and poems celebrate the idyllic union. The whole country
starts dreaming. The politicians, of course, lend a hand
to this idealizing enterprise. It's important to make sure
nobody questions the perfect world of appearances! Actually, neither the boy-king nor the queen-infanta give a
thought to questioning it themselves. He, because he's been
raised to submit to it, and she, because she believes in it.
But in the invisible recesses of their souls, they're equally

alone and lost, both of them, equally prey to emotions that baffle and ravage them.

Louis XV climbs back into his coach and sets off at once for the Louvre. There he will receive the infanta and escort her to her abode. He looks miserable and angry. Inside the carriage, which he shares with the regent, the Duke de Chartres (all of whose voices remain silent), the Duke de Bourbon, called "Monsieur le Duc," who supervises the boy's upbringing, the Count de Charolais, known for his unbridled licentiousness, and the Prince de Conti, a luxurious aesthete, a lover of art and patron of artists, the king says not a word. M. le Duc observes, as if to himself but loud enough to be heard, "This infanta is certainly an infant!" Nobody comments in return.

The infanta's coach leaves after the king's. The little girl is about to make her solemn entry into Paris. She sits on Mme de Ventadour's lap. On her own lap, she's holding Carmen-Doll, who like her is wearing a silver and sea-green dress and who, like her, stares at the Parisian people. The infanta and her doll are aware of the moment's historical importance. The other dolls also perceive that a page of history is being written. This is to their credit, crammed into a trunk as they are. In the darkness, they must evaluate the event according to the level of sincerity audible in the ovations received. They're difficult to fool, those other dolls, with their painted eyes, their sweet, impassive little faces, their miniature presences, and they'd like to be in Carmen-Doll's place so that they could observe the more or less orchestrated outbursts of cheering, the more or less purchased enthusiasm of the jubilant public, the people who can be found in the front ranks of the spectators at every royal entrance into Paris. Besides the infanta, her governess, and her red-eyed favorite, the other occupants of the carriage are Madame (the Princess Palatine) and the *princesses du sang*, the royal princesses. This is a coach-load with the potential to amuse or to terrify the infanta and her doll. For a second, the child is arrested by Madame's improbable facial features, but she doesn't dwell on them. She's yearning with all her might toward the Parisians, toward the wonders they've created for her, toward the magnificent spectacle of the capital transformed for its queen.

The cortege enters through the Porte Saint-Jacques and heads up the street of the same name, continues past the Petit Châtelet and along Rue de la Lanterne, the Pont Notre-Dame, the Rues Planche-Milbray, des Arcs, des Lombards, Saint-Denis, de la Ferronnerie, de la Chaussetterie, Saint-Honoré, du Chantre... The procession passes under triumphal arches and between buildings whose facades are covered with tapestries and festooned with little lamps. On the Place de Grève, acrobats dance in midair and throw bouquets to the infanta. The ovations are deafening. There's an enormous crowd everywhere she passes. People fight to get closer to her carriage. Bodyguards intervene roughly, so much so that the infanta cries out at the top of her voice, "Oh! Don't beat those poor people who want to see me." And she shows herself, all smiles, blowing kiss after kiss. The Latin inscription on the banners is read and translated for her: *Venit expectata dies, felicis adventus ad Lutetiam* (The long-awaited day has come, the happy arrival in Lutetia). The cortege reaches the courtyard of the Louvre late in the afternoon. Once you've been lifted up on the wings of happiness, there's a good chance you'll stay aloft through what follows, at least for a time; and so the ensuing ceremonies carry the infanta to the upper regions of rapture, for the king is there again, waiting for her. She kneels, he raises her up and kneels: "Madame, I am delighted that you have arrived..." Is this scene going to keep replaying itself over and over? Let it, let it, begs the infanta, aglow with the sacred flame, the child madly in love. She's moving in a world of enchantment. Everything that happens to her from now on she will desire for all eternity.

MADRID, MARCH 1722

Regaled with an Auto-da-Fé

In Madrid, the atmosphere is festive: everyone is thoroughly gratified by the young princess's recovery. People pray, people sing, people dance. There's even been an announcement that Louise Élisabeth is finally going to make a public appearance. And she, who hasn't understood the first thing about what's in store, has agreed. Faced with this sudden display of goodwill, and still hopeful that they've brought a normal — that is, docile — young woman into the family, the king and queen decide to give her a splendid celebration, a purely Spanish treat, an awesome spectacle directed by their supreme artist of terror and votary of death: the grand inquisitor. She rejected the animals' dark blood; she's going to be taught to appreciate the blood of heretics. The planned treat is nothing less than a *general* auto-da-fé, a grand exhibition of the triumph of Christianity. Forty-two years earlier, on June 30, 1680, Louise Élisabeth's aunt, Marie-Louise d'Orléans, first wife of Charles II of Spain, was regaled with a similar extravaganza—as a gesture of welcome, as a rite of initiation, and above all as a way to "cheer up" her husband, *El Hechizado*.

An auto-da-fé? Louise Élisabeth wonders what that could be. Her experience—as a young girl of twelve raised in Paris in an environment only tepidly religious—hasn't provided her with any real notion of what the expression signifies. Philip V enjoins her to listen attentively, to observe and admire the effects achieved by the providential mission of the Holy Office, to share in the exaltation of finding herself suddenly uplifted practically to the grand inquisitor's side, as it were, in his combat against heretics. These words fail to enlighten her. When the day has come and she steps onto the balcony in Plaza Mayor with the king, the queen, the Prince of Asturias, the infantes, and the ladies of the court, she's struck by the gigantic architecture of the Theater of Crime and Punishment that has been erected during the night. Her eyes grow wide. The grand inquisitor's chair, complete with armrests, is raised a little higher than the royal loge, so that he dominates the king. The wide platform awaiting the arrival of the convicted heretics has been built at the same level as the royal balcony, thus allowing its occupants a good view of the different characters in the drama: the officiants, the executioners, and the condemned. An amphitheater for the Supreme Council of the Inquisition also overlooks the platform, and somewhat lower but still perfectly conceived as far as visibility is concerned, there's an amphitheater for the general public. The people must not miss an iota of the horror either, and they must rejoice in it with their masters.

What with fear (enormous), excitement (total), and compassion (minimal), the entire Plaza Mayor is in the grip of a terrible impatience. It makes children fight in the aisles, horses whinny, mules become agitated, and beggars grow bold; a legion of the blind and the crippled, of monsters with fantastic deformities, assails the powerful strutting about the loges. The agitation proliferates, rising from the depths if not the dregs, presenting a briefly tempting invitation to chaos that runs through the Plaza Mayor and which Louise Élisabeth, wedged between her repulsive husband and her resentful mother-in-law, inhales like a heavy scent. It's allowed to go on just as long as necessary, this temptation to rise up, to perish very fast but not without having revolted against the order that has eternally encompassed your annihilation. The uproar is part of the spectacle of the auto-da-fé, of its flamboyant vehemence, of its absolute violence. It's the naive preamble to that spectacle, incorporated so that subservient minds will be all the more indelibly imprinted with the terrorizing image of the Inquisition.

A confused impression of music, of hymns, and of the color yellow. That's what Louise Élisabeth notices first, the yellow of the tunics the condemned prisoners are wearing. The tunic is the *sambenito*, the garment of infamy, made of yellow sackcloth and decorated with two St. Andrew's crosses, one on the back and one on the front. The condemned proceed in order, led by the *reconciliados*, those who renounced their heresy under torture. They're going to get off with a public flogging, and then they'll be exhibited in Madrid, bound and riding on donkeys, each naked back scored with the marks of the whip. Next come the heretics who have been sentenced to prison, followed by those sentenced to the galleys. Finally the prisoners who are the real actors in the drama move forward, the ones who are to be burned at the stake. Burned, but with this nuance of difference, evidence of the tribunal's clemency: some of the condemned, namely those who confessed their crimes after their convictions, will not be burned alive; first they'll be strangled to death. The yellow splotches, those infamous silhouettes, those demon's henchmen, shuffle along, heads bowed, with no sensation in their tortured limbs but the sting of the hot wax that drips onto their hands from their lighted candles.

"That last group, who are they?" the princess asks, pointing to the barefoot prisoners at the end of the procession; each is gagged, and each carries a candle.

"Those are the irredeemable, the ones who persist in their blindness and persevere in their evil, the obstinate, the recidivists, the heretics, the damned. They're the *no-reconciliados*, the unreconciled."

"And what's going to be done to them?"

"They will be burned alive, Your Ladyship."

And accompanying his gesture with a thin smile, the speaker indicates the row of pyres, the accumulations of firewood. He waits for her to express her admiration. She merely nods her head. The prince her husband, adding a bit of detail—is this some special attention paid to her, to her femininity?—declares that there are eleven women in this auto-da-fé, eleven convicted female heretics.

On the evening after the auto-da-fé, while a supper presided over by the grand inquisitor and the king is going forward in the salons of the Royal Alcázar, the smell of the heretics' burned flesh wafts up from the plaza. The common people are encouraged to relish those fumes, to conflate them with the succulent tastes of the grilled meats they're getting ready to consume in the bosom of their family, feeling closer to one another than ever before. For the mixture of affection and resentment that unites them, the everyday realities of birth and death, of toil and want, have all been supplemented and eclipsed by hatred of the heretic, hatred of the Jew. Compassion is one of the devil's temptations; denunciation is the proper course. False converts, witches, libertines, dissolute women, brigands, sodomites, usurers must be tracked down, located, and then denounced—in secrecy and anonymity—to the Inquisition, so that the party may continue, so that the procession of the punished may resume and increase, ever longer and longer, and so that (this never hurts) more confiscated goods may be enjoyed. The people eagerly devour the animal they're feasting on. At intervals, they exchange greasy kisses.

PARIS, SPRING 1722

An Abundance of Duties and Festivities

The king is a twelve-year-old boy of normal size. The infanta, soon to turn four, is rather small for her age. Visually, however, the discrepancy isn't so obtrusive. They're both so beautiful. The child-couple they form gladdens the hearts of all who see them. The king holds his fiancée's hand. He walks at her pace. "The apartments where my great-great-grandmother, Anne of Austria—" he begins. The little girl repeats the name like an echo. "She was a great-great-grandmother to you both," Mme de Ventadour specifies. *But Mme de Ventadour can't be a mother to us both*, the young king thinks to himself. And he continues on his way, as gallantly as possible. He's received the mission of installing Mariana Victoria in her residence. He does so with the same assiduous application he brings to every ceremony. The infanta reads this diligence as the equivalent of her own ardor. She trots along at his side, too excited to look at the apartments that have been renovated to receive her. She sees red, red everywhere, here and there a streak of gold, and that's all. They walk over to a window; someone picks up the infanta and shows her the Seine and its boats. "The Bidasoa?" the child asks, giddy from travel and love. The king returns to his apartments in the Tuileries. The infanta, magnetized by her king, would like to accompany him. The parting kiss has been exchanged, the tutor and the governess have said their goodbyes, it's time for the infanta to leave the king, yet she follows his footsteps. Marshal de Villeroy reacts sternly: "Madame," he says to the pink, distraught little girl, "the king asks that you go no farther, indeed commands you as your lord and master."

The gazetteers pick up the incident: "When His Majesty departed to return to the Tuileries Palace, the Queen-Infanta wishing to accompany the King to the royal coach, His Majesty desired her to remain in her apartments." The expression "lord and master" is judged excessive by the Spanish. The infanta's status, although she's married on paper, is de facto preconjugal and will remain so until she reaches the age of twelve. She's a fiancée whose marriage contract has been signed in advance. As far as the infanta is concerned, what pains her is that her impulse has been thwarted; she has and will have but one desire: to go farther. The terms "lord and master" fill her with delight.

A ball that same evening reunites her with two of the regent's daughters, the Princesses de Beaujolais and de Chartres, both distinctly older than the infanta. She's in high good humor and treats them like children younger than herself. She worries about whether they're tired, holds them by the pleats to keep them from falling. When they leave, she kisses them and declares, "Little princesses, go to your houses, and come see me every day."

The king goes to bed frightfully depressed. The prospect of festivities adds the finishing touch to his despondency. To be sad by yourself is no fun, but to be sad in the middle of a city wildly celebrating your supposed happiness, a city where hundreds of people congratulate you on your good fortune, makes you wish you were dead.

At the same moment, Cardinal Dubois is in his study, dictating the following letter to Elisabeth Farnese in the disgusted boy's name:

> I have just seen with my own eyes, infinitely better than I could have done from descriptions or portraits, how charming the Queen-Infanta is; I am moreover convinced that her charm will grow with each passing day. I have no doubt that Your Majesty will be pleased to learn from me personally the extent of my satisfaction and my joy, for Y.M. would be unable to perceive it amid the imminent festivities, wherein Paris and the Court will vie with one another in celebratory zeal. Expect from me, Madame, the warmest and most affectionate sentiments that a son-in-law can offer you. For them, the Infanta's charms are your assurance.
>
> Louis

At that very hour, the infanta, who has been tenderly tucked into a brand-new bed, is too titillated to notice she's tired. She can't fall asleep. But on that night, the night of her entrance into Paris, there are others who aren't sleeping either. The little queen fires people's imaginations. Starting with the toy merchants. At the Green Monkey on Rue des Arcis, at the Purple Monkey, and even more so at the Royal Chair, on the premises of Juhel, purveyor to the royal children, morale is excellent. A four-year-old queen of France, what a godsend! They can hear the louis d'or clinking at the mere thought of the orders they're going to be assailed with. In these circles, the royal child's passion for dolls is already common knowledge, in the same way that, when such and such a great lady cannot resist jewels, it quickly becomes known. The place reserved for Carmen-Doll has not passed unnoticed.

But also, at the other extreme, as far as you can get from cute, pricey toys, poor children who will never own a toy of any kind are tossing and turning on their pallets; the unprecedented situation — their queen is a little girl — has set them spinning. Is the reign of children at hand? Might not Louis and Mariannine, now in power, bring about their liberation? Poor children, exploited, starved, beaten, the last of the lowliest — are they to be first, as it says in the Gospel? The wind is cold, the darkness total. Hidden in a corner of an attic, or shivering under a bridge or in the doorway of a church or on a building site, they dream awake. The chimney sweeps, the street sweepers, the shuckers and peelers of vegetables, the kitchen hands, water carriers, floor wipers, shoe scrapers; the waiflike spinners, the watery-eyed menders, the unwashed goose girls, the laundresses with chapped hands; the mistreated, clubbed, whipped, trampled, harassed cohort of little beggars and beggaresses — they dream in the darkness with wide-open eyes. Will the world turn upside down? Will the boy-king and the queen-infanta accomplish a swift coup d'état? Is society going to set poor children free from servitude, from the little labor camps where they wear themselves out toiling away everywhere? The born slaves, the unpaid laborers, the infinitely exploitable, the barely surviving gird their rags about them and begin to hope.

The infanta familiarizes herself with the Louvre Palace. In fact, she finds her apartment too small and expresses the fear that her bedchamber won't be able to accommodate the great number of courtiers who are coming to celebrate her. Mme de Ventadour holds her writing hand as she inscribes a letter to her parents: "I have the prettiest things in the world." For her part, Mme de Ventadour adds, she's sometimes concerned because "after a journey of some 400 leagues, it's still necessary to make so many appearances, but she does all that and tolerates it marvelously and is the admiration of all France, our King loves her passionately but he's busy at every moment." It's certain that he won't be coming to play with the infanta, and the ardor she brings to arranging her dolls as she settles in is not something he desires to share.

Once again, the regent has failed to follow the Duke de Saint-Simon's advice. Saint-Simon had advised him to keep the children apart in order to arouse their curiosity about each other, to stimulate a wish to know each other better. He'd suggested that the king continue to live in the Tuileries and that the infanta should be shut up in the abbey of Val-de-Grâce with a severely reduced entourage — no ladies-in-waiting, no officers, no guards. She should be allowed to leave the abbey once or twice a year for a fifteen-minute visit with the king, which he would reciprocate, and she should have no public role. Let her remain mysterious so that her future husband may dream about her. Well, "dream"—Saint-Simon doesn't really go that far. It's enough for him to propose a system of upbringing that will give the boy-king and the queen-infanta the possibility of escaping the unhappiness of knowing each other too well, and of being condemned to mutual boredom, or mutual contempt, or even mutual loathing. Should they see each other often as children—and therefore as weak, error-prone, always ready to do something "childish"—their vision of each other would be forever tarnished, according to Saint-Simon, by the absurdities and imperfections characteristic of extreme youthfulness. His arguments prove utterly fruitless, but at the moment, Saint-Simon couldn't care less. Although ultimately captivated by the Spanish countryside and the Spanish sense of honor, and though he's socially enhanced by the title of grandee of Spain, he's returned to Paris much diminished financially and even reduced to less than nothing. That rascal Dubois has skinned him alive. Saint-Simon's embassy has ruined him. The disastrous state of his finances makes other matters quite secondary, including that of how a slow and sure blossoming of love in the hearts of the future bride and groom might best be arranged.

The infanta has therefore been lodged not in the same palace as Louis XV, the Tuileries, but just next door, in the Old Louvre, which amounts to the same thing. She's occupying Anne of Austria's former apartments, whose renovation has required months of relentless work. Between Anne of Austria's death and the infanta's arrival, those apartments, situated in the gallery directly overlooking the Seine, have never been lived in, except by Louis XV during the summer of 1719, when the Tuileries was in dire need of being cleaned from top to bottom. Apart from that brief interlude, the apartments served as a meeting place for various academies of fine arts and shortly before their renovation for the infanta's use were requisitioned for the so-called *Opération Visa*. Holders of banknotes issued by the Scottish banker John Law were granted a final extension of the deadline for exchanging them — at a loss, of course — for valid currency. It was here that such people were to apply — in the gallery, under the handsome coffered ceilings painted according to the wishes of Anne of Austria. The *Visa* offices must have resounded with cries and serious altercations between the swindled and the government's representatives, between the victims of theft and the thieves' employees.

A few weeks before the infanta's arrival, the *Visa* offices closed. The gallery in the Old Louvre was prepared to receive her. For her, nothing would be good enough. She's lodged on the ground floor (the upper floor being reserved for the numerous domestics in her service), and that's a sign of kindness, or of practicality, since she's thus exempted from having to climb stairs. Between the Louvre and the riverbank, the rectangular garden created by Le Nôtre has been restored. The delicately sculptured flower beds have returned to their original design, and at the extreme eastern end of the garden, the water fountain set in a pretty circular basin is flowing again, refreshing a green arbor adorned by four statues representing "Diana's Companions."

The apartment—doors, drapes, screen—is covered with red damask embellished with gold stripes. The same fabric covers the carved and gilded wooden chairs, the large and small armchairs, the folding stools, the large and small tables. In the bedchamber, there are twin beds: the infanta's, surrounded by a balustrade—which it is forbidden, on pain of lèse-majesté, to touch—and Mme de Ventadour's, with no balustrade; both beds are covered in the same red damask. For the infanta's wardrobe, eight tall armoires have been built, their dimensions contrasting with the "little low stool or kneeler" and the "little oaken prie-dieu, two feet tall, with twisted uprights." The best silversmiths have decorated the silver and vermeil tableware all over with the arms of France and Spain, and flourishing between them the fleur-de-lis. The painter Antoine Watteau's powder boxes, adorned with children at play, represent his final tribute to the fugitive grace of the things of this world.

On Tuesday March 3, the infanta is brought to the ceremonial hall. She spots the king at once; he's standing in the middle of the room with a doll in his hands. She goes up to him and kneels; he raises her up and hands her the doll. The infanta takes the doll and curtsies. The doll's as big as she is, but nothing can hinder her movements at this moment. A charged silence greets the event. The courtiers observe the two children, and especially the doll, with dismay, for the doll is not simply a doll but a baby doll, and a ghostly baby doll at that. It's dressed in princely garments, and the delicate features of its waxen face exactly reproduce those of Louis XV's older brother, the Duke of Brittany and dauphin of France, who died at the age of five from smallpox, the same disease that killed their mother and father. The king, only two years old at the time, cannot remember his brother, but the people on hand recognize him. Looking a bit awkward, the king remains where he is, his hands still on the cumbersome doll, while the people before him restrain their emotion. They see again the delightful little boy who was the Duke of Brittany, and some of them even remember the pathetic incident that occurred on the day following his death: the child's favorite dog climbed the stairs to the tribune where his young master was wont to attend Mass and there in the chapel, in the middle of the religious service, began to howl.

The courtiers stare at the tiny face, the slightly turned-up nose, the big eyes, the round cheeks. Madame nearly faints. Mme de Ventadour would like to cry aloud. Everyone wonders who could have had the idea of making a doll with the late prince's death mask. As for the king and the infanta, they content themselves with going through the ceremonial motions. Mme de Ventadour frees the infanta from the doll. Louis XV and Mariana Victoria take each other's hands and go with great pomp from the Louvre to the Tuileries, where the young king shows his companion the park of his palace. Mme de Ventadour, half-paralyzed, follows close behind them, holding the cadaverous effigy at arm's length.

In Paris it's related that the king has made the infanta the gift of a doll that cost thirty-five thousand livres. The macabre resemblance receives no mention. Those Parisians with a taste for death, in addition to the quite satisfactory number of executions that follow the arrest of Cartouche and often take place at night, have yet another bizarre public spectacle to take in. An eighteen-year-old girl, with an annual income of thirty or forty thousand livres, the most beautiful body, and the loveliest skin, but topped by a death's-head, wishes to get married. She's exhibiting herself near the Porte de Saint-Chaumont. People fight one another to get a look at the girl with the death's-head.

On Wednesday, the infanta, in accordance with the honors due to a queen of France, receives the foreign ministers of various countries, followed by the representatives of the principal institutions and the highest officials of the realm.

On Thursday, it's the parliamentary deputies' turn. At first, miffed at not having been invited to the wedding celebrations, they wished to avoid this audience. They were recalled to their duty and obliged to betake themselves to the Louvre. The representatives of the *Parlement* make a declaration to the little infanta: "The King's letter, Madame, has informed us of your arrival; his example and his order encourage us to offer you the respects that are your due." The infanta responds to these insinuations of hostility with an ingenuous smile. The deputies of the *Parlement* are followed by those of the *Chambre des comptes* (the Court of Accounts) and the *Cour des aides* (the Court of Aid).

On Friday, the infanta receives the deputies of the Great Council; those of the *Cour des monnaies* (the Currency Court); the Duke de Tresme, governor of Paris; and the provost of merchants.

On Saturday, the final day of this implacable program, the infanta receives the rector of the University of Paris and then a delegation from the Académie française. She's favored with a speech both spiritual and erudite, to which she listens while sucking her thumb, with Carmen-Doll lying on a purple velvet cushion at her feet.

All the deputies have been introduced by the Count de Maurepas, secretary of state, and ushered with the usual ceremoniousness by the Marquis de Dreux, grand master of ceremonies. The infanta grants her audiences in Anne of Austria's grand study. On the other side of the partition wall, in an as yet undesignated room, the dolls shut up in the trunk beat on it with their nonexistent fists. They demand: (1) to see the light of day; (2) that the infanta be let alone; and (3) a distribution of *horchata*. Their mouths dried out by the journey, the unhealthy air of Paris, and the dust of the Old Louvre, the dolls hallucinate the delights of the sweet white beverage.

Through ignorance or by choice, the infanta remains deaf to those demands. Now she must cope with an entire week of festivities, as meticulously planned as the endlessly repeated compliments.

On Sunday, March 8, from eight o'clock to midnight, the king gives a ball at the Tuileries Palace, in the so-called Hall of Machines built by Vigarani for Louis XIV. The young king opens the ball. The lords and ladies who aren't dancing sit in the tiers of seats, the lords dressed in cloth of gold and silver, the ladies wearing court dresses and diamonds. Liqueurs and hippocras are served. The infanta wets her lips in a glass of hippocras and makes a thousand faces. Thirty dancers launch into a *branle*, followed by a *menuet à quatre* and then a contredanse. The king dances every dance. The infanta dances with the king. At the end of an hour, she goes off to bed, despite the beginnings of a fairly spectacular tantrum.

On Monday, she's feted with a fireworks display in the garden of the Tuileries. The lighting arrangements are magnificent; the Grand Parterre is illuminated by little lamps, and yews sculpted into wooden candelabras augment the light's effect. The fireworks display seems extraordinary even to the pyrotechnist, who takes fright and runs away.

On Tuesday, the celebrations continue with an immense bonfire and a ball at the Hôtel de Ville. The king, the infanta, the regent, and all the court are there. The people drink to the infanta's health, again and again. In the Hôtel de Ville, some people throw their wigs onto the chandeliers, a tumult breaks out, the boats moored next to the square serve as bordellos.

Wednesday is a day of rest. Mme de Ventadour writes to the king and queen of Spain. She describes the noise and the splendors that have greeted their daughter in Paris. The infanta, still in bed, is watching the latest additions to her collection while they dance. She has her governess write to her brother:

> I got a magnificent reception. I'm delighted that you liked the scented sachet. I do indeed have lots of dolls. I wish you could see their wardrobe and the rest of their pretty furniture. I was very glad to hear that the Princess of Asturias is feeling better.

At this point, the packed dolls foam with anger. They're still waiting to get out of that blasted trunk and drink some *horchata*. Their mouths are as dry as cardboard. They can't even salivate when they imagine the almond taste of the exquisitely thirst-quenching, milklike beverage. The chorus of Spanish dolls threaten to set fire to the French dolls, to their pretty furniture and their sweet little changing room.

On Thursday, there's a Te Deum at Notre-Dame Cathedral, where the infanta touches the hearts of all who approach her. The people want to love her. Witnesses remark on the king's paleness and fatigue, saying his "face looks very bad." That evening, the Palais-Royal is illuminated inside and out by white flambeaux and firepots, and another grand ball lasts until the morning.

On Saturday, a fireworks show at the Palais-Royal. The king and the infanta walk together under the arcades and other structures built for the occasion. A painting at the end of the garden represents the Titans, struck by Zeus's thunderbolt; the two children, the cynosures of the celebration—the king, terribly exhausted, and the infanta, her eyes blinking with sleep—listen to the story of the Titans. The following day, the king and the infanta are allowed to rest, and the regent falls ill. It's said that he became overheated by his fire in the Palais-Royal, unless it was by his mistress.

At the end of the month, the Duke of Osuna, the Spanish ambassador, hosts a celebration of extraordinary magnificence. He has an artificial rock built in the middle of the Seine, and on that rock, directly facing the balcony of the queen-infanta's apartment, a temple supported by many

columns. The first of the temple's four sides represents
Hymen, and in his hands two myrtle crowns, which he holds
out to the king and the queen-infanta. Ceres, Bacchus, and
the Goddess of Peace are painted, respectively, on the other
three sides. A ring of boats illuminated by small lamps surrounds the rock. When the king comes out on the balcony,
the musicians placed on the boats strike up a triumphal concert, which is the signal for a water-joust between gondoliers. Once the combat is over, the temple is burned, which
in turn sets off a fireworks display that lasts nearly an hour.
When the grand finale comes, water and sky reflect a thousand flames back and forth. The Seine glitters and sparkles.
The little girl, the reason for this blaze, cries out in joy at
each rocket, and perhaps also in distress as the temple she
had barely time to glimpse so abruptly goes up in flames.
She pulls the king by the sleeve and points to the blossoming
explosions. If he'd only say something! If he'd make a sign!
She insists: "Oh! Ah! How beautiful it is! Oh! Monsieur,
look!" She rubs herself against him, gets out of her seat, tries
to stretch up to his ear.

At last he pronounces the word "Yes."

Whereupon the radiant child turns to the courtiers and
says, "The king spoke to me! The king spoke to me!"

On the scale of fetes, the infanta has reached the top.

Her fourth birthday is hardly distinguishable amid so many
celebrations. She receives letters and gifts from her parents,
messages from her brothers, more dolls with sumptuous
outfits and furnishings, other toys. The king compliments

her. She hears Mass at his side in the Tuileries chapel. When they leave the chapel, a flight of pigeons takes off, and the king smiles at her. The infanta gathers up that smile like the day's treasure. It crowns her somewhat disparate collection of gifts.

It has rained a great part of the day, but at sunset she's able to look out of a window in the Tuileries and contemplate an astonishing set piece of pink-and-gray clouds, shot through here and there with sunbeams. Even more than this, she admires the king's silhouette as he passes in review the regiment of 160 young people, trained by himself, who perform their soldierly exercises every evening on the terrace of the palace. The regiment is called the Royal Terrace. They see the young king every day. The infanta fiercely envies them. But that's trivial compared to how she feels about the Guards of the Sleeve, the detachment of gentlemen who never leave the king's side during a ceremony and whose duty is to keep their eyes on him at all times. Duty? Can there be a greater pleasure?

Returned from his military obligations on the Tuileries terrace, the king shows the infanta one of his treasures, a singular birdcage: a hamper bound together by silver hoops and filled with all sorts of birds. He reveals nothing of his precocious political activities: his creation of administrative entities — the Department of Freshwater Ports and Harbors, of Terrace Trunks and Chests, of Chicken Coops, and of the Orders of the Salon, of the Medals, of the Mustache, and of the Flag, for each of which he has named grand masters, masters, and assistant masters, and dreamed up complex and varied protocols.

The infanta asks to go crayfishing with the king. The matter must be discussed.

In Paris, as on her journey there, she captivates everyone. Mme de Ventadour writes to the infanta's mother the queen of Spain:

> Even after traveling so long, the Infanta has endured all the fêtes perfectly well...She charms everyone, she attends all the celebrations that have been arranged in her honor as if she were twenty years old. She has had one or two little indispositions, but they have not prevented her from going to everything.

Yes, the infanta goes to everything. She goes with all her heart. In her innocence, in a transport of love.

The king also goes to everything, but he puts as little of himself into it as possible. He is not captivated by the infanta; she's too little, too much of a chatterbox, too exasperatingly cheerful, and the way she's acclaimed by everyone can only add to his antipathy. Not to mention the fact that she began by taking Mme de Ventadour away from him. But maybe all this is only a bad start, a first impression that will correct itself in time. Maybe, in the end, he'll be won over like everyone else. Who knows?

The infanta is interested, the infanta is blithe. In the morning, she gets out of bed dancing and singing and hums while she's being made ready, impatient to throw herself into the new day. She never cries except when she has a bad toothache, or when any attempt is made to curl her blond

tresses. This she unequivocally refuses; there's no way anyone's going to touch her hair, or put a nightcap on her at
bedtime, or decorate her head with flowers and ribbons and
frills during the day. She feels even more strongly about the
bourrelet, the padded, protective head roll, which she regards
as a crime of lèse-majesté. She shakes her hair, bobbing and
weaving in all directions like a doe. She was born to support
nothing on her head but a crown.

Apart from toothaches and hairdressing sessions, everything's blissful for the "future queen–infanta": receiving letters and presents from her parents ("She's always delighted
when Your Majesties and Their Royal Highnesses her brothers are spoken of," her governess writes), opening trunks,
laying out her things, plunging headfirst into her toys
("Rest assured, her trunks are filled with everything she
could want, we hadn't opened them until we reached Paris,
having carried with us whatever she needed for the journey"), playing with her dolls, dressing them, undressing
them, having them served little meals, receiving deputies,
rectors, ambassadors, standing out on her balcony, listening to the boatmen's cries, watching the boats pass, the tree
trunks floating on the Seine, going to Mass in the little chapel adjoining her room, in Notre-Dame Cathedral, in the
royal chapel in the Tuileries, or in the churches of Saint-
Germain-l'Auxerrois, of Val-de-Grâce, of the Feuillants,
of the Daughters of Calvary, of the Ave Maria, of Sainte-
Élisabeth...(she visits the different quartiers of Paris by
going to their churches), walking in her garden. But the
infanta's greatest happiness is to see the king, and to let
others see that they're a happy couple.

She baptizes the baby doll "Louis." On the first evening, not having had time to come up with a better solution, she puts the baby doll in Carmen-Doll's bed (the baby doll doesn't have a good night). The next day, she requests a cradle for "the dauphin Louis." She presents him as her son, *their* son. Although she makes no explicit demand, she expects the courtiers to salute their queen and pay homage to her offspring. And they do it. The courtier's status requires great suppleness, the ability to submit, to bend low before power, to crack your back with bowing, to sweep the ground with the plumes of your hat. The council chamber where Anne of Austria used to hold her audiences is always full of people. They prostrate themselves before the queen of France, they converse seriously about doll-related matters, about mechanical birds, about cockchafers and ladybugs. To what level on the scale of tiny things will she reduce them? At what point will she succeed in turning the Old Louvre into the kingdom of Lilliput? She laughs, acts the clown, plays tag, participates in a masquerade of children disguised as dogs and barks instead of talking for several days thereafter. The embarrassment of the courtiers: Ought they to reply in kind?

The Princess Palatine's Liberties

In May 1722, the Duchess de La Ferté writes: "I cannot let a day go by without paying court to her. When I have not the good fortune of seeing her, I feel I am missing everything. As I have the honor of being the King's godmother, she honors me by calling me her own and does me a thousand kindnesses." Everyone is under Mariana Victoria's spell, or pretends to be, but one person alone truly loves her: Madame, the Princess Palatine. The first time she set eyes on the infanta, Madame recognized the specific genius of the little girl, at once so "lofty" and so funny, and felt immediate and total affection for her. She doesn't find it hard to prefer the child to her own grandchildren, with the exception of Mlle de Beaujolais.

The Princess Palatine is seventy years old this spring. She describes herself without mercy:

> I have always been ugly, and the smallpox has left me even more so; moreover, my waist is monstrous, I have the shape of a large cube, my skin is of a reddish color mottled with yellow; I am beginning to go gray, with salt-and-pepper hair; my forehead and the skin around my eyes are wrinkled; my nose is as crooked as ever, but now festooned with smallpox scars, the same as my cheeks, which are sagging; I have heavy jowls and rotting teeth; my mouth too has changed somewhat, having become bigger, with wrinkles at the corners.

She knows she's very ugly, and she feels very old. She's too fat, she has trouble breathing, her feet are swollen. Lately, at any hour of the day, she has a tendency to fall asleep. In the past, that would happen only at Mass. She'd snore heartily, sitting at Louis XIV's side, and he would elbow her awake. The Catholic liturgy and its Latin chants, with their long, drawn-out vowels, had on her the effect of a sleeping potion. So much so that she'd attend a religious service as a cure for insomnia! But even in her present state, ill and weak,

Madame stands out as the woman with the strongest personality in the Regency period, and perhaps even (with her enemy Mme de Maintenon, whom she qualified variously as "old drab," "old dunghill," "the she-monkey," "the hag") in the reign of Louis XIV. She was certainly the most touching, because her life was a constant battle from the age of nineteen, when she was married to Monsieur, brother of Louis XIV, and delivered up to the Sun King's meticulous tyranny, to his courtiers' mean-spirited nastiness, and to the hostility of her husband's several catamites, who dreamed of a thousand different ways to do her harm. At first she had to fear being poisoned, as Monsieur's previous wife certainly had been; then, after that fear faded, she concentrated her energy on staying alive, not only physically, but also in the full spiritual and moral sense, determined above all else to be free. It was a hopeless battle. One day the Princess Palatine utters this harrowing observation, or cry: "They have clipped my wings!" Far from admitting defeat, she keeps on fighting. She resists until the end, with what remains of her spontaneity, her courage, her intelligence. And what remains is immense.

Despite the importunate crowds, the visits, the audiences, the introductions, the galas of every description, the infanta hasn't failed to notice Madame. She's intrigued by this comical personage. Maybe her initial reflex was to hide her eyes, but with Madame's first visit to the Old Louvre, the infanta discovers in the princess the grandmother she's never had and falls madly in love with her, while at the same time the princess declares herself wild for the infanta: "Our little Infanta is undoubtedly the prettiest child I have ever seen in all my days. She has more intelligence than a person of twenty, and yet she retains the childishness proper to her age: the result is a most pleasant mixture." Furthermore:

> I do not think it would be possible to find a nicer and more intelligent child in the world than our little Infanta. She makes observations worthy of a thirty-year-old person. Yesterday, for example, she said, "They say that when someone my age dies, they are saved and they go straight to heaven, and so I would be happy if God wanted to take me." I am afraid she is too intelligent to live; whoever hears her speak is immediately enthralled. She has the nicest ways in the world. I have won her favor; she runs out into her antechamber with open arms to meet me and kisses me most lovingly.

Madame has to restrain herself from paying the infanta a daily visit: "She is prettier and nicer than ever, and were I to follow my inclination, I should amuse myself with her all day long. But because of my great age, people would think I was entering a second childhood. And so I must rein myself in."

But at the hunt, or anywhere else, Madame's tendency is rather to slacken the reins. She limits herself only moderately in her affection for the infanta. She's filled with admiration for a creature at once so childish and so thoughtful. The little philosopher enchants her, and the infanta doesn't hold herself back either. She loves to open her arms wide and run to the Princess Palatine, and to invent excuses for kissing her again and again. The old lady writes: "I am in Her Lovableness's good graces; she makes me sit in a big armchair, takes a doll's stool, sits down next to me, and says, 'Listen! I have a little secret to tell you.' When I bend down to her, she throws her arms around my neck and kisses me on both cheeks."

Madame never goes anywhere without her dogs. Mariana Victoria skips along in their midst, hangs from their necks, races them.

The Princess Palatine wants to give the infanta some knowledge of the woods; she thinks it important that the child should feel nature's superiority over even the most beautiful gardens of the world. She has the coach stop in a moss-covered place. Madame and the infanta walk along a path streaked with sunlight. They lean over a bed of wild violets. The little girl crouches down and picks them one by one, sticks her nose in their golden-yellow centers, explores the tiny tracery of the moss, strokes its velvety softness. She discovers another forest inside the forest, a forest made to the measure of butterflies and ants—a forest made to her own measure. Madame tells her,

> I would rather look at land and trees than at the most magnif-icent palaces, and I prefer a single vegetable garden to a hun-dred parks adorned with marble statues and water spouts. What is more beautiful than a meadow, what is more moving than wildflowers? Natural things are exciting, they give you energy and ideas.

The two of them gather armfuls of daisies. The infanta lies down on the grass and brushes Madame's wrinkled cheeks with golden blossoms.

This is her wildflower lesson, her lesson in truth. A short time later, on April 26, the infanta says something surprising, which the Princess Palatine recounts: "The dear child put down her doll and ran to meet me with open arms. She pointed to the doll and said, laughing, 'I tell everyone that doll is my son, but I'll tell you the truth, Madame: it's only a baby made of wax.'"

Madame often betakes herself to the Louvre; the infanta, for her part, loves to visit the old lady at her residence in the Palais-Royal. Eight spaniels (of which Unknown Queen, the mother of the irreplaceable Titi, is the favorite) cohabit with her in her salon, along with a canary and a parrot. Every time someone enters and goes to pay his or her respects to the mistress of the house, the parrot cries, "Put out your paw!" The infanta laughs so hard she gives herself a stomachache.

One day the princess surprises the little girl by inviting her into her cabinet of curiosities. It's filled with such treasures as butterflies mounted on boards, stones, snakes preserved in jars, microscopes, glasses for observing the stars and solar eclipses, coral shrubs, giant sponges, an elephant's skull, a group of stuffed ostriches…The child goes from one odd thing to the next. Not long afterward, Madame asks her what she liked best.

"You, Madame."

The Infanta's Garden

The Princess Palatine lends her voice and her gaiety to celebrate everything that grows and flourishes freely. And she proves to be a vital resource for the little queen, who's surrounded by grown-ups determined to put on an act, for one another as well as for her. After a visit from Saint-Simon, the child writes to her parents:

> The duke de St. simon, My dear Maman, gave me the pretty things you and dear papa sent me. I kissed them a thousand times with affection and joy. I made a gift of the nicest things to the king, because he gives me something precious every day, and because we love each other very much. Cardinal de Rôhan came to dine recently with maman de ventadour. she told me it will be the cardinal who will marry me to the king. Mme de soubise plays me tricks sometimes: but she always has a hundred charming things to say to me, and she told me about the finery I shall wear on the Wedding day, and what will happen in the church, at the banquet and at bedtime, and the cardinal said he will also take charge of baptizing the dauphin. We laughed and laughed. The entertainments do not rule out serious occupations. There are hours of catechism lessons and other lessons, too. I always remember what you recommended, and I love you, my dear maman, very tenderly, and infinitely more than I can say. (Paris, May 17, 1722)

"We laughed and laughed..." The conspiracy of compliment givers and flatterers, all of them more or less always lying, goes forward: "The king adores you, you will form an incomparable couple and have many children." Any signs of reticence are denied.

Mme de Ventadour writes:

> Our little queen is thriving, but the night before last, after being perfectly gay all day long, she coughed a great deal, and in the morning she seemed a little upset. Then came a fever,

accompanied by so much drowsiness that she slept fourteen hours in a row, and by yesterday morning her fever was completely gone, leaving only an admirable appetite. Because of this, Madame, we shall not leave for Meudon until tomorrow, so that we can be sure enough days have passed and that we need not fear a return of the indisposition; there is certainly no sign of a relapse.

Her intelligence and good sense charm everyone. The King came to see her with a good deal of affection, but ere he came she was waiting for him so impatiently that I took the liberty of sending him a message urging him to come presto, for he had resolved not to come until after the formalities, but I saw how much pleasure his coming would give our little Queen, and he came straightway, and was most gracious in his manner, and our Queen responded in such a way that we were surprised at all she understood. I cannot stop myself from telling Your Majesty that the night she had the fever, seeing that she had awakened, I rose, desiring to give her some bouillon, and sat undressed beside her bed, and she immediately told one of her women fetch a quilt for maman so she won't catch cold. There has never been a child like her.

P.S. My dear maman, i been a little sick, but it is nothing. I am feeling very fine and packing my doll trunks for Meudon.

The King came to see me yesterday and loves me well, to my grate delite. He sends you and my dear papa his best wishes and kisses your hands, your feet, and your whole persons.

Mariana Victoria

She doesn't forget anything about Spain and Spanish and speaks French at first timidly but then "wonderfully."

She also amuses herself by saying some Italian words she's learned from her mother. Her pleasure in speaking, and in speaking several languages (among them Small Dog), makes the fact of the king's silence all the more glaring.

The infanta's at her best when the king's visit is announced and they walk together in her garden. The onlookers drown in emotion. Mme de Ventadour has tears in her eyes: "She took the King's hand led him into her garden they had a meal just the two of them with no one to assist her...and sometimes [she] let go the King's hand and went and picked some flowers for him they kissed each other warmly."

The infanta prays he will come again soon.

One fine day in May, the two children are dressed in white aprons and straw hats. A gardener teaches them to plant tulip bulbs under glass cloches. This takes place in the garden of the Tuileries, not far from the little billiards room built expressly for the king. A few days later, the infanta reciprocates the favor and invites her "husband." Servants shade the couple under a saffron-yellow umbrella. The king and the queen-infanta approach slowly, as do the select few allowed to share this intimate moment. At the instant when they're about to take some refreshment in a jasmine bower, an oboe and viol begin to play a duet. "They are sweet enough to eat," says Mme de Ventadour. The expression is soon on everyone's lips.

The infanta's garden, however, the microcosm of her brand-new reign, does not completely enclose her. Various excursions are organized on her behalf, to Boulogne, Saint-Cloud, Meudon, or—as in this case—La Muette. It's a hot, sunny day; the infanta is riding in a half-covered calèche, the king on horseback beside her. Normally she would exult in such a situation, but because it's so hot, she grows concerned for the king. She continues to worry during the night and finally orders that a request be sent to her father, asking him to write to Marshal de Villeroy and tell him to "let the King sit in the carriage with her so that the sun can do him no harm."

In June the king comes to tell the infanta goodbye. Together they take a last walk in her garden. Mariana Victoria panics. What can this mean? Is she going to stay here alone while the king lives at Versailles? The king, as always, is polite and hurried. He can't stay long. A great many people have come to bid him farewell. He's extremely busy with preparations for his departure. She doesn't want to cry in his presence, but as soon as he's gone, she throws herself on the ground and sobs.

The king returns to Versailles on June 15. It's been decided that the infanta will join him in two days. She can breathe again. The Princess Palatine, for whom visiting her in Versailles would require a much greater effort than going to the Old Louvre, hides her irritation. She doesn't want to dampen her young friend's joy. The infanta's entourage is disconsolate: "I am indeed vexed," Mme de Ventadour writes to Spain, "that Cardinal de Noailles is making us go to Versailles, we were beginning to settle into the Louvre most comfortably, for the Queen could walk out into her garden from her cabinet and had a beautiful terrace on the riverbank." Her garden, the infanta's garden, that marvelous place made entirely to her measure, the dazzle of her first spring in France, her fairyland of perfect love — Mariana Victoria leaves all that behind without regrets. She has but one thought: to rejoin the king.

On the morning of her departure, amid a great confusion of trunks and furniture, M. le Duc comes in unexpectedly. He desires, he says, to assure himself that everything is in order. What order? grumbles Carmen-Doll. She too was "most comfortably settled in" and loved to hail the boatmen from the balcony. The infanta takes refuge in a corner and watches the terrible fellow bustle about like a madman, surveying what was once her domain. His presence paralyzes her. She whispers to Carmen-Doll, "The one-eyed man has the evil eye."

Did the one-eyed man hear her? In one giant step, he's looming above them, he raises his arm as though to crush them. His shadow covers them completely.

MADRID, JUNE 1722

La Quadra's Bouquets

In those days, Death was mowing left and right. At the slightest sign of weakness, he came a-running. People with that monumental scythe hanging over their heads tended not to waste a minute. There was no time for uncertainties and long apprenticeships. No time for adolescence, which provides a sort of vacant lot for experience. With luck, you moved directly from childish weakness and the traps that beset it to adulthood, and then you had two major tasks: work and reproduction. Work: for the poor, it began when a child was capable of standing upright. Reproduction: for the poor as for the rich, it was a matter to be decided by nature. At around twelve or thirteen, a girl reached childbearing age and was therefore marriageable.

The Princess of Asturias has passed her twelfth birthday, and her illness seems to be truly over. Her head has returned to its normal proportions, her skin eruptions have vanished without a trace. She takes little care of her appearance herself, but she does let her ladies-in-waiting fuss around her. As unamiable as ever, she often shuts herself up with her women. It's thanks to them that she learns Spanish and, perhaps while they're playing with the words together, discovers gaiety. Hers is a spirit bound to clash sharply with the sinister duennas in long black dresses who have been charged with her guidance. Fairly quickly, the princess starts to exist in two registers: one of them, the one she shows to the Prince of Asturias, to Philip V, to Elisabeth Farnese, and to the court, is her old self—glum, uncommunicative, sulky, and made still worse by her present circumstances; the other is her new self, mocking and insolent, which appears only when she's in the company of her women. They are twenty-seven in number, and they're by no means all as wild as her three favorites: La Quadra and the two Kalmikov sisters, twins who have a gift for hysterical laughter. The spontaneous lessons she receives from her ladies make up her entire education. She sees no dancing masters or singing masters or writing masters; and should such persons be assigned to her, she'd have no qualms about snubbing them. The only master she accepts is a "master of equitation," and she proves to be assiduous in her riding exercises. Philip V sees this as a good sign, as he himself never feels right except when he's on horseback—on horseback or in the conjugal embrace. Don Luis gives his bride a phaeton and six little black horses. Every day she gallops up and down the paths of the Buen Retiro and makes some sensational entrances into the courtyards of the convents she visits.

After one riding lesson, she feels painful cramps in her lower abdomen, her legs won't carry her anymore, her back aches. And to top it all, something that stuns and frightens her: she's bleeding from her crotch. Blood is flowing out of her sex, staining her stockings and spreading onto her skirt. She sends her women away and spends the night in terror, lying on a towel with her thighs clamped together. In the morning, her sheets are soiled too. La Quadra forces her to get up. She explains to the girl that she's in no danger of dying, on the contrary, now she's capable of giving life, she has her period, she's a woman. Louise Élisabeth doesn't look pleased at the prospect. La Quadra has her sit on the edge of the bed and puts a basin on the floor between her feet. On her knees, she gently slips off the girl's damp, blood-stained linen. She dabs perfume on her. The princess lays aside her tragic mask, bends down to La Quadra, who's clasping her tightly, and kisses her on the mouth. La Quadra, broad-hipped, very tall, and something of an oddball, with her multicolored mantillas and her long, loose-fitting, décolleté blouses, gains greater and greater authority over the other ladies-in-waiting. And over the princess? Not really; Louise Élisabeth is beyond anyone's control. She's not answerable to her favorite or to anyone else. Nonetheless, she does have some moments of contentment when La Quadra presents her with big bouquets of flowers picked especially for her. She has a fondness for yellow flowers.

Joy isn't necessarily something she's familiar with, but it may be that she feels the suddenness of a happy surprise, a drop in anxiety, a fugitive well-being that lasts for the duration of her pleasure with La Quadra.

The Princess of Asturias is nubile. Should the date of her fleshly marriage to Don Luis be changed? The sooner he produces a successor, the surer the monarchy's future will be. Don Luis begs that the date of August 25 be moved up. But in the end, nothing is changed. The princess is deemed still too delicate — she looks no older than her twelve and a half years — and the prince insufficiently sure of himself. At the Spanish court (and on this point the reign of the Borbones, in spite of its French origins, strictly follows the model of the Austrian Habsburgs), ceremonies or entertainments, weddings or seasonal sojourns, all must take place on the prescribed date. Their Majesties' customary program is as inflexible as a calendar fixed by God Himself. Faced with his father's refusal, Don Luis dares do nothing, but the fear in his eyes becomes more striking.

⁓ III ⁓
Fortresses of Deceit

VERSAILLES, JUNE–JULY 1722

Reclining in the Hall of Mirrors

It wasn't Louis XV himself who made the decision to leave the Tuileries Palace, and it wasn't the regent either, as he feels nothing but aversion to Versailles; it was, once again, Cardinal Dubois's idea. Not that this hardworking, sly commoner feels any particular sympathy for the palace and the life of the court; for him the move is part of a political initiative, an initiative with the specific purpose of allaying the government's growing unpopularity and silencing the talk about how the regent's immorality is likely to influence the king. Moving back to Versailles is also a way of rallying part of the nobility of the old court. Louis cares nothing for any of this; he's simply delighted to return to Versailles, which he left at the age of five, as we know, under lugubrious circumstances. Does he hope to find there some trace of the time before everything came apart? Does he hope to tear away the mourning veil that covers everything he touches? In any case, he's impatient. "Trifles, trifles!" he replies to M. de

Villeroy's objection that work on the palace has not yet been completed. On the day of his departure from the Tuileries, the young boy is jubilant. Dressed in bright pink stockings and an apple-green outfit, he belongs to the spring. He's so charming and supple, he strolls about with so much grace, that perhaps it's not the wily Dubois but rather the elves and fairies — inside the hollow trunks of scattered trees, in the sainfoin's warmth and the palaces of moss, on the water-lily islands — who after many a moonlit confab have come to the conclusion that the passage of seven years means the evil spell has been broken.

"The King's departure for his Palace at Versailles having been fixed for the fifteenth day of this month," the *Gazette* tells us,

> His Majesty set out today at around three o'clock in the after-noon. The King was accompanied in his coach by the Duke d'Orléans, the Duke de Chartres, the Duke de Bourbon, the Count de Clermont, and Marshal de Villeroy. His Majesty arrived here at approximately five-thirty, to be greeted by vociferous acclamations from the people, who filled the avenues of the Palace. He dismounted from the carriage and entered the Chapel, where he said a prayer, and then he went up to his apartments. After having remained there for some time, he went down into the gardens, where he walked until eight in the evening.

Will His Majesty return to Paris for the coming winter? Is this a definitive departure? The king doesn't have the answer. And his entourage waits to see how the boy is going to acclimate himself, or reacclimate himself, to Versailles. All along the route, starting with the wooded avenue of the Champs-Elysées, the king responded joyfully to the public's acclamations. Exceptional behavior on his part. Usually, when faced with a jubilant crowd, his first movement is to hide himself. (Right after his recovery from an illness during the summer of 1720, when he was ten years old, the Parisians thronged the gardens of the Tuileries Palace, shouting out their joy: "Long live the king! Long live the king! Long live the king!" This outpouring of love sent the terrorized boy running from one room to another, trying to escape his subjects. His tutor brought him back to the window by force, whereupon the people's shouts of *Vive le roi!*, and the little king's panic, were redoubled.) The women of La Halle, with their obscene jokes, especially horrify him. But on the day of his return to Versailles, people can approach him, sing, shout, applaud him from the rooftops or the upper branches of trees; nothing frightens him. Children adorned with blue and white ribbons cheer his passage.

In the park at Versailles, Louis XV dashes off to the copses, the fountains, the paths; he wants to see the statues again, and the grottoes, and the labyrinth, and behind him he drags his noble entourage, already fairly worn out by the trip. It's hot, and none of those personages, with the exception of the Count de Clermont, M. le Duc's brother and not much older than Louis, is capable of matching his pace. The two boys far outstrip the others, running off in all directions, hopping over the little streams. In their wake, panting, perspiring, carrying canes and wearing wigs, the small group of worthy gentlemen make what haste they can. They put on smiling faces — it's a fine day, they must reflect it; the king is happy, therefore they are too—even though they're on the verge of fainting. At last the torture comes to an end. From the Fountain of Apollo, the king turns back to the palace, heading for the Hall of Mirrors, and there, oh joy, he stretches out on the floor and orders his tutor, the elderly M. de Villeroy, who's more dead than alive, to tell him the stories depicted on the painted ceiling. M. de Villeroy requests an armchair and a pause to catch his breath. Around him the gentlemen sit on the floor; someone inquires about the possibility of being served some lemonade. The brand-new crimson taffeta curtains are drawn aside and the windows opened to facilitate breathing and let in more of the light from the setting sun. The narrative can begin.

They're in the Hall of Mirrors, lying flat on the floor or propped up on their arms with their heads tilted back. Together with the boy-king, they listen to the marshal, the Duke de Villeroy, as the old man explains the paintings above them. Each is by Le Brun, and each commemorates a victory. M. de Villeroy recounts the Sun King's life of wars and triumphs. Sometimes his voice breaks, for while he's enunciating the emphatic words in the ceremonial tone he always adopts, bits of conversation with Louis XIV, images of him at different ages and in contrasting moods, come back to him. Little by little, because of the marshal's irresistible fatigue, those portraits of the king in armor and on horseback, eternally young and triumphant, like an Olympian god, are overlaid in Villeroy's mind by the insistent, terrible vision of the old monarch as he was in his final appearances, mortally wounded by grief and disease. The ceiling doubtless sang of his victories, but the ruler himself, down there on the floor, with his toothless mouth and gouty limbs and yellowish skin, was nothing but a cripple, a dying man pushed about in a "rolling chair." Louis XV hears nothing but the victory song. He trembles with pleasure as the saga unfolds. Apart from the keepers of the taverns along the route and the merchants and hoteliers of Versailles, no one's as pleased as he is.

For the great nobles of the kingdom, for those closest to him, those reclining on the parquetry, this is not necessarily a good moment. As for the wider circle of courtiers, they're going to have to resume their double existence, shared between Versailles and Paris, or Versailles and their châteaus in the provinces. That will require time and money. Everyone knows that paying court is the quickest way to obtain protection, privileges, employment, *on condition of* winning the king's confidence and finding the way to please him. However subtle one's maneuverings may be, success depends on an unpredictable element: the prince's pleasure. So much so that in the final analysis, the courtiers are in the same boat as the gamblers who devote all their intelligence to working out strategies and figuring combinations when the final outcome is a matter of chance.

M. de Villeroy discourses upon the central fresco, which depicts Louis XIV's assumption of personal power. The boy smiles delightedly. He's certain that the monarch who called himself "the greatest king in the world" knew how to assume power and how to keep it. The noblemen sigh. In their rumpled coats and dusty perukes, with their shirts sticking to their skin and the sweat running under their wigs, dying to scratch themselves, dreaming of being so bold as to kick off their tormenting shoes, they endure the golden legend.

Each of them keeps to himself his mixed feelings, his own memories of the great king, and his expectations from the new one, so young, laughing and wriggling his legs as if physically tickled by the rays of light that emanate from his painted ancestor, fall gently upon him, and encompass him in single splendor.

For the rest of the listeners, it's aching backs, stiff necks, and bitter deglutition, hardly sweetened at all by the lemonade.

Marshal de Villeroy waxes enthusiastic. The mythical reign is on display everywhere. For Louis XIV, the dimensions of human glory could not suffice; he required the gods of Mt. Olympus. M. de Villeroy leads his audience to the painting by Jean Nocret in which all the members of the royal family are depicted as ancient deities: Anne of Austria is Cybele, mother of the gods; the king is Apollo, laurel-crowned and bare-chested, draped in golden fabric and exhibiting his scepter; his wife, Queen Maria Theresa, is Juno; on the extreme left side of the large canvas, Monsieur, the king's brother, also bare-chested and draped in an ample, cream-colored cotton cloth, holds the morning star in one hand and with the other caresses one of the several daughters born of his first marriage.

"And the two babies inside the golden frame in the foreground, who are they?" Louis XV asks.

"Two children of Apollo, that is, of your great-grandfather, who died while still in the cradle."

A shadow passes over Louis XV's face.

The regent rises to his feet. Was there ever anyone more worthless in war than Marshal de Villeroy? Not very likely! Listening to him go into transports over the battle paintings and ceiling frescoes is unbearable. Moreover, the regent finds the fashion for painted ceilings hideous. Plus he needs to change his shirt — the one he's wearing is soaked through. Since he doesn't have any clothes at Versailles yet, he has a young worker borrow some for him from the palace storage rooms. As he's taking off his jacket, a folded note drops from his pocket. With his nose on the paper, he reads these words:

> The king's a child; the monster at his side,
> Renowned for poison, incest, atheism,
> Abuses unrestrained the sov'reign power.
> Thy former greatness, France, for aye has died!
> New kings, new gods besmirch this century's dawns,
> And there beneath thy feet the chasm yawns.

His heartbeat returns to normal. He finds insults of this sort everywhere, under his plate at table, rolled up and stuffed inside his boots, slipped beneath his pillows, daubed in big letters on the facade of the Palais-Royal. No sooner are they erased than they reappear. Every time, the effect on him is like so many stings. It's as if he were walking through a cloud of horseflies or wasps; for a moment, he can believe he's escaped, but they're only gathering in ever greater numbers, vicious and unrelenting.

His neckband and jabot loosened, his shirt billowing out of his breeches, the regent dodges into the War Room, the Salon de la Guerre. He moves a chair and sits down heavily before one of the high, open windows that look out onto the water terrace and, farther off, the Grand Canal, which leads to the bloodred horizon and the setting sun. If he leaned out and looked right, he could see the Neptune Fountain.

The lawns are in bad shape, likewise the groves; the Grand Canal needs to be cleaned; the Clagny pond is an infection. This water feature, the so-called Stinking Pond, located between the Swiss Lake and the menagerie, deserves its nickname more than ever. As for the menagerie, the regent doesn't care to know what may have gone on in there during the past seven years. Dubious couplings between wading birds and cobras, Sultan chickens and leopards, marmosets and their keepers, unheard-of crossbreeding, interesting monsters? Most of the fountains and ponds in the park are dry; in the ones that still have water, the women of Versailles do their laundry. The budget allotted to him for the maintenance of the palace and its gardens has been calculated down to a bare minimum, and even less than that. Had the suggestion of the Duke de Noailles been followed and the palace razed, he would feel no regrets. None whatsoever! Going back to Versailles is going back to the marsh. In the Hall of Mirrors, the king's venerable tutor drones on. The regent is willing to let that mummified representative of the old court, that doddering, ridiculous pedant, that arrant coward in combat, that stuffed jackass Villeroy yammer on at his ease.

He, the regent, has his own version of the Sun King.

What does he see? His father on his feet, assisting at the dinner being served to Louis XIV, who always ate alone. On his feet? Not always. But on the occasions when the king deigned to invite his brother to take a seat, the ritual was conceived in such a way as to be even more humiliating. The king would make the offer; Monsieur would nod and bow. A stool would be brought. But Monsieur had to wait. He couldn't sit down until the king made a gesture, to which Monsieur would immediately respond with another humble bow. Then and only then could he take the proposed place. And if the king "forgot" to make the gesture? Well, in that case Monsieur had to stand there like a sentry with the stool beside him. What else comes back to the regent? The smile on the king's face when he congratulated his brother on his shoe buckles, on a piece of lacework, on some ribbons, on his wig (on such occasions, crazy for wigs as he was, the king would hide neither his displeasure nor his envy...Come to think of it, the regent thinks, what's the best use for the late king's wig closet, what should replace the wigs?). Some things he'd rather forget: his father beseeching the king in order to obtain position or advancement for one of his favorites. And the complacency of Louis XIV, who was all too happy to make his brother a person of no account. Monsieur, an ineffable coxcomb manipulated by his male lovers or by those whom he desired as lovers, a man absolutely without willpower, a purely decorative prince. Monsieur, whom Louis XIV in his later years, when his vigilance had lost some of its sharpness, used as a spy to keep him informed of breaches of etiquette, unjustified absences, botched genuflections before the king's sacred bed-altar, sniggers and scoffs, gossip about Mme de Maintenon, licentiousness.

Louis XIV, a master of castration, had emasculated the nobility as he'd emasculated his brother. There was King Louis XIV, the admirable incarnation of virility and the spirit of conquest, and next to him, there to make him look good and act as his foil, his milksop brother, ridiculously shaking his ribbons, his curls, his jewels, his baubles.

And he, the regent, is that mad, effeminate creature's son.

And there's worse, there's always something worse: *The king's a child; the monster at his side, / Renowned for poison*... The note and its hateful words serve to remind him. When they all died, one after another, in nightmarishly rapid succession — first the grand dauphin, then the Duchess of Burgundy, then her husband the duke, and then their elder son the Duke of Brittany — so much death, it seemed, couldn't be natural, and suspicions were focused on him, the primary beneficiary of the massacre, suspicions that corrode his existence and make him fear, in his darkest hours of generalized doubt, that the young king is not completely indifferent to such rumors; that he too, little Louis, may not trust him, may see in him the murderer of his mother, his father, his brother, and may be afraid for himself... Was that the reason why he asked the boy to stop calling him "Monsieur" and to address him thenceforth as "Uncle," so that the affection implicit in family ties might contribute to discrediting the suspicion of crime? In reality, as the regent knows, the king's upbringing has revolved around death; he's been brought up in the certainty that there are people whose sole desire is to poison him. The arrogant Villeroy, incarnation of ill will, first-class coward, disastrous warrior, and depraved reader of *The Book of Venoms*, has inculcated in his pupil an obsession with cyanide, with powdered glass, with odorless, colorless arsenic.

A delegation of the citizens of Versailles comes to ask the regent's authorization for a fireworks display to salute the little king's return. He refuses. This day, it seems, will not end. He remains unmoving, a heap of weariness and disgust. He stares at the immense pale blue sky above the meticulously designed garden and beyond it the lines of bushes and trees, the jumble of vegetation ready to rejoin the woods. He loathes Versailles. He loathes hunting and has no interest in gambling. He's enthusiastic about opera and painting, he appreciates good conversation and humor, all of them things that can be grafted upon life at Versailles but do not constitute its core. In the beginning and forever, Versailles is a monument to the chase, to the violent pleasure of hunting as a way of relaxing from the exercise of power. With the transition from Louis XIII to Louis XIV and the expansion of the original hunting lodge into the new palace, power had won out over hunting, but the chase retained an extremely important place in the royal schedule. The religious ritual of royalty, on the one hand; on the other, the gallop in pursuit of the deer. Hour-by-hour meticulousness, on the one hand; on the other, the taste of blood. Etiquette versus the distribution of guts.

Night falls at last, and with it the pitiless dark that is the lot of country life. The regent wants to return posthaste to Paris. When he looks back at the palace from his carriage, he sees the windows of the king's chamber shining out of the darkness, sparkling with the light of flickering candles. Those emergent, luminous points, so weak and fragile in comparison to the nocturnal mass surrounding them, bring back to his mind both the fear of going blind and the monarchy's uncertain future.

One thing is certain: he too will be obliged to move back to Versailles. He's going to have to spend many a night in utter boredom. He thinks about the satirical joke that's making the rounds: "The regent has been exiled to Versailles by order of Cardinal Dubois!" Yes, he'll be chained up in that desert of ennui, and not, as now, en route to Paris, already inhaling the rarefied air of pleasure.

The Basket of Delights

It's true, what they told the infanta. The plan is for her to join the king two days after his departure from Paris. The *Gazette* confirms it: "The Queen-Infanta arrived here on the afternoon of the 17th, and the King, having gone to welcome her, escorted her through the Grand Apartment to the one prepared for her use."

She kneels, he lifts her up, kneels in his turn, takes her hand. He repeats the formula: "I am delighted that you have arrived in good health." Or maybe he ventures a variation: "I am glad that your journey has been completed without incident," or even, "I am overjoyed to receive you in Versailles, birthplace of your father, His Majesty the king of Spain." Then again, his mood probably isn't good enough to tempt him into such improvisations; in fact, it would be more in character for him not to say a word. But he's smiling, and the happiness he felt as he trod the paving stones of the Marble Court again hasn't dissipated. This air of joy further enhances his beauty.

The queen-infanta doesn't take her eyes off him. True to herself, she babbles, managing brief pauses for him to make some reply, and then chattering on more volubly than before, all the while being careful not to trip on the carpets.

He escorts her to her apartment. They go through the seven rooms of the Grand Apartment, previously the residence of his great-grandfather. The place where the young king lays his head at night is the same as the one from which the dying voice predicted to him, "Darling boy, you will be a great king..." The queen-infanta is lodged in the queen's apartment, formerly occupied by Louis XIV's wife, Maria Theresa of Spain (the infanta Maria Theresa, whose painted portrait Mariana Victoria couldn't look at) and then by the dauphine, the very young Duchess of Burgundy, married at the age of twelve. Thus young Louis escorts the little girl to the very chamber once occupied by his mother. And whereas in the park he desires to find everything as it was before, and the uncut grass, the uneven ground, the rust, and the cracked or broken statues and basins do not prevent him from believing that nothing has changed, here within these darkly paneled walls, in the room where his life began and where all the furniture and every nook belong to his prehistory, it doesn't seem to him that he recognizes anything. The strangeness is oppressive. A sudden panic seizes him, and he feels the hollow presence of oblivion like an intolerable weight. He goes away. He turns his back on the newly ventilated chamber, on Maman Ventadour, submerged in emotion and distracted by the things she must take care of, on the infanta, on the infanta's ladies — and on a painting titled *Departing for the Falcon Hunt*: three or four women prepare to mount richly harnessed horses. One of the women, in the left foreground, attracts the eye. She has long black hair and is wearing a wide red skirt and a red riding coat. She's as slender as a reed. The necessary immobility of her painted figure appears like an unreal standstill in the life of a creature whose element, like a dancer's, is pure movement. She's the Duchess of Burgundy.

When all is said and done, nobody misses the Louvre. Mme de Ventadour is thrilled with her apartment ("Sire, we are very comfortable at Versailles, I see the King very often and he enjoys our meetings and so do we. He does me the honor of coming to play in my rooms, I have Mme. de Maintenon's former apartment and also the Duke of Burgundy's, which adjoins the Queen's"), and so is the infanta with hers. She's occupying the queen's chamber, which suits her completely. She's also much nearer to the king than she was at the Louvre, and more visible in her role as his wife. Versailles is certainly very big, but not too big for her. In those vast rooms, faced with those immense skies, her being expands. "My house!" she repeats, laughing. At the same time, she must once more start from scratch. She has to take up again the task of adapting, of marking out her territory. As she had during her journey, Mariana Victoria has the sensation of being on unstable ground, of advancing into the completely unknown. She pays attention, strains to remember what's said to her, repeats the new sounds and words. She demarcates the boundaries of her realm. She creates a world to her measure, transports her moss forest to Versailles. And confidently makes new conquests every day.

The king often plays in Mme de Ventadour's apartments. He also spends time in the infanta's. On one occasion, Mariana Victoria has an inspiration. Her governess, still outraged, writes, "She even tried to retire while the King was playing in her chamber because she wanted him to see her in bed." The king looks up from the game of snakes and ladders and feels afraid of this infanta in whom, suddenly, he no longer sees a baby.

The infanta loves her bed. It's higher than the one she had in the Louvre, but that's been remedied; an order has gone forth for a "little ladder made of pine wood in the manner of a footboard, covered in red damask," so that she can "climb up to her bed." The infanta becomes maniacal about her little stepladder, which raises her to such a queenly height. She spends a great deal of time climbing up and down that ladder. She also uses it as a miniature, multilevel theater to display her favorite dolls, according to their current hierarchy. Those that have fallen into disfavor and find themselves buried in the trunk are enraged. Some of them break their wooden heads against the wood that imprisons them.

The carved and gilded balustrade that surrounds the infanta's bed has had to be solidly attached, for she loves to lean on it and watch the passing parade of men with multicolored calves, the pageant of pleats and flounces and trains sweeping the parquet.

To the sum of her delights, her small pleasures and great joys, she can also add the boat trips along the Grand Canal, and the marble corridors where she takes off with all the strength in her little legs and runs or slides until she falls down. (Mme de Ventadour panics. The infanta is picked up and laid down, her temples rubbed with eau de cologne.

The moment her guardian angels get distracted, she dashes away again.)

She loves to accompany the servants when they close the shutters in her chamber and draw the curtains and bring night to the Palace of Grandeur.

She loves to bend over the fountains and pull algal blooms closer to her with the aid of a hook.

She loves to be tickled by the lace frills of Maman Ventadour's "fontange coiffure," and just before she falls asleep, she likes Marie Neige to sing her a Spanish song while caressing her cheeks with the heavy tresses of her hair.

She loves the Water Avenue.

She loves to stop in front of the fountain with the statue of the little girl and make faces at her.

She loves to crawl on all fours under the table in the council chamber, and in the park to slip out of sight, into the darkness of the many bits of forest that have been left standing and marked off by wooden fences. She prefers the bamboo forest for the music of its foliage.

She loves to be the center of the world. She loves to slip out of sight.

She loves rainbows and fireworks.

She loves to watch herons take flight and is fascinated by hedgehogs.

When, for the thousandth time, she's pressed on the subject of Spain and asked if she misses her country, she loves to pick up Carmen-Doll, hide behind her, and reply in her shrillest doll voice, "Yes and no."

She loves it when, at the turn of a path, in the morning light, at sunset, or anytime, anywhere, the king appears.

She loves the idea that the king loves her, she loves to be able to write to her mother, "My dear Maman, the King loves me loves me with all his heart."

In Versailles, as previously in the Louvre, the infanta never goes to sleep without first being sure she's left enough room beside her in the bed for her king. Tiny as she is, she sleeps close to the edge on her side.

The king's schedule has become more studious. Under the direction of the regent and Cardinal Dubois, he receives lessons in the politics of the kingdom, in economics, and in diplomatic relations with foreign countries. The infanta, under the same teachers who taught the king as a young child, learns to read and write. She's burning with impatience to be able to read and answer her parents' letters. At the bottom of her governess's letters, she adds samples of the present state of her writing skills. When she sits at her little desk and copies her lines — Com bi na tions of vow els and con so nants form syl la bles: KING DOM DO MI NO PA RIS BI DA SO A — she fully accepts the seriousness of her task. To be illiterate in a situation of exile is a terrible thing. The infanta is conscious of that.

One Tuesday, which is the day when the king receives ambassadors, he brings her his own writing notebook. With her fingertip, she follows the letters drawn by the beloved hand. She redoubles her efforts, doing her utmost to write exactly like him. An excess of tender feeling gives her a tendency to bear down too hard on her pen.

She also takes lessons in dancing, music, singing, deportment, and drawing, but in her eyes they count as mere amusements.

When she's good, her reward is permission to pay a visit to the king, sometimes even during his morning study hours. In such cases, she sits quietly in a little armchair while he repeats his history lesson or does equitation exercises on a wooden horse. She's constantly on the point of asking a question.

The king is handsome, elegant, attentive, clever; he promises to become an excellent horseman. To say nothing of his religion: he's the Most Christian king, and she, the queen, accompanies him with fervor. "Her love for the King only continues to grow," writes Mme de Ventadour.

As instructed, the royal pair have revived the ritual of traversing the Hall of Mirrors on their way to the royal chapel: "All those who saw her with the King, as he took her hand for the entire length of the gallery, were in ecstasy" (Mme de Ventadour). The courtiers on both sides make their bows. The "charming couple," as Cardinal Dubois refers to them, delight the spectators. And those who remember Louis XIV's remark about the severe geometry of Le Nôtre's gardens — "They lack childhood" — can believe that Versailles, with a twelve-year-old king and a four-year-old queen, is going to be rejuvenated, that the stone walls will be replaced by an intangible softness: the down of childhood...

The king and queen of Spain are depicted in two portraits that hang by the entrance to the chapel. The infanta bows and crosses herself before each of them. She blows them kisses and makes "little loving gestures." She does the same with the statues in the park, which look as bare to her as French religious statues. (Spanish religious statues, by contrast, are covered with precious fabrics and bedecked with jewels.)

If the promenade through the Hall of Mirrors is one of the infanta's delights, religious services in the chapel, all white marble and gold and flowers, are pure elation. In the royal tribune, their prie-dieux touch; angelic voices soar; the dove hovers. Peeking between her white-gloved fingers, Mariana Victoria checks to make sure that the king hasn't flown away with the Holy Spirit.

July is delicious. The exploration of the palace and its park takes up most of the infanta's time. In certain rooms the floors need to be redone, and there are several broken windows. A number of lowly and destitute people have taken refuge in the attics, while others more insolent than they have settled into princely ground-floor apartments. These squatters are the first to be chased out by the army of floor polishers who flood the whole palace with wax. Other guests will perhaps never be spotted, like the family of white owls nesting in a study. Outside, the grass has grown randomly. The perimeters of the lawns have disappeared, absorbed into large meadows. With a resolute gesture, she tosses the wide-brimmed hat meant to protect her head onto the greenery and starts picking poppies. It's as if the park has been transformed according to Madame's wishes, as if her lesson on wildflowers created this new landscape. Alas, Madame's health is in decline. She's often obliged to cancel visits. Instead of the dear lady herself, Mariana Victoria receives a basket of cherries. She eats them sadly. When she doesn't have the heart to eat them, she wears four of them as earrings.

One stormy afternoon, Madame reappears. She's far from being as exuberant as her dogs, but she has enough energy to carry off the infanta in the direction of the Trianon. The little girl congratulates her on the return of her health, whereupon Madame replies, "Thank God, I was able to neutralize my doctors' initiatives, otherwise I would be dead. I told them a long time ago: 'My health and my body are mine, so I intend to govern them as I please.'"

"They obeyed you?"

"They obeyed me. And you too, my dear child, you must never forget that: your health and your body are your own..."

"...so I intend to govern them as I please. I am queen of France, and of my body."

The Princess Palatine stays for supper. No tutors, under-tutors, preceptors, masters of ceremonies, or experts in good manners are at the party. Madame eats—like King Louis XIV, she recalls—with her fingers and a knife. It's much better to touch your food. She has no patience with affected people who show off by using forks. The infanta plunges both hands into her green pea puree.

Fetid Dampness

When they're away from bad influences like the Princess Palatine, the boy-king and the queen-infanta handle their forks perfectly well. Sometimes they take their meals in public. They perform as successfully at table as they do in church or in the passage through the Hall of Mirrors. Louis XV and Mariana Victoria are little model persons, perfections in miniature.

Our King tires everyone but is never tired himself. He is growing and gaining weight at the same time. I do not believe that there is a countenance in the world more agreeable than his, without any trace of complacency. We shall have a King and a Queen worthy of their subjects' admiration. When your dear child was at table yesterday, there was a large crowd of people come to see her eat. She said, "It is hot, but I prefer to have this trouble and let myself be seen by all my people." Her words filled everyone with joy.

P.S. from the Queen: The King my husband thanks you and my dear papa for all your kind words in maman Ventadour's letter; he said so in front of me and I am happy to know it, for I feel for my dear papa and my dear maman infinite affection.

Mariana Victoria

The infanta charms all with her good humor and her rejoinders. For example, when the Portuguese ambassador, having inquired about her health, asks her if "she finds France and Versailles more beautiful than Madrid," she replies, "It was very hard for me to part from my father and my mother, but I am delighted to be queen of France." Her intelligence, it's said, verges on the prodigious. People admire, they go into raptures. And what if it's all too much, what if she's too intelligent to survive? People laugh, they applaud her, but they whisper to one another a prediction by Nostradamus:

A little after the match is made,
Before the day is solemnized,
The Emperor shall all disturb,

And the fair new bride,
By fate linked to the land of France,
A little thereafter shall die.

Under the pried-up floorboards, in the empty armoires, the shadowy corridors, the uninhabited children's rooms, the cradles of agony, Death is lurking. The "new bride" sometimes cries in her sleep and has inexplicable bouts of fever. She wraps her dolls in shrouds and lines them up in the Salon de la Paix, the Peace Room.

Returning from a rabbit hunt, the king catches cold. His stockings are soaked, but he's so accustomed to being dressed, undressed, and served on all occasions that he says nothing, despite his gelid feet.

On another day, he faints at the Mass.

The infanta turns pale, would like to take him in her arms.

The rumors about Versailles's bad air come back, the talk about the miasmas, about the multifarious corruptions fostered in that former marsh.

The infanta is thought to be too intelligent to live long, the king too handsome to keep his virginity for any length of time. Louis XV is the object of seductive maneuverings by persons of both sexes, who plot to gain power over him through the enchantment of sensual pleasure. While still in the Tuileries, the young boy sometimes had the surprise of seeing extraordinarily beautiful young girls—peasants, princesses, sultanas—emerge from the half-light of an adjacent room and cross, as if by chance, his field of vision...Such apparitions were sometimes staged to give them an air of verisimilitude, as when two shepherdesses, one blond and one brunette, exquisitely got up and partially naked, burst onto the royal pall-mall course in pursuit of a sheep. Play was stopped by the shiver of desire that ran through all the players except the king, who was vexed because a sheep had dared to disturb his game. The plots to make him succumb to feminine charms were all the more relentless in that the would-be seductresses were counterattacking a very solid offensive position held by a small group of nobles in the king's inner circle, young men certain that their efforts to ensnare his royal and virginal body would succeed because of his implicit consent, his vague collusion in his own exploitation. According to hearsay, which for the moment had not spread beyond the court, Louis XV seemed uniquely susceptible to masculine charms, to the beauty, reflecting his own, of companions little older than he. According to the custom established for future kings of France, at the age of seven he had "passed to the men," that is, he'd been snatched from Maman Ventadour's hands and given over to an entourage of tutors and instructors, all of them men. The question was, had that passage been *definitive*? The doubts and suspicions were confined to a small group. It was essential that nothing be disclosed for however long it took to correct the king's tendencies. But what remained unnoticed in the Tuileries is on display at Versailles and provokes public condemnation.

They bear great names and have quite naturally been designated as the king's favorites. They are the Duke de Boufflers, the Duke d'Épernon, the Duke de Gesvres, the Marquis de Meuse, the Count de Ligny, the Marquis

de Rambure, and M. d'Alincourt, the Marshal de Villeroy's grandson... Most of them are married, no older than
twenty, fond of laughing, and inclined to find forbidden
caresses and furtive bonks in convenient corners of the palace more exciting than conjugal embraces. They surround
the king, gain access to his chamber, sneak into his closet,
where they caress him, guide his hand, and set about teach-
ing him to come without concern for women or pregnancies. Their words are surreptitious, semen-stained.

The king's wearing nothing but a white satin dressing
gown and long stockings. M. d'Alincourt takes Louis's sex in
his black-gloved hand, on which several rings are sparkling.
He makes the boy moan and slide softly against him. The
very pretty Charles Armand René, Duke de la Trémoille,
sixteen years old, first gentleman of the king's bedchamber,
observes the scene from the stool he's sitting on. He too is
breathing heavily, his hands are likewise trembling. On his
knees is his interrupted embroidery work. He's not jealous;
the king's progress along the path to pederasty should turn
to his advantage. At the moment of orgasm, he swallows
one after another three round fruit pastes drenched in pear
liqueur.

It's hot. The fetid dampness their elders find so trying suits
the favorites. It makes them feel like embracing, biting one
another, frolicking naked in the copses. Night after night
they gather in the darkness and fornicate under the statues
of Diana the Huntress in her short chiton and Louis XIV in
his armor. The park belongs to them. They have the audacity of the satyrs. The garden side of the palace isn't enough;

they venture into the guarded areas near the big gates and even into the Marble Court, where they wind up under the Duke and Duchess of Boufflers's windows. Awakened by the noise, the couple go to the nearest window and discover their own son with his ass in the air, trampling on all the laws of propriety and offering himself to the young Marquis de Rambure. Other windows are flung open, and the light of the full moon catches the joyful group in flagrante delicto of the vilest sort, on the very ground where Molière, during the previous reign, produced his comedies. The king, God be thanked, is sound asleep.

The young libertines are severely berated. Some of them get sent to the Bastille, others exiled by lettres de cachet requested by their families. In Paris, the jokes and gibes proliferate. Louis XV is surprised that he no longer has about him some of his most entertaining friends. The explanation he's given is that they've been punished for wrecking fences on the grounds of the palace. The notion of "fence-wreckers" enjoys a good success both among the courtiers and beyond the court. The king accepts it without comment. Perhaps it's the gentle Duke de la Trémoille who undertakes to explain the expression to him. He may even clarify the various positions for the king by embroidering the scene into one of the idyllic landscapes he's working on.

However that may be, shortly after the scandal of the fence-wreckers, and in conjunction with it—though the king doesn't know it—he becomes aware of a new disappearance that touches the very core of his existence: the Marshal de Villeroy, his tutor, is gone, he who was appointed by Louis XIV and never left the young king's side, neither by day nor by night, convinced as he was that his little charge might suddenly die, poisoned like his parents. For Villeroy, the enemy was Philip d'Orléans, who reciprocated the sentiment, as we've seen. The regent detested Villeroy. The limit was reached when Villeroy tried to prohibit private meetings between the uncle and his nephew; Villeroy had overstepped his prerogatives. But the regent couldn't simply relieve him of his duties; he needed a pretext. The fence-wreckers furnished him with one, thanks to the presence among them of the marshal's grandson.

Everything happens very fast. One afternoon, M. de Villeroy is carried in a sedan chair to the regent's study, which opens onto the gardens. After an unpleasant exchange, he gets back into his chair, but the porters, instead of returning him to his apartments, charge off in the direction of the Satory pond. They pass under the queen-infanta's windows and run along the Aile du Midi, and soon the old tutor finds himself inside a carriage, all doors bolted, all curtains down, being whisked away at a gallop into exile.

The king watches for M. de Villeroy's return. He sends people to look for him. Hours pass. M. de Villeroy cannot be found. The king goes into a panic. Without M. de Villeroy's protection, he's going to die. The very air he breathes seems baleful. When night falls, his fear grows uncontrollable. He begs for his dear tutor, "Grandpa Villeroy," to be returned to him. The presence of the regent, who has hurried to his bedside to reassure him, increases his terror. The boy has a hallucinatory vision of the poison's icy path through his body. He believes he's dying, even believes himself already dead. He continues to act and to be treated like a living person, whereas he's been poisoned to the marrow of his bones and has departed this life — like his great-grandfather, he sobs, like the dead man who addressed him and promised him he'd become a great king, and now he's dead in his turn, without having had the time to become anything.

Two days later, when M. de Villeroy's replacement Bishop André Hercule de Fleury arrives, the boy stops eating, won't drink, avoids touching papers or letters addressed to him, is wary of breathing the scent of flowers and indeed of breathing at all...In his imagination, he dies dozens of times. The elegant prelate, a man of great gentleness already familiar to the young king, strives to save him from his nightmares. In Paris, word circulates that "the King appears cheerful enough in public, but in private he is sad and given to complaining and weeping at night."

SPAIN, SUMMER 1722

"Saint Ildephonse"

The heat and the difficulty of tolerating the stench of Madrid, which permeates even the park of the Buen Retiro Palace, have induced Philip V and Elisabeth Farnese to relocate to a cooler climate. They're at Valsaín, in a hunting pavilion in the middle of the forest, chosen by Philip V for its proximity to the chief subject of his thoughts and the single outlet for his energy: the royal property known as La Granja de San Ildefonso—or "Saint Ildephonse," as he calls it in his correspondence, in a Gallicized spelling indicative of his expectations for the palace (including a church) he's building there. Philip V and his wife supervise the work from Valsaín. They have themselves transported to the site every day, climbing up the cedar-lined path that opens onto the foundations of the church. It will be magnificent, the jewel of his secret dream: to pray to God under the richly decorated ceiling, surrounded by frescoes of angels and glistening marble; and outside, to go upon the rocky, piney slopes of the Sierra de

Guadarrama. And between the two? Between the Lord's glorious temple and barren nature? There will be the royal palace of San Ildefonso. Out of pure nostalgia, King Philip has modeled his conception on Versailles. He inspects the terrain and chooses the locations of the fountains of Diana, Latona, and Apollo; there will be rectilinear paths and statues of giant turtles identical to the ones he used to sit on as a boy. He pressures, hounds, verifies. His impatience delights no one close to him, especially not, for different reasons, the queen and Don Luis.

The *Gazette* offers some royal news: "On the 8th day of this month, the King and Queen are due to return from their château at Balsain [*sic*] to El Escorial, where the Prince and Princess of Asturias and the Infantes are expected on the 6th." Some days later, a notice informs the readers that the king and queen have changed the date of their return. They're going to stay longer at Valsaín. The decision has been made by the king, who wants to be there to accelerate the work on his new palace. The queen is discovering a bad side to her symbiosis with the king: his obsession with his rustic retreat. Nevertheless, in her view, delaying the start of their sojourn at El Escorial is not a disagreeable prospect, at least not for the foreseeable future. She feels no attraction to that monastery/palace, and despite her efforts to introduce comfort and decoration in the wing they live in, she doesn't like it there. Besides, the more time she spends away from her daughter-in-law the better, because the girl's company is nothing short of unbearable.

Louise Élisabeth doesn't dance with her husband or anyone else, nor has she developed any interest in hunting, nor does she even pretend to like music. Thus she absents herself from all three main activities of the royal family. "The Goiter Girl" has nothing in common with them. After barely six months, has she withdrawn from life at court, ignored the regular daily schedule, eschewed the seasonal relocations from one palace to another? Not yet, but she's getting there, she's well along the way. The bridges between the crown of Spain and the lost waif are fragile structures, but they're not down. They can't be, because the project that's her reason for being there—namely her marriage to the Prince of Asturias and the royal offspring she's expected to produce—is still in its early stages. The official messages lean toward the effusive. The good Father de Laubrussel writes to Cardinal Dubois:

> In carrying out Your Eminence's instructions to the very letter, I shall not find it necessary to weary you with a long and detailed report, for nothing is less subject to diversity than Her Highness the Princess of Asturias's style of living; everything in that regard is so well ordered and her hours so well divided that no gaps remain…It has hardly cost her more effort to learn the language of the country than to breathe its air, and I have heard her speak to her ladies-in-waiting as if she had never lived anywhere but Spain…The King, the Queen, and the Prince continue to cherish her dearly, and she knows too well where her true interests and her duties lie to do aught but preserve so precious a treasure.

The Jesuit in Spain and the cardinal in France compete in rosy-colored depictions. The Jesuit, because he's blinded by the conviction that God's order and the order of the realm necessarily entail admirable, well-behaved personages, and the cardinal because he works with a cynical duality that allows him to report in all tranquillity the opposite of what he sees with his own eyes.

The Anguish of El Escorial

It's true, Louise Élisabeth blithely chatters with her ladies in their language. The evening before they leave for El Escorial, all these girls are in a state of excitement that makes them especially noisy. They're celebrating summer and their departure. The two Kalmikov sisters, their blond hair disheveled, give Louise Élisabeth fandango lessons. Dancing the fandango is just as easy as speaking Spanish, they tell her, trying to overcome her reticence. La Quadra has got hold of a guitar. And how about wine? There's no wine? Louise Élisabeth sends a couple of her companions to the kitchens to fetch some, but when her door is abruptly pulled open, it's not by ebullient young girls carrying pretty carafes but by the extremely haughty Mme de Altamira. The high spirits dissipate at once. In the frightened silence, Louise Élisabeth keeps on dancing; her snapping fingers make a dull, cold sound.

"El Escorial is a monastery, a place of prayer—a quiet place. Their Majesties do not deem it proper, Madame, that you should be accompanied by your ladies-in-waiting. You will find the necessary services already in place."

"And the prince my husband, what does he deem proper?"

Mme de Altamira withdraws without responding.

They leave at dawn for the three-and-a-half-hour trip from Madrid to El Escorial. The Prince of Asturias's coach is occupied by Louise Élisabeth, Mme de Altamira, and Father de Laubrussel. The infantes and their tutors are in the following coach. They traverse the hard-packed earth surfaces of Madrid's few broad avenues. The thoroughfares are already clogged with vehicles, flocks and herds of animals, carriages, sedan chairs, donkeys laden with enormous bundles, street vendors, beggars...The prince is silent, as is his wife. Mme de Altamira is dozing. Only Father de Laubrussel is in a talkative mood: "What city can compete with Madrid? What capital can boast of being greater?"

"Paris."

"I meant, my dear princess, more Catholic. Look at all the churches and monasteries and convents, look at all the spires! Madrid is literally bristling with them! What a joyous sight for the eye and for the soul! All those crosses pointing up to heaven! My God, I thank thee!"

Louise Élisabeth would like to sleep, tries, can't, resigns herself to contemplating the harsh landscape, the shriveled oaks that come into view as they exit the city. Nothing to see, she observes. And she closes her eyes again so that at least no one will speak to her.

She must have fallen asleep. The sun is blazing, and the air feels almost as hot as the air in Madrid. Her throat tightens at the appearance of an enormous edifice of gray granite, isolated in the middle of a desert horizon. You can see it

from far away. Its endless walls, its paltry windows, its sur-
roundings. Like a prison for homicidal highwaymen.

"El Escorial has one thousand two hundred doors and
two thousand six hundred windows," the prince announces.

"Two thousand six hundred windows, and no one standing at any of them!" says Louise Élisabeth.

"You belong to a world, Madame, where one does not
stand at windows," Mme de Altamira lectures her. "Unless,
of course, when duty requires one to respond to ovations."

"Alas!" the prince sighs.

Louise Élisabeth is sorry she woke up.

"A grand edifice born of a grand design," says Father de
Laubrussel. "This admirable royal monastery was built by
Philip II, son of Charles V, to commemorate his victory in
the Battle of Saint-Quentin."

"A victory against whom?" Louise Élisabeth asks without
thinking.

"Against the French," the prince and the Jesuit answer in
chorus.

"How jolly."

"Philip II," the Jesuit continues, "had another, more pious
motive: to establish a royal pantheon."

"Jollier and jollier."

An ashen monk is standing at the entrance. Louise Élisabeth would like to go back the way she came. The interior
confirms her premonitions. A succession of inner courtyards offers no vistas. The intensely blue sky adds no note
of hope but rather serves as a reminder of an inflexible
law, Louise Élisabeth confusedly thinks. Meanwhile, she's
made acquainted with the part of the palace reserved for

the Bourbons, whose spirit is as contrary as possible to that fostered by Philip II. But like the blue sky, the embellishments — the tapestries and silken carpets, the scenes of shepherds and shepherdesses, the painted or fresh flowers — all leave intact (where they don't exacerbate it) the prevailing severity.

Their Majesties at Valsaín maintain a daily correspondence with the Prince of Asturias. The king writes: "I was well pleased to read in your letter of yesterday, my dear son, that you have arrived without incident at El Escorial, and I await news of your hunting..." On the same page, at the end of the king's letter, the queen repeats, with very minor variations, her husband's words.

The prince replies: "This afternoon after dinner I missed a rather fine fallow deer and we saw five very big deer, two fine and two others passable, but I was unable to get a shot at them..."

"I share your distress at the ill success of your first hunt, my well-beloved son, but perhaps you have been able to compensate for it today..."

And indeed there are good days that compensate for the bad: "I returned from today's hunt with three deer. Let me tell Your Majesties everything that occurred..."

Philip V replies, "I am delighted, my well-beloved son, to learn of your fine hunting yesterday...," and Elisabeth Farnese corroborates: "I am infinitely delighted by the fine hunt you enjoyed and hope that it will be followed by many others."

While the prince hunts, Louise Élisabeth goes horseback riding. She ventures farther and farther upon the slopes and folds of the Sierra de Guadarrama. Taking risks distracts her. She urges her mount through masses of fallen rocks and forces it to jump over crevices. Until one day her horse slips and sends her flying, and she strikes her head on a rock. She bleeds a great deal, but the wound isn't very serious. As the bandage wrapped around her skull makes it look deformed, she thinks that her head is, once again, a fright. Immobile, her arms and feet covered according to Spanish custom, she lies with her eyes fixed on the eternal azure. She's bored with her women. She's bored with the gossip from Paris. She'd give several of her diamonds to hear the thin voices of the lemonade vendors under the trees of the Champs-Elysées, or the worn, enticing patter of the tarot card readers around the Palais-Royal. She's bored. She'd give everything she has if only a great bird, one of the vultures or hawks that incessantly trace circles in the sky above El Escorial, would carry her away.

The princess's accident allows Don Luis to enhance his correspondence with a novelty. "As for other news," he begins his account, in the same style employed by Their Majesties on the exceptional occasions when an event unrelated to hunting has occurred.

To change Louise Élisabeth's ideas, and to satisfy his own curiosity, Father de Laubrussel proposes a visit to the Habsburg Apartments, the Austrian part of the palace—a zone long since abandoned to dust and to the vestiges of a pitiless faith. Following a servant carrying a torch, the girl and the Jesuit, she leaning on the priest's arm, walk down long, constricted corridors that end in chambers of limited size with narrow or even blocked-up windows. Priest and princess feel the sadness inherent in abandoned rooms. The light of the flaming torch picks out a few objects: furniture, beds, desks, screens. They accentuate the effect of emptiness, but the walls, for their part, are overloaded, hung with wooden, ivory, and silver crucifixes, with innumerable painted canvases recalling and glorifying the tortures suffered by martyred saints. Severed heads, lopped breasts, gouged-out eyes, broken, torn, nailed limbs, bodies chained, beaten, buried alive, pierced with arrows, devoured by lions...Louise Élisabeth and Father de Laubrussel find it hard to go on. The mute cry of those faces, disfigured by suffering and yet ecstatic, strikes them like a whiplash.

"That one there, the one we keep seeing, the one broiling on a gridiron, who's he?" Louise Élisabeth asks.

"Saint Lawrence. El Escorial is dedicated to him. In fact, the floor plan is in the form of a gridiron. Do you mean to say you didn't know that?"

"A torture palace!" the girl cries, and considering her pallor and her injured head, she sees herself as El Escorial's most recent martyr.

Don Luis comes bearing a gift for his wife: a new edition of Baroness d'Aulnoy's fairy tales. Louise Élisabeth is happy with the present. They remain silent together, afloat in an atmosphere of unusual calm. Then they hear the sound of carriages, running footmen, Elisabeth Farnese's authoritative voice giving orders. The charm is broken, the sweet spell vanishes. Don Luis declares that he must go and welcome the king and queen.

"Please stay a little longer. I feel bad in this palace at night."

"And during the day?"

"Days are easier."

"Then, Madame, you are in luck, thank God. For me day and night are identical."

He kisses her hand with his habitual respect and, using one finger, dares to caress her cheek.

VERSAILLES,

AUGUST–DECEMBER 1722

A War Game

Before long at the Palace of Versailles, all rumors, illnesses, wicked spells, and scandals have been swept away. The "charming couple" has triumphed over the forces of evil. In the royal chapel, the king receives the sacrament of confirmation from the hands of Cardinal de Rohan, the grand almoner of France, who has first favored him with a most eloquent exhortation. The ceremony takes place in the presence of the regent, the Duke de Bourbon, the Count de Clermont, the Prince de Conti, and a great many lords and ladies of the court. In the afternoon, the king attends vespers. Mme de Ventadour marvels:

> August 9. Sire, Your Majesty—filled with piety as you are—would have been pleased to see with what modesty and devotion our King received confirmation yesterday, everyone was moved to tears, and Cardinal de Rohan gave an admirable address. My little Queen was placed somewhat above

the King. Her little hands were folded, praying to God for him, and she said admirable things all day long. The Duchess de B. came to pay her court and was astounded by her grace and by the thoroughly charming manners she has when she wishes to please.

Two weeks later, the king makes his first communion. His reverential demeanor arouses praise. He visits several churches in Versailles. The infanta, wearing a sky-blue dress, bedizened with medals and crosses, throbs for joy. The king is celebrated more than she, as one would expect on such an occasion; why would she take offense at that? She knows that the sacrament of first communion is a serious matter, and in her ingenuousness, she's convinced that everything which adds value to the king redounds to her own.

The regent himself is sensitive to this breath of virtue; he thinks about separating from his mistress so that his immorality won't act like a gangrene, corrupting the purity of the space in which the innocent couple moves.

Madame comes to pay court to the infanta as often as possible. The ceremonial is always the same. As soon as Mariana Victoria hears the announcement of Madame's arrival, she drops everything and runs to throw herself in the old lady's arms. Next, holding her by the hand, the infanta leads her into her chamber. She takes a doll's chair for herself and directs Madame to an armchair. And then their endless conversation resumes. But in high summer, Madame stays in the Château of Saint-Cloud. She comes less often. The infanta yearns for the days when they were neighbors.

It's been explained to her that Madame will go back to the Palais-Royal in the autumn. Before September's over, the child starts expecting her, but in October she learns some news both good and bad: at the end of August, Madame suffered an attack of jaundice. She's back in the Palais-Royal, but her feet are so swollen she can't move. She lives in her memories. She contemplates a map of the Palatinate, which she has had placed near her bed. A "lovely map," she writes, "in which I have already done a great deal of roaming. I have already gone from Heidelberg to Frankfurt, from Mannheim to Frankenthal, and from there to Worms. I have also visited Neustadt. My God, it makes me think about the good old days that will never come again."

Something's lacking in the king's education. He needs — without putting his life in danger — experience in war. His mentors could have him observe battles from afar, but France is at peace. Well then, let's put on a show! Let's build a fort for the occasion, let's take some soldiers from the royal battalion and divide them into two groups: attackers and besieged. Let's call the besieged the Dutch. The battlefield will be at Porchefontaine, right next to Versailles. The spectacle of this imaginary siege attracts a large audience and the soldiers play their parts vigorously, all the while taking care not to injure one another. The king leads the attack. He throws out at random, but very earnestly, such terms as "bastions," "moats," "ravelins." The queen-infanta, from her seat in the grandstand, observes the fighting, shuddering at the sound of cannon fire and trembling if she loses sight of the king, be it only for a minute, as he caracoles at the head of his army. The Dutch hold out just long enough. Toward the end of each day of the siege, the imperious infanta reminds the warriors, "Gentle soldiers, count the dead, spare the wounded." (At one point, she notices a certain carelessness on the part of the slain combatants lying on the battlefield — some of whom are taking advantage of the opportunity to chew a little tobacco — and sends them a message, by order of the queen: "The gentlemen who have been killed will please conduct themselves accordingly.") She slips away so that she can be the first to congratulate the king. Victory is approaching, the Dutch are going to waver. Young boys in greater and greater numbers have been arriving to observe the battle. They've brought their weapons: slingshots, sticks, stones. These add a touch of reality to the exchanges. A Dutchman whose face has been broken open by a large stone howls at this violation of trust.

Trenches are dug, battle lines come into contact and attack one another, cardboard bombs explode, spies are hanged in effigy, the intrusive young rascals are run off, and the show goes on as it should. Fort Montreuil, the Dutch stronghold, capitulates on September 29 after more than ten days of resistance. Near the end, the fighting grows more intense, and the king is brought to the battlefield at night, too; the wounded are crying out, and in the light of the campfires that add even more drama to the scene, the boy squeezes his pretty gold-and-mother-of-pearl-encrusted bayonet with all his might. Between two assaults, he snacks on muscat grapes and roasted chestnuts.

He plays at war. She plays with dolls. What more perfect balance could there be? Everything seems in order. In *their* order. Are adults not but puppets at their disposition, role players for balls and children's battles?

"The king touches you, God heals you"

The infanta demands explanations. The king's coronation, the great event that she's been passionately anticipating, will take place without her. She won't go to Reims. Mariana Victoria sobs loudly. At Versailles, the coronation is all anyone talks about. Preparations for it constitute the only occupation of the moment. The infanta is shown the clothes the king is supposed to wear. She touches them, feels their weight. It worries her. She's afraid her "husband the king" will be exhausted merely by putting on such heavy garments. How is he going to be able to stand and walk, wrapped up like a mummy in those gold and silver capes, and with that crown on his head? There are two crowns, someone explains to her: a massive gold ceremonial crown, called the Crown of Charlemagne, that he'll wear only briefly; and the other, much lighter vermeil crown, a crown for everyday use...But she thinks that even the vermeil crown is too heavy for Louis's head. In an aside to the king she says, "That crown, Monsieur, is going to give you frightful headaches," takes her own head in her hands, and groans. She's exaggerating and she knows it. "I was just being dramatic," she says, correcting herself. And together they admire the crown in detail.

On the eve of his departure, the king comes to present his compliments. The infanta is pale and frustrated, but dignified. She adopts the polite tone the king uses for every

occasion. A tone that he calibrates between kindly distraction, frank boredom, reserve, and pointed exasperation.
With the familiar blindness of the unloved, she perceives
bows as equivalent to kisses, hand kisses to embraces, a kind
word to a passionate declaration.

During this particular visit, amid so many fittings and
rehearsals for the coronation, kindly distraction wins the
day. The king bids the infanta farewell, she kneels, he raises
her up and kneels in his turn. The ballet of their love is staged
again, as before, unchanging. At supper, the infanta appears
cheerful. She eats everything, even the soup, to please the
king her father, her mother, and the king her husband. She
accepts a second plate so that she can grow faster. But on the
day of the king's departure, she can no longer contain herself. Drums, trumpets, and fifes are deployed to accompany
the king on the way to his coronation. Painful music. Suffering pierces the little girl like a skewer. Mme de Ventadour
writes:

> The departure of the King for his coronation touches her as if
> she was fifteen years old and suffering from a keen and seri-
> ous hurt and she never wanted to go to the window to see
> the King's household and everything else that accompanied
> him and thrust her fingers into her ears for fear of hearing
> the timbales.

She weeps with a pillow over her face. The touching passion, now that it appears unshared, leaves the public behind.
She weeps. And queen though she may be, her distress isn't
treated with any more consideration than what's appropriate

for children, whose "great sorrows" elicit laughter from grown-ups; the fillip of an unhappy romance makes her case even funnier.

The king plays the game, or he feels forced to do so. He hastens to write to the infanta. Mme de Ventadour is able to reassure the child's parents: "Early this morning, mail from the King arrived with a small gift. The letter which he did me the honor of addressing to me is charming for our queen and had she been willing to give it back to me I should have sent it to your majesty."

When she goes to bed that evening, the Infanta slips the purloined letter under her pillow, not forgetting to respect the place reserved for her husband. The empty place.

The whimpering choir of dolls—trunk shut-ins, muffled mourners—accompanies the king's fanfare.

With the first little notes, the first presents, the infanta is consoled: "The King my husband wrote to me from his first stopping place I cried very much when he left wherever he goes he will think of me and I of him."

The fable has regained its rightful place. The king loves her as she loves him—for eternity. And when she finally reaches the age of twelve and is old enough to give France a child, they will love each other the way her parents do, without ever leaving their bed. The infanta asks, "But where will we sleep when the time comes? In the king's bed or mine?"

She poses this question to Mme de Ventadour, to Marie Neige, to Abbé Perot, her writing master, to her master of deportment, to her ladies, to her servants. Someone finally answers her: "You will sleep in all the beds, Your Majesty."

"All the beds in Versailles?"

"Yes, all of them."

"And the beds in Meudon, Marly, Fontainebleau, Chantilly, and La Muette, too?"

"Yes, you will sleep with the king in all possible and conceivable beds. Featherbeds, greenery beds, hanging beds, floating beds, mossy carpets..."

The infanta smiles.

She has her governess write to her parents for her: "I am waiting impatiently for the King my husband everyone admires him."

The beauties of the coronation ceremony, the different stages of that age-old ritual, are described to Mariana Victoria. She particularly appreciates this part: a cortege headed by the Bishop of Laon goes to the archbishop's palace to fetch the king. The Cantor of Reims, wielding a silver baton, knocks once upon the door of the king's bedchamber. The Bishop of Laon asks for Louis XV. On the other side of the door, the grand chamberlain replies, "The king is sleeping." Another blow from the silver baton; the request is repeated, receives the same reply. Only after the third request—"We seek Louis XV, whom God has given us as king"—is the door opened.

"So the king's not still asleep?" the infanta wants to know.

"No. His Majesty is on the bed, dressed in a red satin tunic, but he is not asleep."

The infanta wonders whether she too will eventually be able to find the magic words that will make him open his door to her. She sees clearly that the king isn't very effusive; he loves her, but he remains silent. She'd like to be able to change him. She prays for him to become talkative.

On the day of the king's return to Versailles, the infanta receives a gift from him, a pretty basket lined with white silk and containing three oranges, two limes, and a lemon. Her complaints, already weakening, dissipate altogether. She's all his, she can't stand to wait for him any longer. With her basket on her arm, she strolls between her apartment and Mme de Ventadour's. The next day, having observed the good effects of this gift, Mme de Ventadour has the same basket filled with flowers and presents it as a little thought from the king.

A contemporary, a lawyer named Mathieu Marais, notes in his diary:

> The Queen-Infanta was pleased to see the ambassadors when they returned from the coronation, and she said to Mme de Ventadour, putting her hand to her forehead, "I should like to say something to them, but nothing is coming to me." Then after making the same gesture several times, she said to them, "I shall speak to you on three points: first, I am very glad to see you; second, I would be gladder to see the King; and third, I shall do everything I can to please him and merit his friendship." A few days previously, she had heard a sermon based on three points, which gave her this idea.

And above all, practically since infancy she has heard her father, whenever he feels called upon to perform, exhibit consummate rhetorical artistry, an eloquence that surprises

Saint-Simon and elicits comparisons to Philip's grandfather Louis XIV.

At last the king comes to pay her a visit. He is the anointed of the Lord, and adorably so. He's miraculous. In Reims, at the Abbey of Saint-Remi, His Majesty touched more than two thousand people suffering from scrofula, Mme de Ventadour proudly announces, her hands crossed over her chest. "The king touches you, God heals you," the king confirms. "I touched each sick person's face with my right hand and repeated those words. Two thousand times." The infanta swoons with admiration for a being capable of such things. A being with supernatural powers. Her husband. She repeats the number and starts to count: 1, 2, 3, 4, 5, 6, 7, 8, 9, 10, 25, 43, 200, 2,000.

"Did all two thousand crofulous people get well right away?"

"Scrofulous," Maman Ventadour corrects her. "Of course they got well right away; after all, His Majesty had touched them."

The king bows and goes out.

"The king doesn't speak to me. Why doesn't he ever say anything to me?"

"Because he loves you. That's a real sign of love."

Madame's Fir Tree

Madame has returned exhausted from her journey to Reims. She takes to her bed, perfectly aware that her "little hour" is approaching and resolved to be well prepared to die. In the period of time that elapses between her still bearable weariness and the first symptoms of angina pectoris, she receives, at Saint-Cloud, a visit from her "dear little queen." The ceremony is reversed. Madame, lying on her bed, is lower than the infanta, who's perched on an armchair. Therefore the child's the one who has to lean down to kiss the damp forehead, the wrinkled cheeks. The parrot cries, "Put out your paw!" The infanta and Madame burst into laughter, which for the old lady ends in a choking fit.

She catches her breath and in a voice made low and gravelly by illness says to the little girl, "You have always thought me worthy of hearing your secrets, so today it's my turn to tell you one. But remember, don't be sad. In a few days, a few weeks at the most, Almighty God is going to call me back to his kingdom. I shall never again have the happiness of coming to pay you court, but I wish you to know that I have never loved any of my granddaughters as much as I love you. And not because I am old and weak and my faculties are declining, but because you are exceptional, Madame. Without allowing the consciousness of your merit to render you arrogant, do not let mediocrities humiliate you and make you doubt yourself. The court is an appalling mechanism. Like all the foreign princesses who come here, I was celebrated and then mistreated, slandered, wounded. In the beginning we are young and amusing, some of us are pretty, the court caresses us and seems to fawn upon us. But in fact it's a devious vampire, and it sucks our blood. Pregnancies do the rest. The young bride quickly dwindles into nothing more than a poor thing, dragging herself along and soon forgotten."

Mariana Victoria can make out only that she won't see Madame anymore, and that's awful. The Princess Palatine comes back to herself and adds, "God be thanked, your destiny will be nothing like that. You will be happy, because the king your husband..." Madame turns her face aside. She interrupts herself. She hates falseness too much to echo the official lies, but she's not cruel enough to disclose what she ascertained very early on. It doesn't surprise her, given her opinion of the boy's personality and character, which she has always considered diametrically opposed to any form of candor.

At the end of her strength, Madame still has enough to write a letter to her half-sister, the Raugravine Louise:

> My dearest Louise, today you will receive only a short letter from me, for in the first place, I am more ill than I have ever been before—I could not sleep a wink last night—and in the second, yesterday we lost the poor Marshal's wife. She died suddenly; it's not that she had a crisis, no, her life simply faded away. They say she caught cold in her stomach from drinking too much orangeade. Her death truly grieves me, for she was a very intelligent woman, and gifted with an excellent memory; she was very learned, but she never let it show. She never displayed her knowledge unless someone asked her a question. They say she has designated the son of her eldest brother as her heir. Although there is nothing surprising in the death of a person who is eighty-eight years old, it is painful all the same to lose a friend with whom one has spent fifty-one years. But I shall stop here, my dear Louise, I'm too miserable to write any more about that today. All the

same, however miserable I may be, and until I receive the final blow, I shall love you, dear Louise, with all my heart.

Between consciousness and unconsciousness, in the acute suffering caused by a cough that shreds her lungs, she keeps on gloomily rehashing all the things she hasn't had the time to pass on to the little infanta. She has told her—and it's important advice—not to yield to mediocrity, to the petty atmosphere of a society totally dependent on the king, of a court that destroys all spiritual aspiration and drags you ever downward, but she hasn't been able to reveal to the child the essential thing, her recipe for survival, for escaping the general dissolution of character and the leveling of personalities: to make writing her true life, to transmute ordinary, trivial events into words all her own, to know, my dear, my darling little girl, the music of your being, your own true tastes...

It's frigid and rainy. At Versailles, Mariana Victoria has a cold. Like everyone else. The subject of taking her to visit Madame is avoided. The infanta has the same impression she had before the coronation: something's going on without her. If her exclusion from the trip to Reims caused her profound chagrin, being kept away from Saint-Cloud and Madame's chamber fills her with anxiety, makes her suddenly stop playing, makes her call Maman Ventadour and cling to her skirts so persistently that the governess complains in a letter to the child's parents about how difficult it is to find time to write so much as a word. She adds a hasty note: "We are expecting Madame to die at any moment."

In the afternoon of December 5, Louis XV goes to see Madame. He excels in all ceremonies, especially those that have to do with death.

On December 8, Madame dies.

Saint-Simon describes the grandiose and mute scene of the ceremony known as the visit of condolence. The courtiers, more than five hundred strong, "each dressed in a coat with mourning bands on the sleeve, a hat adorned with crape, a pleated rabat, worn-out shoes, and a cloak with a train four or five feet long," come and bow to Louis XV, wearing a purple mourning suit, to the queen-infanta, to the regent, his eyes red with tears, to the Duchess d'Orléans, lying on a sofa, and to the Duke de Chartres.

The moments when the infanta finds herself at the king's side for a ceremony are joyful moments, no matter what that ceremony may be. They're the king and queen, united and together, as the medals, engravings, paintings, and prints celebrating the royal couple show them to be. She stands very straight and with a furtive caress grazes her prince's cuff. He's there, he's hers, everyone can see it. Condemned to play the role of the neglected wife despite her tender age, the infanta is at the height of her powers of presence and charm in every official situation. Even today? Even for Madame's burial? Yes, for she doesn't truly comprehend the nature of the event.

She sees only that she's occupying the central place with the king, that it's *the two of them* before whom the immense procession of courtiers, the 534 long cloaks with long trains, file past and bow. Yes, she loves this moment, and may it last. The ceremony goes on for hours. The infanta is thrilled.

At least this time, she's sure the king isn't going to slip away as soon as the greetings are over. And therefore she stands firm, dressed like him all in purple, though her fur collar tickles her chin and her nose runs; at regular intervals, Marie Neige discreetly applies a handkerchief. That makes her feel like laughing, and there are some funny things she'd like to whisper to her Neige, but Marie moves away too quickly. So the infanta remains alone with her joy, alone but within reach of the beloved who is its source. In writing about Madame's funeral to the infanta's parents, Mme de Ventadour doesn't hide the joyful excitement exhibited by their daughter. She describes it as a sort of worldly fever, a frenzy of clothes and movement, carriages and corteges, music and singing — unseemly, but excusable in so young a child as Mariana Victoria. The implication of that excitement — the brief happiness of a woman revered as the official wife of the marvelous young man on display in her company — remains veiled to Mme de Ventadour. On this occasion, she also writes, "[Madame] loved our little queen more than her children, and as Madame was truthful, she found her prettier and said so truthfully."

In spite of the disparity in their years and the differences in language, experience, reasoning ability, and maturity of judgment, the old lady and the little girl had recognized and mutually reinforced each other; they were true, they were lively, they were incapable of inhabiting the same asphyxiating spheres as people devoid of feeling. The old lady and the little girl: an encounter absolutely poetic and profoundly right. Madame had paid tribute to Mariana Victoria's genius for being both child and adult at once, but she was the same, provided we reverse the terms: at once adult and child. It was enough to observe her face, to read her smile, when, bedridden by age and disease, she traveled by finger across the map of the Palatinate and pointed unhesitatingly at the magical cherry tree of her youthful summer dawns.

After the old lady's death, the little girl is the only truthful person left. The manufacturers of lies redouble their zeal, trumpet to the world outside the fable of the dream nuptials, the myth of the children born to love each other, while inside the stern law of survival rules. Madame used to say about herself that she withstood the courtiers' malice because she was a hard nut to crack. How can the infanta, so little, so tiny a nut, succeed in doing the same? On the other hand, some little nuts don't crack so easily. And innocence, without being a weapon, possesses a strange power to disarm — at least for a while.

Madame's death creates a void, even for those who weren't especially attached to her. The young king, however, is not particularly bereft. Madame made no mistake when she suspected that he was hostile to her, that he felt aversion to her outspokenness, her impetuosity — her "big mouth," as Louis XIV would say, referring to the people of the Palatinate but putting her in the same category. Louis XV doesn't pretend to weep for Madame or to be affected by her absence. Once the ceremonies are over, he keeps the color purple but abandons his funereal demeanor. The scandal of the "fence-wreckers" has taken some of his friends away from him; enough are left to make up opposing teams for snowball fights in the foggy park, enough to have a target installed at the northern end of the Hall of Mirrors for the young people to shoot arrows at. At such times the infanta prefers to remain invisible at the other end of the gallery; she occasionally has the door of the Salon de la Paix set ajar so that she can assess the situation. The boys are gathered in the Hall of Mirrors, their backs turned to her. They draw their bows, their entire attention concentrated in the direction of the orange-gold target. What if the group should break ranks with their leader, what if they should all turn against him as one man? Frightened, wedged between the two leaves of the half-open door, she sees the arrow penetrate cloth, pierce flesh, and strike not the little golden sun but the king's heart.

The infanta still has a bad cold. She's not allowed to go out. She watches the snow fall from inside the palace. Sometimes she stations herself at a window in her chamber, facing Satory Hill, sometimes in the Hall of Mirrors, and sometimes, but more rarely, in one of the smaller rooms in the back that overlook an obscure courtyard, because from there she has no chance of seeing the boys engage in their brutish games. But one bright sunny morning, the kind of morning when Versailles sparkles, a dogsled is made ready for her. The sled takes off—it seems to her it takes flight—and in a breath she passes up the king and his friends, who are departing for a hunt. She's so completely wrapped up that she doesn't have time to free one of her hands and wave, but he salutes her as she goes by.

In an all-out crusade against the truth, Mme de Ventadour writes, "It appears to me that his penchant for our little mistress is steadily increasing, he would be in the wrong were that not so, for she is prodigiously lovable."

During all those hours, and during many others, the infanta doesn't miss Madame. Besides, the little girl is used to going for weeks without seeing the old princess. Except that eventually she would always reappear...Madame loved to tell stories of her childhood Christmases and promised the child a decorated fir tree, something completely unknown at the time. Mariana Victoria makes a deal with herself: if she gets that tree, it will mean that Madame's alive and that she has managed to send her the promised gift, which will further signify that Madame, wherever she might be—swollen feet, loud voice, kind eyes, and all—is going to come back and take her in her arms.

On Christmas morning, after midnight Mass, the family is gathered in the king's chamber. Enormous logs stamped with fleurs-de-lis are crackling in the fireplace. Like the others, the infanta is fascinated by the blaze. It's beautiful, irresistibly beautiful, totally spellbinding. She sees fantastic images emerge from the flames, but she can't help thinking it's her dismembered fir tree that's going up in smoke.

MADRID, JANUARY 1723

"If wild boars could reason" (Louise Élisabeth)

According to a notice in the *Gazette*, dateline Madrid, December 29, 1722: "The Princess of Asturias was indisposed for several days by erysipelas of the head, but after being bled a few times, she has completely recovered her health." This trivial bit of news doesn't hold the attention of anyone in France, not even her parents. Especially since she's said to have already recovered. Nobody in Spain is interested in the state of her health either, with the exception of the prince, who frets about it. With reason, because no sooner is Louise Élisabeth cured than she has a relapse. Her condition changes the royal program for the month of January, which included a hunting sojourn in El Pardo, a few leagues from Madrid. The planned hunt goes on, of course, but Louise Élisabeth is not in the company. She remains in the palace in Madrid with the infantes, Don Fernando, Don Carlos, and Don Felipe. Ever since her arrival, the princess and the infantes have formed a single, anonymous, vaguely childish, often sickly unit. And so, no Pardo for Princess Erysipelas. A happy respite for her. It's cold in the forest, it will be pleasant to remain close to a fire and play riddling games with her women.

Her only obligation is to write to her husband. And curiously enough, her juvenile words, her raggedy little notes, have been preserved; first by the prince himself and then by someone else, no doubt out of consideration for a royal personage. The prince would awaken each morning, hoping to receive in his mail one of those cream-colored envelopes addressed to *Monsieur le Prince* in the princess's capricious handwriting. If one came, he'd open it excitedly and read it with a contented heart.

Madrid, January 9, 1723
I received with joy Monsieur the signs of your remembrence and the news of your hunting success — continue to enjoye yourself and know it will help me get better.

Madrid, January 13, 1723
I congradulate you Monsieur on your hunting explots and send you many thanks for kindely remembring me. If the cold wether or my recovery would allow me to go and pay my respects to their Majs and see you in el pardo I would do so with pleasure.

Madrid, January 16, 1723
...make war on wolfs, don't spare those horrid animals...

Madrid, January 19, 1723
You did me the kindeness Monsieur of coming to see me in such a thick fog that I am in concern for your dear helth...I lay myself at their Majs feet and believe me infinitely sensible of your frienship...

Madrid, Jan 20, 1723
Monsieur I have enjoyed myself pretty well in my way which is not to kill boars but to savor don alonço's regalo [a gift from Don Alonso, a personage whom, incidentally, the prince suspects of jinxing his hunts] I congradulate you on your explots...

Madrid, Jan 23, 1723
I am glad Monsieur that my letter gave you pleasure that is indeed my intention kill many wolfs and may joy rain down upon you today the fine wether has come back but do not put too much trust in fine days in winter I saw as you did the chevalier Dorleans—the noble infantes send you many compliments my very deep respects to their Majs and believe me always very sensible of your frienship...

Madrid, January 29, 1723
...continue to give your game no quarter until next Saterday to which I count the moments, I believe that if wild boars could reason they would very much look forward to the truce that you shall grant them...

He puts down the letter, draws the curtain aside, and looks out at the landscape, which the mist has erased. If wild boars could reason...and why not bucks and does, wolves, dormice, moles, rats? He loves Louise Élisabeth. Her character — sometimes despondent and desperate, sometimes playful and jocular — pleases him; there's something about it that also disturbs him, like this crazy notion...if wild boars could reason...He picks up the note, reads it again, and carefully puts it away with the others.

VERSAILLES, JANUARY 1723

The End of Regency

The regent is stricken. He tries to struggle against the superstitious idea that with the death of his mother, a knell has rung for him. Cardinal Dubois is getting visibly thinner, and his leaden-gray complexion frightens people. The Duke de Saint-Simon, incapable of deluding himself about the way in which his duel with the contemptible politician has ended, doesn't come often to court. No one is in good spirits. Minds are dozing, bodies going numb. Apart from the end of the plague in Marseille, there's hardly any news to comment on. Chimneys draw badly. Eyes sting. Because of the cold, the king and the queen-infanta are kept in their respective apartments as much as possible. They make the passage through the Hall of Mirrors to the royal chapel in sedan chairs, side by side, with their feet on hot water bottles. To their right and left, scattered courtiers, their backs against the mirrors, are wearing fur-lined cloaks over their dark clothes.

The infanta has been placed on a rug. Her ladies sit around

her and work on their tapestry. Mariana Victoria plays with some wooden toys sent from Nuremberg by the crate: châteaus, horses, elephants, carts, farms, princes, peasants, huts, fish, roosters, trees, boats, priests, nuns, soldiers, peacocks, turtledoves...A miniature world that reflects her own universe. She lowers a drawbridge and with infinite patience has crowned heads, dwarfs, dignitaries, and clergy cross over it in proper order, followed in disorder by pages, laundry maids, chambermaids, grooms, ducks, and dogs — everyone and everything that can walk. Next come trees, fountains, turrets, and other bridges placed end to end, for the drawbridge can hold no more. There's an enormous traffic jam. No one can enter or leave the bridge. The infanta howls.

During this time, the king is busy with his great army of toy soldiers. He much preferred the real soldiers in the siege of Porchefontaine. It was great, he thinks, when he gave the order to start the attack and the battalions went into motion, like waves stirring the surface of still water. It was even better after the fighting was over and he went upon the battlefield in person, bent over the wounded, and heard the last sigh of a soldier who was a particularly good actor. He remembers the death agonies, the sometimes comic efforts of soldiers all too pleased with the recreation. To one of them, who wasn't even trying to pretend, the king said, "Monsieur, you have not earned the Cross of the Order of the Moribund." And the soldier, shaken by the boy-king's contempt, searched his mind in vain for something historic to say. The king abandons his toy soldiers and lets himself slide toward the morbid sweetness of melancholy.

He wonders—he who hates to talk—about the final, fatal seconds of life, about whether some defining phrase may be reserved for each of us to speak at that moment. As in the case of his mother, the Duchess of Burgundy: "Today princess, tomorrow nothing, after two days forgotten."

Mme de Ventadour was the person he questioned about his mother, back in the days when she was indeed Maman Ventadour. Now, because their apartments in the palace are so close, he has become her darling little king again and enjoys spending time in her rooms, dining there, possibly even making her his confidante. Mme de Ventadour's love for the infanta doesn't bother him so much. He's grown used to it, or maybe he has obscurely perceived that Madame's death was a blow to the infanta's self-assurance; maybe he sees that Versailles, where he feels at ease and sometimes even happy, represents a movement toward his ascension and toward her decline. In any case, whether the confidential relationship between him and Mme de Ventadour is reestablished or not, he no longer interrogates her about his mother. He no longer needs to. By virtue of the stories his governess has told him, his mother is forever the singular young woman whose whims were sufficiently strong or piquant to subjugate the will of the Sun King, as inflexible as ever, but lacking in vitality and in the ingredient for which no fine exterior can substitute: a zest for life. The Duchess of Burgundy possessed that treasure and shared it with all who came near her.

She loved lights at night, loved dancing by those lights, and constantly desired the king to throw new parties for her delectation. But she also loved the night for the night, for its shadows, for the fear and the refuge they provide.

Louis XIV accorded her every right, as did her husband. The boy would never tire of hearing tales of her eccentric behavior. Like running alone through the gardens in the dark, jumping with both feet onto a carriage seat, or dancing on the tables at a banquet...And today, in this palace where he's treated like a king only in order to teach him to obey, his mother's frail ghost continues to run through the mossy undergrowth and the deserted groves. When he's too bored, he appeals to her Etruscan dancer's grace to invent for him some strange gesticulations, some dances of rebellion. When she died, the Duchess of Burgundy took her zest for life with her. She didn't have time to pass it on to her son.

The infanta asks for her sewing scissors and some white paper. She cuts it into narrow strips that form strange designs when they fall to the floor. The daylight is fading, and what's left of it is concentrated in the whiteness of those sheets of paper. The infanta cuts faster and faster, the strips pile up on the parquet. The ladies admire her fine work.

The king catches cold while hunting. All the same, he attends Mass, where he faints. In the conflict-ridden and crepuscular period that is the end of the Regency, the young boy's illness, now when he's so close to his majority, causes the beginnings of a panic. "The King our master is in good health now but he almost made me die of fright yesterday when he fell ill at the end of the mass he was in the royal tribune with the queen...there was a crowd of people around him" (Mme de Ventadour).

The day of the final Regency Council meeting arrives. The king attends without visible emotion. The participants put on cheerful faces and display full confidence in the reign that's about to begin. Tomorrow is the king's thirteenth birthday. Tomorrow he will reach his majority.

MADRID, FEBRUARY 1723

Carnival

The princess is having fun. Masks give her an exciting freedom. She and La Quadra are dressed up as men, the two
Kalmikov sisters as peasants. The princess and La Quadra
harass them and pelt them with confetti. But the daughters of the people, supported by some other followers, fight
back. The battle degenerates. Louise Élisabeth is ready to
unsheathe her sword.

Don Luis keeps his distance. He stays in the palace and
writes laconic notes to his father, such as, "after supper there
will be a water fight and sugared almonds the Queen casts
herself at His Majesty's feet as do the Infantes…"

VERSAILLES, FEBRUARY 15, 1723

"I want" (*Louis XV*)

On February 15, Louis XV turns all of thirteen and is henceforward an absolute monarch.

In jest, Cardinal de Fleury shows the king a flea that has had the audacity to laze around on his pillow and says, "Sire, you are now of age, you can decree this creature's punishment."

"Hang him!"

The clever retort makes people laugh, but not exactly wholeheartedly. What if the king should decide, on a whim, to apply to those around him the punishment he decrees for a flea? "M. d'Ombreval?" — "Hang him!" "M. de Romaine?" — "Hang him!" "Mme d'Ambran?" — "Hang her!" At such a rate, the branches of the great oaks in the park would soon be weighed down with macabre fruit.

The king takes pleasure in saying, "I want." Sitting on every chair as though upon his throne, he assumes a reflective attitude. Long silence. Then he begins: "I want..." Everyone waits for what's next, including him. He's surer about what he doesn't want. Thus he agrees to go to Paris, but in spite of all Philip d'Orléans's persuasive efforts, the king will go neither to the state theater, the Comédie-Française, nor the Opéra. And when compliments are addressed to him, he replies not a word.

The first meeting of the King's Council takes place on the appointed day. The youngster appears as stone-faced as ever. He hasn't brought his little cats with him and so has no handy distraction, no living creatures snuggled against him, no warm fur to stroke. He will never again bring them along when he has to appear in his official capacity. He'll have to find in himself the solutions for his boredom. Not that he has any. Perhaps at some point the judgment he pronounced back when he was still a little boy crosses his mind again. A cat had killed one of his pet birds, and as in the case of the flea, he was asked, "Sire, what punishment must the cat suffer?"

"Have him attend a meeting of the Regency Council."

The king announces that he wants to create an Order of the Mustache, reminiscent of the games he used to play at the Tuileries and his organization of secret governments. Those to whom he grants the order will have access to him. Work on drawing up the order's statutes is hastily begun, even though everyone bears in mind that the whole thing may be a joke and participation in it risky. In particular, the nobles of the Order of the Holy Spirit (known as the Knights of the Blue Ribbon) cannot bear the thought of being mixed up with members of the Order of the Mustache.

After the attempt to establish the Order of the Mustache, Louis XV makes a more concrete decision: he has the most beautiful interior courtyard of his apartments decorated with twenty-four plaster deer heads. He's very proud of his Deer Courtyard. He stands at a window, contemplates his Cour des Cerfs, and tells himself that "I want" can sometimes produce effects. And then he shuts himself up in the little room with the dogs' heads and caresses them one after another, seized by a deep despondency.

Only the urge to go hunting really touches him. It prevails over all the rest, over his duties as well as his diversions. In someone who must soon assume power, this dominant taste seems rather troubling. The public has already noticed it. Philip d'Orléans deplores it as well. Without directly contradicting his charge, the regent does all he can to make the occupation of king intellectually attractive to him. But between a series of lectures on past wars or on the meaning of history and a bird hunt in the forest of the royal château at Marly, the boy doesn't hesitate. Even though from the outside, and even in reality, the king's attainment of his majority hasn't changed the actual functioning of the government, and even though it's true that Philip d'Orléans is still master of France, he knows he's lost ground. The enemy faction, led by M. le Duc, never stops nibbling away, if not at his prestige, then at least at his ascendancy. M. le Duc respects the limits of his role, his conduct is beyond reproach. He contents himself with inviting the king to splendid hunting parties at his Château de Chantilly. And Louis XV is delighted to accept. How can he, Philip d'Orléans, stand between the king and his desires? They're desires typical in a boy of his age. "We are here to wait upon the king's pleasure," the regent declared at the beginning of his regency, and he's convinced, deep down, that it's the truth.

In the king's carriage—ritually occupied by the same persons, whose conversations vary little—the level of hatred between Philip d'Orléans and M. le Duc goes up a notch. There are no changes in the usual tone, but the air is heavy with homicidal impulses. The king, without ever going very far away, has absented himself from his palace throughout much of the spring. His returns to Versailles last only for the time it takes to arrange his next sojourn in some different château.

Like a clock that's been stopped for several years but found intact, the mechanism of Versailles has been put back into working order. The king's comings and goings basically disrupt nothing. In his presence as in his absence, the courtiers are obliged to make a reverence when they pass in front of the royal bed. The infanta is kept informed of all the king's movements. She plainly expresses her displeasure when she's not invited along—which is often the case when the invitation has come from M. le Duc. However, as when she wasn't allowed to travel to Reims for the king's coronation, it doesn't take much for the infanta to regain her confidence. A message, a jewel, a flower, and she welcomes the king back with demonstrations of affection. He persists in not talking to her. Mme de Ventadour insists that his reticence is proof of love. Can the infanta really believe that? She'd very much like to, but it's becoming more and more difficult for her. There's not only the matter of the king's silence—always his most immediate reaction—but there's also the expression that accompanies it, the annoyance he doesn't hesitate to display ostentatiously.

The infanta tells the king about her visit to the labyrinth in the gardens, moves on to one of Aesop's fables, mimics the rabbit with the big ears, leaps from her chair to demonstrate how it scurries away; Louis XV seizes the opportunity to sneak off. The perfect image is starting to reveal some defects. A few shadowy areas are hiding in the brilliant mirror. And as for the portraits where they're depicted as a couple and where the miracle of such a lovely union is documented for posterity, the infanta doesn't fail to notice the fact that they never pose together. The painter begins with her, because she moves around so much that it takes a long time to capture her. But throughout those long sessions, she can't stop believing that the king is going to join her, that the two of them will pose side by side for Jean-François de Troy or Alexis Simon Belle or Hyacinthe Rigaud. Eventually, Mariana Victoria's disappointment puts her in a bad mood, which she takes out on the artist. As he has no desire to lose a royal commission, the painter is careful not to snap back at her. The infanta grows angrier and storms off the set, scattering paintbrushes in her wake. Mme de Ventadour catches up with her, implores her to take up her pose again. The infanta calms down and allows herself to be reinstalled on the velvet armchair. Her hairdo, her makeup, the folds of her dress, her gesture toward the crown—everything is properly adjusted once again. The sitting ends well. The infanta is happy and relieved, because these portraits are destined for her parents, destined to nurture their memory of her. And if there were no more portraits, or if they were failures, then she would fall into the hole of oblivion, and as far as Madrid was concerned, it would be as if she hadn't existed. A comment by Elisabeth Farnese in a letter to Don Luis gives a just idea of this fragile survival, so closely linked to the pictorial talent of the infanta's painters: "Mariannina's portrait has arrived. If it resembles her, she is very much changed, and not for the better."

And in Versailles, where she in any case lives, does she really exist? Is her existence taken seriously? Her will is rarely opposed, and when it is, she's willing to recognize that it's for her own good; so well has she learned the lessons instilled by Mme de Ventadour. The child proudly reports her good conduct to her parents: "I am quite reasonable. I hardly ever get into moods anymore. Everyone loves me madly," or, "My dear and much beloved Maman, I have been charming all this week," or again, "To please you, I am as nice as can be." For those around her, her desires are orders. The infanta's charm ("everything she says," "her little ways," "her endless antics," in the words of Mme de Ventadour) continues to work, except on the person she adores. There are certainly a few problems in the sphere where she reigns, but they seem insignificant. For example, on the days when she holds audience, her room is less full than it once was. There may be something of a drop, even a noticeable drop, in the general eagerness to see her. It's that she's no longer an event, and also that the Princess Palatine's enthusiastic support of her was infectious: since she found her extraordinary, it was plain that she was. In the courtiers' eyes, the queen-infanta has been trivialized. She's still as remarkable as ever, she still seems older than her size indicates, but that's just the point; some are beginning to worry about her size and the rumor that she's not growing starts to spread.

She's measured more and more often, with less and less deference. Mariana Victoria feels a violent urge to modify the course of things. Wearing an undershirt and a petticoat, she stands barefoot on the floor. She rises on tiptoe under the measuring rod. The second physician thwacks the floor with the wooden rod and brings her back to reality. He announces the verdict. The third physician notes it down. The first physician sums up: same height as last time. The queen-infanta has tears in her eyes.

"I want to grow," she says to Louis-Doll. "We must grow." She gives him a three-point speech on the said necessity and undertakes to find out about magic potions. She invents some herself: decoctions of sand, water, fern roots, peppercorns, and orange blossoms. Carmen-Doll takes charge of producing the potions. Louis-Doll's job is to taste them.

SPAIN, SPRING–SUMMER 1723

Toledo: First Time Alone Together

The Princess of Asturias, who gets on with no one, gets on with the climate. To unanimous disapproval, she has realized that she has to dress — or rather to undress — according to the temperature. When the first warm days arrive, she can no longer keep still, she demands new activities. She likes the Spanish summer, she likes the scorching air, the breathless nights, and at the first signs of the relentless heat to come, she comes to life. Her health is pretty good. Of course, she suffers constantly from indigestion because of the "vilenesses," as the Prince of Asturias says, that she stuffs herself with. She never eats anything hot. When she's supposed to make an appearance at a meal, the excuse she gives is that she has already dined. She eats sporadically, whenever the mood strikes her, which can be at any time. She gorges on vinegared vegetables and salted meats. Afterward she's dying of thirst and swallows every liquid within reach. Her body makes disgusting sounds.

She laughs about them after she's finished vomiting. These indispositions, for which she herself is responsible, don't prevent her from growing taller and heavier and gaining energy. This spring she's wild about gardening, taking walks, and riding horseback. It's hard to follow her. Some of her ladies drop out. Louise Élisabeth hadn't even noticed they were there.

In contrast with his wife's burst of growth — peppered though it is, after her fashion, with bad moments — Don Luis's health is by no means glowing. He's losing weight and constantly catching cold. Louise Élisabeth is no more seduced than she was in the beginning by the gray-skinned young man to whom her father has joined her, but in spite of herself she's responsive to his love for her, and most of all, she wants something to happen. Never seeing him weighs on her. And the fixed, immovable date of their wedding night, the consummation scheduled for August 25 without any preliminary meetings beforehand, strikes her as absurd. To a French diplomat, she expresses her surprise at the distance established and so strictly maintained between her and her husband. The Frenchman reports to Cardinal Dubois that she asked him, "blushing very much," how the king was living with the infanta and whether they saw each other often.

"Very often," responded the envoy from Versailles, playing his part in the high-level lying. "And there's no doubt that their frequent interviews have resulted in a perfect understanding."

"Indeed, I am sure that the king of France has nothing to reproach himself for on that account."

M. de Coulanges explains that Louise Élisabeth smiled when she said that. A sad smile, because she's comparing her fate to the queen-infanta's happiness? Or a purely formal smile, because — unlike Philip V and Elisabeth Farnese, who believe what they're told in the letters from France — she has her doubts? She knows her cousin, and she wonders whether M. de Coulanges isn't obliged to stick to the official version. However that may be, her conversation with him has an effect. Philip V and Elisabeth Farnese arrange a trip for themselves and the young couple. The reason for the trip is a pious one: the royal family is traveling to Toledo Cathedral to hear a "Mozarabic" Mass, a rarity only to be found in that city. Louise Élisabeth hadn't had any notion of what an auto-da-fé might be (now she knows; she still has the smell of burned flesh in her nostrils), and she isn't any more informed concerning the existence of Mozarabic Masses. Makes no difference. At least it will be a distraction.

The characteristics of the Mass, celebrated in exact accordance with the liturgical forms and practices in use before the conquest of Spain by the Moors, don't make much of an impression on her. Neither the dances nor the music draws her attention. Masses follow and resemble one another: so many blocks of time to get through, so many somnolent and often frigid hours. The real novelty is that the prince and the princess are authorized by Their Majesties to dine together, just the two of them.

The dinner goes well. Louise Élisabeth devours hers. She says two or three words to the prince. He eats nothing and contemplates her. He's absolutely charmed. She doesn't vomit.

Frog Fishing

After their return to Madrid, Philip V and Elisabeth Farnese leave for Valsaín and the prince and princess for El Escorial. She's going to resume her hazardous horseback rides. He's going to insist on scouring the terrain, gun in hand, anxious to obtain some good hunting trophies to present to his father. All things considered, it's not a good season. The prince laments having repeatedly missed his targets; the king reassures him: "One can't kill without shooting, my well-beloved son, and thus you must console yourself for yesterday's bad hunting. You will perhaps be able to make up for it today."

But the results remain mediocre. "I am vexed, my well-beloved son, that you did not have better partridge hunting...perhaps you have made up for it today by killing some large beast..." And when for lack of anything better Don Luis begins to go frog fishing, the shame is great. For although such hunting delights the princess and the infantes, it does nothing at all for Their Majesties: "If you have been able to kill a stag today, my well-beloved son, or even a fallow deer, I believe it will have meant more to you than yesterday's twelve frogs."

The frog fishing amuses Louise Élisabeth. She and others put on a play, a comedy (Philip V's comment to his son: "In spite of what you wrote to me in your letter about the comedy yesterday, a half-pound carp would probably have given you more pleasure in fishing..."), and at the end of July, a *jeu d'anneau tournant*, a rotating ring game, is installed. "I am very glad, my well-beloved son, that you have such a lovely *jeu d'anneau tournant* as the one you described in yesterday's letter," writes the king, immediately followed by the queen: "I was very happy to learn from your letter yesterday that you and the Princess and all the others enjoyed the rotating ring game, and I am quite delighted that it is beautiful, desiring infinitely as I do all that can contribute to your satisfaction." Louise Élisabeth doesn't have her mother-in-law's lively pen. As she's incapable of dilating indefinitely upon racket or ring games, she avoids answering her mail as much as possible. The queen: "When the letters came this morning I wondered if the Princess was indisposed, because we haven't heard from her at all, even though yesterday was her writing day, but I see from the Duchess de Montellano's note that the Princess is well, thank God."

After the hunts for large and small game, the prince tackles garter snakes. Philip V approves: "I rejoice with you in your destruction of the garter snakes," and Elisabeth Farnese is even more supportive: "I am very glad that you have destroyed so many garter snakes, because as you know they are no friends of mine."

The outside world rarely manifests itself in these inter-palace exchanges; sometimes Philip V mentions the arrival of news from France. Don Luis, for his part, writes to his half-sister Mariana Victoria. Their father passes the missive along: "Your letter for the Queen my daughter, who is very well, will leave with the next mail" (July 11, 1723).

Besides that, there's nothing to report.

MEUDON, JULY 1723

He Will Never Be Pope

The drought in France extends its ravages. What storms there are bring no rain; the Seine is very low. In Paris, to breathe is to poison yourself. In the country, fires break out on their own. Flocks of sheep die in place, on cracked, white-hot earth. Branches of trees — those that still have leaves — are cut off to feed animals. Landscapes of stones and skeletons. The peasants have nothing to offer that might appease the wrath of God. They drag themselves along on their knees across the countryside, getting scratches from roadside thorns, flogging and bruising themselves. They chant their guilt and beg for pardon. Priests, their faces turned skyward, their hands lifted up in the torrid air, call for rain. The processions thin out between one wayside cross and another, the hymns break up, bit by bit. There's not a cloud. Not a drop.

The peasants, who would like to murder the priests, slip at dusk into witches' shacks, utter occult formulas, try crucifying victims other than, or rather lesser than, the son of God. The witches thrash about. The peasants support them in their paroxysms. Not a cloud. Not a drop. The distress is total. People turn to the church. People speak to Philip d'Orléans. In this emergency, what's needed is a remedy of the last resort, a divine intervention. After some tense negotiations (it's important that the ceremony be regarded as an exception), the bishop of Paris agrees to announce a procession and most importantly grants an authorization (hitherto unheard of) to take Saint Genevieve's reliquary out of its church and carry it about the streets. Not a cloud. Not a drop. The drought provokes epidemics. The desolation gets worse.

Cardinal Dubois is not a lovely sight. One can't accuse him of wearing the cardinal's purple unctuously. For unctuousness, it's best to turn to Cardinal Fleury. He's the incarnation of courtesy and mildness of manner. A constant affability suffuses his regular features, and age has not tarnished their beauty. He belongs to the race of the ambitious who dissimulate their passion. Instead of furiously hurling himself into the melee, which is Dubois's style, he contents himself with waiting—and with making himself loved. Like everyone else, Fleury observes that Dubois is visibly wasting away. Fleury's smooth face displays the appropriate level of compassion.

That Dubois continues to play his part in working sessions is already no small feat. But he rises to heroic levels when he decides to accompany the king as he passes his troops in review. The crowd witnesses the bizarre way the cardinal bumps and jerks while on horseback. Laughter breaks out. The cardinal, will he fall, won't he fall, the cardinal? He doesn't fall. But his riding ordeal pierces the anal abscess he suffers from. Once the review is over, he's put on a stretcher, mad with pain. In keeping with the chasm separating the vision of persons in good health from the vision of those who are ill, the days are long, long gone when Dubois, at the height of his political intelligence, legislated without the slightest concern for the physical consequences of his decrees.

Using the work of cleaning the Grand Canal either as a pretext or as a genuine reason, the court leaves Versailles and moves to Meudon, where Cardinal Dubois is already installed. Meudon is halfway between Paris and Versailles and therefore much more convenient for Dubois. The cardinal looks like a dying man. He suffers atrociously. He's finished. He will go no farther, he will never be pope. Bursting with fury, vilely abusing each and every one, Cardinal Dubois goes to his death ranting and raging, flailing about him in a battle long since lost. His conduct is devoid of all panache. "It's the urchin coming out in him," some people snigger. Traveling by carriage causes him to cry out, and even from his bedroom cries can be heard, the echoes of his rage at having to suffer and die. Philip d'Orléans and the king take up positions at his bedside so that work can go forward. The cardinal approaches death not as a Christian, but as a worker. Philip d'Orléans and Cardinal Dubois discuss financial affairs, alliances, ministers, and the future. The king, maintaining his habitual silence, peers into his chief minister's emaciated face and sees there the glistening perspiration, the dark greenish circles under the eyes, the deep wrinkles, the spasms that shake him and send the ink spattering from his pen. The youth is captivated. If every working session were to coincide with the progress of death, politics would begin to excite him.

At the other end of the palace, at the farthest remove from the cardinal and his final turmoil, Mariana Victoria sits in a rosewood carriage drawn by a single pony and rides up and down the paths in the park. She sings the refrains of the Protestant hymns she learned from Madame.

She writes — under dictation — to her brother Don Luis:

> My honored brother, no birthday festivities could rejoice me more than the recent proofs of your dear friendship, to which do not doubt that I respond in kind, with the most affectionate sentiments of my own. The King amuses himself marvelously in this place. Hunting occupies much of his time. As for me, when I do not accompany him, I spend my time in most agreeable pursuits. I often visit you in Spain and wander around other countries as well on my map. Nothing is wanting to my satisfaction. I trust that yours too is entire, and that you remember me as much as my kind thoughts of you deserve. I am
>
> my honored brother,
> your most affectionate sister,
>
> Mariana Victoria
>
> Meudon, July 26

Like Madame, she has enough imagination to travel just by moving her finger over a map.

Dubois has reached the end. Another stretcher will bear him from Meudon to Versailles. He's placed in one of those enormous black coaches called *corbillards* (the name would later come to mean "hearse") that are normally used to transport a high-ranking nobleman's servants. Dubois's *corbillard* is followed by three vehicles: the first filled with chaplains, the second with physicians, and the third with surgeons. The cardinal is going to die in a few hours, not without first being subjected to a real butchery of an operation, against which he will struggle in vain, reduced to beastly behavior by beastly suffering. Cardinal and chief minister, man of pleasure and subtle politician though he is, he bellows in despair, calling out for some relief or only for a little air, because the August night is stiflingly hot. A storm is prowling around; white lightning streaks the sky. The baleful flashes light up the exposed, muddy bottom of the Grand Canal, where dying fish are wriggling. Philip d'Orléans, who has joined Dubois at Versailles just before his death, returns to Meudon to inform the king. That same morning, the regent appears in the king's chamber and announces the passing of his chief minister. He then proposes to replace Dubois himself, despite his rank.

The king says yes.

Philip d'Orléans kneels at his nephew's feet and swears the oath.

MADRID, AUGUST 25, 1723

Wedding Night

On August 25, a date that has long been set, Louise Élisabeth and Don Luis at last have permission to become man and wife, completely. The princess is thirteen years old, the prince sixteen. Exactly sixteen, because the king his father has thought about such things; he has authorized his son to consummate his marriage on the feast day of Saint Louis, which is also the prince's birthday:

For the feast of your patron St. Louis, my well beloved son, here is a gift: your wife in the same bed as you. You have experienced that already, I know, but today you may enjoy the additional right of sleeping with her. The right, or rather the duty. Do not forget, either of you: we await an heir. Spain awaits an heir.

That day — so long desired, fantasized, feared — is incredibly hot. Fortunately, there's a Mass; churches are cool places. Upon leaving the service, Don Luis feels dizzy. Louise Élisabeth fails to notice. Afterward, they have the day to kill. Don Luis goes hunting. He trips over a root, suffers the

beginnings of a sunstroke, and spends the rest of the afternoon playing solitaire. His frustrated desires and the bully-
ing he's undergone have made him lose his confidence — *all*
his confidence. The intellectual incapacity he's always felt
and to which he's grown accustomed is complicated by sexual anxiety. Louise Élisabeth, for her part, gorges herself
on tomatoes while someone reads stories to her. She bursts
out laughing at the cruelest passages, always from tales of
kings and queens victimized by curses, of little princesses
abducted from their palaces, of princes paralyzed by the
spells their wicked stepmothers have cast. "What could
be truer?" she asks. "These tales show the world as it is!"
Around ten o'clock in the evening, the king and queen
arrive at the royal palace of Madrid. Philip V is suffering
from an attack of gout. He limps heavily on the parquetry,
and he's in a gloomy frame of mind. The queen, a veteran
at dissembling, has no trouble hiding the contempt and
hostility she feels toward the young couple — this pair of
losers — and silently offers up her most heartfelt prayers for
their sterility.

The Prince of Asturias is undressed at the door of the
bedchamber, where the princess has been undressed in
the presence of the queen. When the princess is in bed,
the queen escorts the prince to the bed in his turn. The
bed curtains are closed. Don Luis feels ill. He can't get
hard. Louise Élisabeth, feeling not the slightest twinge of
desire, mutely observes him. They have the sheet pulled up
to their chins. Don Luis moves his hand over his spouse at
random. He grips a shoulder, grazes her navel. She doesn't
move. He attempts some fondling but doesn't dare touch

her sex. They embrace, and an onlooker might think they like it. It has all the features of a sin. The prince makes the sign of the cross. The princess moves away. He lights a candle. He reflects. They *must* copulate, *must* produce an heir. Right, but how? Neither of the two gets a wink of sleep. Toward dawn, the princess, with her back to her husband, begins to hum; it's a malicious sound, the low buzz of a bee thoroughly resolved to produce no more honey. She bites her nails without interrupting the buzzing in the back of her throat.

The following day, the princess hastens to return to her quarters. The symptoms of erysipelas are coming back. The headaches, the swelling, the red, deformed face, one enormously swollen cheek. The prince comes to inquire about her health. For a sufficient answer, she shows herself.

The prince writes to his father:

> I am very vexed about your gout, because I cannot communicate my doubts to you in person, and that is the reason for my writing you: because yesterday evening I told the princess what you had said to me, and she told me that she knew no more than I did about what should be done, because she had been told only implicitly...

A few days later, he writes again to his father; his note ends with these words:

> ...nothing at all; and for the rest, we love each other more and more every day, and I try to make her as happy as I can,

I very much wish to see you again and hope that you will soon be well, answer me as soon as possible and farewell until another occasion.

In any case, he's chained and bound: in Spain, any spouse who doesn't share his or her conjugal bed is excommunicated. From now on and until one of the two of them dies, they're condemned to sleep, or to prevent each other from sleeping, together.

VERSAILLES, AUGUST 25, 1723

A Successful Day

It's also Louis XV's saint's day, but without any conjugal urgency on the horizon. The Feast of Saint Louis goes forward with the usual ceremonies. Masses, congratulations, the king's music. After having a strawberry sorbet in the Bosquet de la Salle de Balle, the infanta is blowing soap bubbles. The king allows himself to be acclaimed by the Versaillais, the people of Versailles. A gondola ride on the Grand Canal concludes a successful day, successful because the official schedule has been strictly adhered to.

EL ESCORIAL, AUTUMN 1723

Opera Interlude

The princess rarely smiles, except for bad reasons. Nothing besides the facetious nonsense that occupies her days makes her laugh. A rumor about her face, too serious for a girl so young, is spreading. In the hope that such apparent seriousness may be a good sign, odes to the virtues of the Princess of Asturias circulate among the people. Like them, the prince would prefer to delude himself; night after night, however, the fiasco is repeated. Not without variations, of course. Once they even reach climax, not together, not in one another's arms, but in the same bed. He strokes her hand. Her eyes are closed, as if she's sleeping. He keeps her hand tight in his until morning. He tells her he loves her. She doesn't withdraw her hand. He takes this as a confession. Louise Élisabeth finds the whole thing funny, and like a child who becomes infatuated with a new toy, she takes pride in responding to him and seeks to outdo him in the demonstration of feelings. In the austere setting of El Escorial, scenes

take place that leave the courtiers wondering. Louise Élisabeth accompanies her husband everywhere—almost everywhere, because she draws the line at hunting—kisses him,
lets herself be embraced, spends days thinking about what
gifts to give him. If he has to absent himself from the palace for two days, at his parting they act out a great scene of
despair. They clasp each other, weep, move apart, rush back
together with cries of "*¡Mi marido!*" and "*¡Mi mujer!*" The
princess has to be supported. During this same period of
time, she declares to her confessor that she wishes to reform
her life and learn Latin.

The first noun declensions bore her as rigid as her role of
loving wife does. She demands that those of her women who
have remained in Madrid be brought to El Escorial. They're
hardly in El Escorial before they all, including the princess,
proclaim their desire to go back to Madrid.

"There is nothing new here," writes the prince to his
father, "and the women have already asked me when we will
return to Madrid."

Among the things that aren't new is the meticulous
exchange on the subject of hunts good and bad, marked by
such confessions of discouragement as "my hunting goes
from bad to worse" (November 6). In this period of disastrous weather, the sources of the prince's disappointment
even include a sermon he's heard: "the best thing about it
was that it lasted only twenty minutes" (November 28).

VERSAILLES, DECEMBER 2, 1723

"I hope for a crisis that will carry me off by surprise" (Philip d'Orléans)

Death has his eye on Philip d'Orléans. He feels it, knows it. It excites him and terrifies him. He has apprehended the demise of his daughter and his mother and Dubois as so many premonitory signs. Death appreciates that sort of consent, preferring as he does to work in collaboration. Perhaps that's why, after the regent declares, "I would not want a slow death; I have no wish to undergo the torments of a fatal illness. I hope for a sudden death, a crisis that will carry me off by surprise," his wish is granted. The evening of December 2, when a large part of the palace is plunged in darkness and things outside are much worse, Philip d'Orléans, on the point of going to finish some work with the king, decides to grant himself a respite. He sends for Mme de Falari. He's sitting in an armchair beside a fire, and he wants her to amuse him with a little story, one of the thousand bits of gossip that make up the daily life of Versailles. She begins cheerfully, leaning toward His Lordship. And then stops in horror.

Philip d'Orléans has fallen forward, his chin on his chest. Mme de Falari rushes out of the apartment and calls for help. She finds the corridors empty, doors closed, no servants, certainly no doctors. She hurries up and down stairs, passes through deserted antechambers. After running around and crying out for more than half an hour, she finally manages to unearth someone. Philip d'Orléans is laid on the floor. In accordance with contemporary medicine's first reflex and key remedy, the physician bleeds the patient. If the effects of this procedure upon the living are dubious, there's no chance it will resuscitate a dead man. M. le Duc hastens to the scene and receives a double satisfaction: he sees the lifeless corpse of the man he detests and almost immediately obtains the post of chief minister. For he quickly betakes himself to the king, informs him of his uncle's passing, and in the same sentence petitions to take the deceased's place. After Cardinal Fleury gives his approval, the king, his eyes wet with tears, nods his head in affirmation.

M. le Duc likewise takes over the apartments formerly occupied by Philip d'Orléans, on the ground floor, facing the Orangerie.

~ IV ~
Woe to the Vanquished!

EL ESCORIAL, DECEMBER 20, 1723

Defenseless

The Princess of Asturias is again afflicted with erysipelas. Her whole face swollen, her head like a stone, she sinks into a lethargic life. Whether because of her illness or through indifference, she isn't told of her father's death until nearly a fortnight after the event. She has no notion of politics, but she instinctively knows that once the head of your clan is dead, unless he leaves behind an eldest son or widow of exceptional caliber, you lose and the enemy clan wins. Her despair is frightening. Elisabeth Farnese goes so far as to kneel down next to her daughter-in-law to talk sense to her. That the queen has made this gesture, that she has literally lowered herself to her knees beside Louise Élisabeth, whose face is swollen by sickness and chagrin — this is considered most remarkable.

Louise Élisabeth's sister, the Duchess of Modena, is quite simply not informed. She discovers her father's death only by obtaining a copy of the announcement sent to her father-in-law, a letter whose contents he had not the slightest intention of revealing to her.

VERSAILLES, JANUARY 1724

The Real Coming of Age

Concerning the late Duke d'Orléans, the *Gazette* writes:
"This Prince was particularly devoted to the maintenance
of the peace he found established in Europe when he came
to power; he solidified it even more by new treaties, and
later by the formation of the happy bonds that unite France
and Spain and are today the source of our dearest hopes."
The infanta, it seems, can continue to be joyful and sure
of herself. "She asks only for joy," as Mme de Ventadour
noted upon the girl's arrival in France. Any sort of music
makes her feel like dancing, even a requiem. Nonetheless,
there's something irreparable in the air. The death of Philip
d'Orléans means the end of his policies, the burial of his
projects. It propels the young king into a new atmosphere.
It definitively separates from power all those, men and
women, whose presence or whose functions were dependent on Philip d'Orléans. They are now out of the running,
Saint-Simon among the first of them. The little daughter

of Spain transformed into the queen of France and her French ambassador both belong to the same lot: those who are to be, or have already been, disposed of. Saint-Simon has hardly glanced at the queen-infanta since her arrival in France, but if he would, he could see in the tight parabola of her triumph and decline the mirror image of his own political destiny. Saint-Simon will go into exile from Versailles of his own accord. The infanta will maintain some of her momentum and continue as long as possible to contribute heartbreaking fragments of joy to Mme de Ventadour's obstinate lies.

Louis XV's thirteenth birthday liberated him in the abstract (and the most significant symbol of that pseudo-liberty may be seen in the king's decision, once he came of age, not to sleep in the same room as his tutor anymore; except that the said tutor had in fact stopped watching over his sleep, only to be replaced by the undertutor!). Louis XV's uncle's death liberates him concretely, physically. In spite of his sadness, the young king feels the same new rapport with his body and its urges as he did on his tenth birthday, when M. de Villeroy gave him permission to abandon the corset of whalebone stays that trained him to hold himself erect.

Discreetly, but with implications that Louis XV grasps immediately, M. le Duc absolves him from any feelings of obligation toward the person whom the king's new tutor refers to as the "pygmy" infanta. Mariana Victoria is still there, but the king can live as if she doesn't exist. So much for the project — which has proved to be highly unrealistic — of getting the king to love her. The appearances of affection are done away with. All that remain are the forms of courtesy and ceremony.

At his grand château in Chantilly, M. le Duc organizes fabulous hunts, diurnal and nocturnal spectaculars, for the king. The boy's apprenticeship to the kingly profession is about to retreat into the background—unless one thinks, as M. le Duc does, that enjoying the pleasures of life and delegating professional matters to others constitute the proper occupation for a sovereign. At Versailles, nothing less than icy conditions can keep the king from his hunting. The courtiers curse his energy, which obliges them to spend all their time galloping in pursuit of some animal; and as the beast jerks and twitches in its death throes, those noblemen—drenched, freezing, suppressing nasty coughs—sometimes wonder whether, instead of delighting in their exploit, they shouldn't see in it a version of their own approaching end. But as for the king, he's growing, and his health is a marvel. And even in the coldest temperatures, when frost turns the locks that escape from his headgear crisp and white, there's something Dionysian about his young beauty. It cheers the hearts of the gouty and the rheumatic and sweeps away in a carefree gallop the princes closer to his age.

Must Christmas at Versailles be preceded by a death every year? Does the celebration of the fabulous event, the birth of the infant Jesus, necessarily imply some sort of counterbalancing, macabre pact? Mariana Victoria doesn't go so far as to think anything like that and, no doubt unconscious of the repetitive aspect of those December bereavements, doesn't even make the connection between one Christmas and the other. She scampers through the winter from day to day, cherished by Mme de Ventadour and advised by Carmen-Doll. She passionately follows the king's every act and gesture, sends him kisses and prayers. But it seems as though the elusiveness of her beloved, the gray skies, and the tardy mail deliveries, hampered by bad weather, combine to act upon the little girl's morale. She's no longer recognizable; she's grouchy, ready to snivel at the slightest pretext, given to complaining without being able to say about what.

On one particularly dismal morning, she wakes up aching all over; while she's being dressed, she eschews her usual humming and her usual comments on the different articles of her clothing. She doesn't admonish a foot that's too slow to get into a stocking or a clumsy arm that won't slip into a sleeve. All the same, she goes to morning Mass; afterward, however, she needs to be put to bed. Her nose and eyes are running, light hurts her. In her room with the curtains closed and her heart beating fast, she lies curled up under the eiderdown and awaits the intervention of the doctors. The sounds of footsteps outside her room, amplified by fever, give her a headache, through which she senses the physicians' arrival. And suddenly they're there. They move toward her bed. The flame of the candle placed at her bedside accentuates their dreaded silhouettes. With her burning eyes, the little girl perceives the visitors: gigantic noses, hunched backs, long arms ending in hands prepared to crush her. They're carrying the lancet they'll bleed her with. Mariana Victoria shrieks and howls. The bleeding must be postponed until later, but the doctors manage to examine the child. On her face and behind her ears, red blotches have appeared. Smallpox! The scourge that strikes children first, infects their eyes and eyelids, transforms their soft skin into a mass of pustules; the hemorrhagic plague that causes them to die in streams of blood! As soon as the physicians formulate their diagnosis, they abandon the infanta and turn their attention to what's most important.

M. le Duc flies into a rage; "Not only is this alliance bloody ridiculous, it's also threatening to cost us the king." The latter is covered with a fur cloak and thrust into a carriage that deposits him at the Trianon a few minutes later. The cold is glacial, and the teenager, standing before a fire that's taking a while to catch, is at first disoriented by his exile. The protective cocoon of his habits has been ripped apart. Louis curses the way in which, one more time — the last, he swears to himself — he's been summarily dealt with, the way his opinion has not been consulted. Is he the king or isn't he? His Majesty is indeed the king. And it's precisely because of that, because of the sacred character of his precious person, that it was necessary to act so quickly, to ensure that the disease infecting the queen-infanta doesn't have a chance to reach him…The fire has caught. The king spreads out his cloak and lies down in the crackling warmth. The road between the palace and Trianon is noisy with the barking of dogs and the laughter of his friends. Louis lets himself give in to a surge of good humor. All of a sudden he likes this impromptu excursion. It allows him to forbid the place to people who bore him and to keep only his playmates near him.

Throughout the morning of January 1, a ritual of long standing is renewed; in a long procession, the courtiers file past the king and offer him their good wishes for the New Year. The king has played his part in this annual scene since the age of five and has always been resigned to submitting to it as a matter of course. Generally, he simply doesn't listen. When he was younger, the only effort he made was to remain still. As he grew older and became more compatible with the patient and imperturbable ceremonial mannequin he was supposed to incarnate, he might have lent an ear to at least some of the many auspicious felicitations. He has refrained from doing so. Because he didn't believe them, and because he was afraid that if he stopped playing deaf, he could be induced to reply. But on this January 1, 1724, in the little Trianon palace he so much loves, at a time when he's just starting to have a sense of real freedom, the courtiers' good wishes become clear and audible utterances, words he can believe in, expressions of his own desire to live.

The young people leap from their mounts to the pink marble paving stones of the Trianon. At the supper that awaits them, outpourings of friendship will take the place of etiquette. And the champagne will provide the king with his first discoveries of the newborn year: the ease of drunkenness, the euphoria it engenders, the heat that rises to one's cheeks and loosens one's tongue.

MADRID,

JANUARY–FEBRUARY 1724

Conjugal Hell

The king his father has carefully explained to him what one does; his professor of natural sciences has — with the approval of the church — commissioned illustrated plates that show the male and female reproductive organs. In addition, he has been able to see some anatomical wax sculptures sent from Italy, in particular one of a very beautiful brunette woman with a long braid. Her smooth belly could be dismantled to reveal an imbroglio of vital organs inside. Don Luis shuddered. But in spite of everything, he is resolute. The princess never plays the game of *"Mi marido, mi amor"* anymore. In bed, she doesn't allow him near her and kicks at him when he gets too close. She threatens to break his skull with a candlestick. Don Luis persists. And one night, he gets his little wife in a tight embrace, his hard, taut sex just at the entrance of her vagina. He's practically there. But all of a sudden she frees herself, bites his tongue bloody, and escapes to the other end of the bed, ready to fight. The prince, propelled in equal measure by fear and despair, takes refuge in the chapel. He thinks, "I would rather be sent to the galleys."

VERSAILLES,

JANUARY–FEBRUARY 1724

A Defeat for the Infanta

Mariana Victoria's bedroom is the equivalent of what the city of Marseille used to be, a hotbed of pestilence. It should be walled up, except for a tiny opening her doctors could slip through, though they would still get none of the infanta's blood. For the present, they have yet to obtain a drop. In spite of her fever, her fatigue, the spread of the red rash to her upper torso and then to her arms and legs, she holds out. With a fortitude that arouses respect, not at Versailles, for her star is fading there (what Mme de Ventadour admires as her "strong will" is more and more disparaged as the result of a bad upbringing), but beyond the narrow, twisting corridors where calumnies are born and nourished and virtues shrivel up. Outside the gates of the palace, the infanta's courage demands sympathy.

The physicians have tried everything: gentle urging, the allure of rewards, appeals to reason; they undertake to explain to the child why she must be bled and what the immediate benefits of bleeding are, she must get well, it's obvious, Her Majesty wishes to get well, does she not? For herself, for her people, because the health of the queen of France is important to her subjects, to the twenty-three million French who adore her. Twenty-three million, repeats the little girl, still curled up and tense, twenty-three million, twenty-three million; she chants the number of her people, the population of France, like a litany. She possesses 347 dolls and twenty-three million French people. Three hundred and forty-seven dolls, not counting the dolls that are shut up in the trunk...For the first time since her arrival in Versailles, she remembers them. She thinks she'd like to have them with her. Those uncouth dolls would know how to stand firm against these bleeding doctors. The infanta—lying on her side, her arms wrapped around her knees and her knees against her chest—wishes she could change herself into a bundle of thorns. She feels a burst of fierce energy. She yanks her limbs out of the physicians' steely hands and curls herself up even more tightly. Marie Neige rushes to assist her. The men in black withdraw. The infanta's worn out, but she has won. She recalls Madame's voice, very close to her, repeating, "Your body belongs to you, you are its mistress, you are not a pig whose blood can be drawn to make sausage." They've gone; they'll come back. The little girl would like to block up her room's two doors and two windows. The rumor that she's been badly brought up begins to be augmented by the insinuation that she's mad.

The infanta is prepared to defend herself against the physicians' return, but she's stunned to be awakened by a deafening uproar in the Salon de la Paix. Some travelers who proclaim that they've been sent by the king of Spain intrude into her bedchamber. They're roguish-looking fellows, wearing boots and traveling cloaks and enormous mustaches that partly hide their faces. The first of them declares in Spanish that His Majesty Philip V has been informed of his daughter's illness and desires most affectionately that she recover and live; and for this reason, therefore, he *orders* her to let herself be bled. Mariana Victoria is about to capitulate. However, she's not completely convinced. "Show me the letter from His Majesty my father and I will obey." When they cannot produce the substantiating document, she dismisses them with uncontestable authority.

The doctors have not spoken their last word. They return to the attack. Their monstrous silhouettes writhe above her and conspire in Latin. She feels alone, desperately alone. While two of them force her to relax her arms and extend her legs, the third brings down on her, like a club, the final argument: "And the king your husband, have you thought of him? You have smallpox, one of the deadliest of diseases, a disease most readily transmissible; for the person of Louis XV and consequently for the throne of France, you represent a mortal danger." The infanta is astounded. The bleeding doctors have gone too far. Reeling from the blow of such an accusation — that she's putting her dear husband's life in danger — she sobs, crushed by a sense of guilt, unable to react otherwise. A physician takes advantage of her state to draw a pint of blood from her. When the operation is over, she says to them in a very small voice, "Since the king need only touch someone to heal them, let him come, let him touch me, and I shall be healed."

The smallpox turns out to be nothing but a case of measles. The red blotches fade. The newspapers announce: "Ever since the 5th day of January, the Queen-Infanta has continued to recover from her illness, and she is at present in perfect health."

The king returns to Versailles. He is spared the chore of paying a homecoming visit to the infanta; a question of elementary prudence, according to M. le Duc, who sent constantly for news of her when her sickness was at its most serious. Had it carried her off, as it did thousands of other children, that would have sorted out everything.

To have fallen ill from a disease, whether measles or smallpox, which threatened to infect the king has humiliated the infanta. In her ensuing weariness, the humidity, the drafts, the gigantic rooms, the exhausting corridors make her suffer more keenly than ever before. As she lies in bed and stares up at the somber canopy, she grows afraid of the dark and listens motionless to the night birds' cries. She weeps in silence at first, then a little more loudly, so that Mme de Ventadour (who has just fallen asleep) will get up and take her in her loving arms. Like a baby? Yes. Like her baby? Like the way she used to hold Dauphin-Doll in her arms. But that was before she got sick, before the insolence of the doctors, when it was fun to pretend and to see the greatest dignitaries accept the game. Today Dauphin-Doll is still marked with the red spots she daubed on him, but on one part of his face—the part she tried to wash with soap and water—the irruption has become a bloody stream, which has stained all his clothes. He disgusts her, gory thing that he is, like an incurable sickness. He has fallen off the bed. She doesn't touch him, doesn't ask for anyone to come and help her. In the state he's in, who would dare return him to her? She waits for a chambermaid to sweep him away and throw him on the fire. "I tell everyone that doll is my son, but I'll tell you the truth, Madame: it's only a baby made of wax."

The men in black lift up her chemise, maul her lumbar region, pinch her spinal column with their violent fingers. They track down, they invent her infirmities. They shake their headgear and dismiss her, wipe her out, her and her descendants. The infanta is malformed, no doubt "obstructed." Her pelvis is afflicted with a crippling narrowness, and as for the organs of procreation, those of Her Majesty, unfortunately, are definitively atrophied. There's nothing to be done. Except to bleed her, of course, to bleed her and thus to liberate her malignant humors.

For her convalescence, M. le Duc gives her a fool. At first, she asks to have the Duke de Chartres, son of the late Philip d'Orléans, as her fool, because of his unstable voice. The Duke de Chartres as the infanta's fool? The request is met with guffaws. She is given Bébé IV, a dwarf from the Polish court. He wears a red wig, has big, round, bulging blue eyes, and will pull as many faces and perform as many antics as you please. When he doffs his wig, he reveals a nearly bald pate with very sparse tufts of pale blond hair. That pate and those scattered tufts intrigue the infanta, who has only ever seen heads covered by wigs. She'd like to touch the dwarf's hair.

"May I?" she asks Bébé IV.

"My pate belongs to you, queen of my heart!"

"Why do you have all those holes in your hair?"

"It's age, age without wisdom, queen of innocence."

"They gave me an old fool," the infanta concludes peevishly.

"It's a simple matter, Almighty Queen, you need only exchange me for a young, hairy fool."

"Well, I was exchanged."

"For what, peerless wonder?"

"For Mlle de Montpensier, a French princess. She married Don Luis and I married King Louis. She's becoming a Spanish girl and I'm becoming a French girl."

The infanta's resting, sitting up against her pillows. Her face is tense. It looks contracted somehow. Not only is she not growing, hiss the vipers' tongues, she's actually getting smaller. She observes Bébé IV's monkeyshines gravely. Under the pretext of supervising her convalescence, her doctors torment her. They listen to her chest, remove her clothes, palpate her. They bruise her and humiliate her. Her ability to reproduce is not only declared to be many years off, too many years off, but she is suspected of being incapable of ever giving birth because of a malformation that will, they say, condemn her to sterility. A badly brought-up child, slightly crazy, too little, deformed. In her governess's loving eyes, the infanta is radiant with grace and beauty. Likewise in the eyes of the artists who paint her portrait. But insidiously, venomously, within the restricted space of Versailles, a different creature born of hatred and rejection is being substituted for her. A puny, disagreeable, wan, wildly chirping little girl, an unbearable child about whom only one question can be asked: How do we get rid of her? The king's antipathy is supplemented by the political bias of the Duke de Bourbon, head of the House of Condé, which has not yet finished settling scores with the House of Orléans.

The infanta, however, regains her strength. She is authorized, between two rain showers, to take a turn in the park. Her ladies enthuse together over this lovely break in the bad weather. Bébé IV accompanies the infanta's first outing with a comical dance, possibly Russian, requiring much vigorous leg-thrusting. The child is hardly visible at all, protected as she is by scarves and coats — except for her lively eyes.

Today, February 1, those eyes are wide with surprise and shiny with welling tears. "That is not true," she says. "It isn't possible. My father is the king of Spain and always will be. A king can't stop being king."

The Spanish ambassador has the thankless duty of announcing to the infanta the news of Philip V's abdication. "You must believe me, Your Majesty," he says. "His Highness Philip V has decided to renounce his throne."

"You forget my mother. She's too cunning, she's as clever as a hundred devils, she would never let Papa abdicate. You are lying to me, it's a plot to make my head spin."

"The ambassador is speaking the truth," Mme de Ventadour assures her. "His Majesty the king of Spain has handed over his crown to your brother, the Prince of Asturias."

"My mother is the wife of the king of Spain as I am his daughter, and that cannot be changed...La Savoyana's son...," the infanta sobs.

Louis XV, extraordinarily enough, corrects her: "The son of Maria Luisa of Savoy, sister of Marie Adélaïde of

Savoy, my mother. Maria Luisa of Savoy was, like her, an exceptional woman."

Trying to overcome the affront inflicted on her by Louis XV, the infanta has the situation explained to her: Don Luis is the son of Louis XV's mother's sister, and therefore these two Louises are first cousins, Louis XV and Luis I...but that's not the problem. Can she, the infanta of Spain, today be nothing more than the daughter of a dethroned king?

"Since you have your doubts, listen to this," says Mme de Ventadour, and she reads the end of the letter from the infanta's mother: "Moreover, you will perhaps be surprised to learn that we have abdicated, and that we are withdrawing from this corrupt world."

Mme de Ventadour, writing in the infanta's name, addresses the new king of Spain:

> My Royal Brother, although I and all this Court admire the generous resolve of the King my father, I cannot but be pained by it, and my only consolation is that you will be raised to the throne. Your Majesty brings to the government all the virtues that one could desire for the welfare of your realm. I congratulate you with all my heart; rest assured that your friendship is extremely dear to me, and that I shall always answer it with all the sentiments of the most loving and devoted sister who ever was. I am, my Royal Brother, Your Majesty's
>   Very affectionate sister
>
> Mariana Victoria

On the sly, the infanta slips into the envelope a few lines of her last writing assignment and some peony petals for the palace ladies.

LA GRANJA

DE SAN ILDEFONSO,

MADRID, FEBRUARY 1724

"It having pleased God in his infinite mercy, my well beloved son, to make me sensible for some years past of the nothingness of this world and the vanity of its grandeurs..." (Philip V)

To those close to Philip V, his decision came as no surprise. Elisabeth Farnese, like the Prince of Asturias, knew that the king would abdicate as soon as San Ildefonso became habitable. On the day when he signs his act of abdication, Philip V experiences true sovereignty, the kind that places one above all he surveys. It's the dead of winter. The mountain passes are closed. The lines of communication between him and Madrid have been cut. He walks through his park, roams around his palace, and yields without restraint to the joy of having freed himself from the cares of the world. He contemplates a portrait of Louis XIV, well placed on the wall of the vastest room in San Ildefonso, and finally feels bold enough to meet his eye and say to him, "The crown you charged me with, Majesty—I renounce it. And see, you for whom no enjoyment equaled the business of being king, see what I dare to do: I abdicate. I abdicate a kingdom that cost thirteen years of war and more than two million dead. And to keep nothing hidden from you, I will confess that it took me but a short time after the end of that same war to resolve, in secret, to step down. You always thought me incapable. I surpass your worst judgments. You despise me as you, a man whose hauteur is legendary, have never despised anyone. I am, in your opinion, a pathetic king, a coward, a religious zealot, and the gardens of La Granja reflect my miserable destiny. That I compare them with your gardens at Versailles, what buffoonery! It's like trying to compare the 'Great Century' of your reign with prehistory! The dimensions, the harmony, the infinite horizon…Nothing about your gardens is comparable to mine. The paths in La Granja mimic those in Versailles, but they end in walls of snow. Life here is naked and savage; one bumps up against it, no doubt about that, but prick up your ears, listen to that music, that perpetual streaming. Here water flows in abundance, it meanders, seeps, gushes, cascades…water is everywhere, it fills my pools, my ponds, my canals, it makes the glory of my fountains. At La Granja, Majesty, I have water with me. Mountain water, running forever, inexhaustible. To receive it, I need only dig out a shallow basin. My Great Water Spectacle, my Very Great Water Spectacle, suffers no interruption. You smile, but God tells me I would be wrong to bow before that smile, and that this alone is the right way to build, not by declaring war on nature, His Creation, but by humbly thanking him for It, the source of every Good."

From now on, it's undeniable that the king and queen do everything together, they don't leave each other for a minute, but also that *they don't think together*. The queen hides her pique: she loves the corrupt world she's withdrawing from; the retirement to San Ildefonso horrifies her. Her childhood and youth were filled with mortifications, and now they're going to start again. In the silence of La Granja, a stillness broken only by the muffled thuds of masses of snow falling from the trees, she reflects bitterly on her vitality, on her intelligence, on all those talents of hers that are going to be interred...She speaks and writes several languages, she dances and sings admirably, she draws, paints—for whom? For what? In her letters, she offers no glimpse into the storms raging inside her; at most, she permits herself an ironic point or two, such as, "Forgive me if I use a rustic term, but as I have become a rustic, I employ the terms of my fellow rustics."

Nowadays the royal palace of La Granja de San Ildefonso is a tourist site, and several works by Philip V's wife are on display there: portraits of saints, in full-face, profile, and three-quarter views. Her line is sure, her color sense subtle, she was obviously gifted. Her pictures are flawless, yet they leave the viewer indifferent. The thing is, they have no soul. It doubtless exists, but like that of Elisabeth herself, it's too deeply hidden to show through. These are facade saints, perfect, decorative, and insipid. Nuanced watercolors put up as screens to conceal the devastating rage inside her.

The people of Madrid are jubilant. Their hearts go out to Don Luis, La Savoyana's son, a child nourished on chocolate, a real Spaniard! "*Viva, viva, viva! Viva Luis I, el Buen Amado!*" (Long live Luis I, the Well Beloved!). The people's joy spreads from street to street until it reaches El Escorial. "What is that noise?" asks the Princess of Asturias. Her ladies have no idea. A message signed "Luis I" and delivered by the Duchess de Altamira informs the princess that she's the queen. She gets dead drunk that night. She swallows everything La Quadra pours into her glass. She offers some dreadful toasts. Her twenty-seven ladies-in-waiting, all disheveled, cry out, "*Viva la reina! Viva la reina!*" Faced with their gibes, the Duchess de Altamira scuttles away.

Louise Élisabeth staggers to the royal bedchamber. The Kalmikov sisters, each bearing a torch, open the door wide and announce, "Her Majesty the queen!" Louise Élisabeth, with a woolen blanket draped across her shoulders, a sort of coronation cape for a shepherdess, mumbles, "*Estoy borracha como una cuba*" (I'm as drunk as a skunk). The king parts the bed curtains and holds out to her a white, fragile, exceedingly delicate hand, a hand limp and impotent.

VERSAILLES, FEBRUARY 1724

Spies in the Queen of Spain's Household

M. le Duc rejoices. Philip V's abdication is excellent news. The daughter of a dethroned king is easier to send back discreetly, without risking a war. He's going to make sure the Princess of Asturias, henceforward queen of Spain, is closely spied upon. He must know whether or not she has any influence with King Luis. Decidedly, ever since the death of Philip d'Orléans, good fortune has smiled upon M. le Duc. This doesn't prevent him from strolling around as rudely as ever, with the same expression of discontent, of fury about to explode—or in fact exploding. His passage is marked by invective and blows from his cane. Valets, servers, chambermaids, and even pages, who because of their high birth should be better treated, all fear him. The panic that overcomes the infanta as soon as she catches sight of him is felt by everyone who's in a position of weakness. For that's his talent: to put you in a position of weakness. Ever since her illness, Mariana Victoria feels like a target. The daughter of a king who's not a king anymore, the wife of a king from whom she never stops waiting for a gesture of attention, a word of love, she's able to hold out because of her pride, and because the force of her will has not been in any way diminished; but the source of her vitality is no longer the same. She's lost her carefree attitude and her self-confidence, as well as her desire to dance in place, to sing upon awakening, to win every heart. Mme de Ventadour is her refuge. The infanta tries with all her might to believe the duchess's letters, according to which the king is overjoyed to hear her spoken of and loves her more and more with each passing day. Letters in which Mme de Ventadour assures her correspondents that the couple formed by Mariana Victoria and Louis XV is a miracle of harmony. The infanta manages to delude herself again, but a new need, redoubtable because insatiable, has begun to grow in her: she wants proof. Just once, outside of well-ordered ceremonies and courteous exchanges, formal congratulations and condolence visits, she wants an impromptu look, an impromptu gesture from the king, she wants him to feel an irrepressible urge, she wants something that will say to her, just once, "I love you."

MADRID, CARNIVAL 1724

Flying Pebbles

In the correspondence between Don Luis and his parents, the most noticeable effect of Philip V's abdication is that now there's an exchange of majesties: the royal son continues to address them as Your Majesties, whereas now the royal father and royal stepmother, Elisabeth Farnese, refer to the royal son as Your Majesty or His Majesty.

In celebration of the new reign, the Carnival is especially brilliant, featuring masked balls, comedies, sugared almond battles, bullfights, and an auto-da-fé on a par with the other festivities. Louise Élisabeth never sobers up. She displays herself in La Quadra's arms. They're both wearing scarlet mantillas and identical white masks, adorned under the eye slit with a heart-shaped beauty spot. The men send them armfuls of flowers and shout full-throated obscenities at them.

The king avoids displays of public joy—and joy in general. At court, the celebrations are rather more formal:

equestrian shows, ballets, operas. Don Luis and his wife attend a performance of Calderón's *Fieras afemina Amor* (Love Effeminates Savage Beasts). She sleeps; he, looking lost, observes the exploits of Love, who like Orpheus's lyre tames wild animals. Luis doesn't tame them, but he hunts them whatever the weather. It even seems that bad weather exacerbates his passion. He writes to his father: "It was so windy that little stones came flying up into our faces and blinded us, the hunt ended before I could shoot anything except two partridges" (February 14, 1724), and then a few days later: "At El Pardo this afternoon, I fired at a deer from a distance, the ball went through him and we followed him for nearly a league, he leaving a great abundance of blood in his trail and even leaving a clot of blood as big as a hat the night came we had to go back and so he was lost."

He entered into his night.

Luis doesn't weep. It's not weakness on his part if the world flings stones in his face and forces tears from his eyes.

VERSAILLES, SPRING 1724

The Enjoyment of Terror

Louis XV prepares to leave Versailles, where he's been dreaming of the festivities to come in the summer — the summer of his fifteenth year — that are going to make a glittery saga of his sojourn in the Palace of Fontainebleau. He's in a hurry to step onto the White Horse Courtyard, to run up the stairs four at a time, to admire the Deer Gallery, decorated with deer hunted in the forest of Fontainebleau. He will embellish with his own trophies the gallery built by Henri IV. He'll cram it with dozens, hundreds of sets of antlers, with innumerable stuffed heads. In the end, no one will be able to penetrate into the gallery anymore. He'll go there alone, in secret, at dusk. He'll slip through the intricate tangle. The massive antlers, the heads, rising up everywhere and multiplied by the mirrors, will neither wound nor hinder him. They'll remind him of the only *lived* moments of his existence. Since his first hunt with hounds, last spring at Rambouillet, he can conceive of no stronger sensation than that of galloping along the trail of a deer amid the loud barking of the pack, the calls of the hunting horn, the ecstasy of speed, and the shafts of light piercing the foliage, that fever of power and risk, the joy of a hand-to-hand struggle with nature, of a loving combat with animal life. To destroy it? No, the hunter thinks, he's bound to his prey. The fear he causes it can turn around very quickly. It's the matter of a second, a fall from a horse, the charge of a wounded boar, or like the accident that befell the young Duke de Melun at Chantilly only a few weeks ago, an antler that rips you open. The young man was wounded in the side, so deeply that his liver was pierced. He'd been carried into one of the rooms of the château. And the king had witnessed his friend's death agony.

Some thought that the youthful monarch would suffer emotional repercussion from this tragedy. He no doubt did, but not enough to calm his frenzy. For the dark side of that activity, so readily defended by appeals to fresh air and good health, is not unknown to him. It is even, perhaps, what he was first taught in the course of the bizarre shooting sessions during which he'd be placed, pistol in hand, inside a gigantic aviary and instructed to shoot without even aiming. The slaughter would end in a dizzying whirl of flight and demented rustling and falling birds, while the boy, without ceasing his fire, would cry that he had had enough. But his master-of-arms would reply, "You have to savor the enjoyment of terror right to the end." Those sessions, had they really taken place? Did they form part of his old dreams? Marked for death from the start, Louis has grown up in fear.

It constitutes his deepest connection to all the events of his life. And perhaps he remains indifferent when fear doesn't intervene. On the other hand, his interest is aroused whenever an event, an activity, a person has anything at all in common, however remotely, with the panic in the aviary — with the enjoyment of terror.

Scandalous Girl

Louise Élisabeth needs La Quadra's fingers, but they don't suffice to calm her. She's not in love with that girl. It just so happens that La Quadra and the Kalmikov sisters are more indulgent than the others, and they have fun ideas. They know how to cool her down properly.

She's lying stretched out with her thighs spread; one of the girls fans her crotch.

She's lying stretched out with her legs pressed together; one of the girls penetrates her with little flicks of her tongue.

She's lying with her limbs in disarray, arching her back and crying out as if possessed; one of the girls, or the three of them, rubs her labia with pieces of ice.

Louise Élisabeth teaches them some lewd French words, words spoken in the fairgrounds theaters of Paris or by the prostitutes of the Palais-Royal, words she didn't know she knew but which occur to her in private, just as the little infanta, in public, finds herself naturally inclined to rhetorical emphases that date back, through her father, to Louis XIV.

King Luis makes an effort to remain deaf to the rumors, to cut off Mme de Altamira's complaints or other well-intentioned persons' attempts to inform on the queen. But there's a limit, and it's crossed when Louise Élisabeth allows herself to ask La Quadra, in front of witnesses, "Would you agree to pimp for me?"

Shocked, the king, who is on the point of going to Valsaín, writes to his father that he'd prefer to see him alone — without Louise Élisabeth:

> As for the rest, I told the Queen that I wished to go to Valsaín and she said that she too would like to go I answered that the journey could be bad for her the road being long and full of snow I say this to Your Majesties so that I can tell the Queen that I have written to you but certainly I have always wanted and still want to go without the noise of those women who all too often make my head spin. (March 18, 1724)

He's resolved to travel alone so that he can really talk to his father.

Once he's in Valsaín, he perceives the impossibility of a private interview and resolves, despite his embarrassment, to reveal to both the king and the queen a small fraction of the abyss he's sinking into. They listen to him with similar expressions of disgust and incredulity. Their Majesties extract from him a promise to conduct himself with firmness. On the eve of his departure, the former king, in accordance with the rite, gives his son his hand to kiss, but the queen, not for the first time, refuses to offer hers. Luis finds this refusal, at a time when everything is slipping out of his control, intolerable.

As soon as he's back in his palace, he informs Their Majesties of Louise Élisabeth's behavior: "Although the Queen is better, she is not yet what I wish her to be but I promise Your Majesties never to desist in my undertaking" (April 13, 1724). He has a moment of optimism:

> I write to Your Majesties with great joy because of what happened this day with the Queen. For in the first place she was given a written list containing every instance of her extravagant behavior and having then told her that my patience was at an end and that if she did not mend her ways it would be necessary to move *ex verbis ad verbera*, she trembled and begged my pardon and promised to mend her ways as I have no doubt she will do. Today I went out looking for quail saw three and fired three shots and killed all three of them. (Aranjuez, May 22, 1724)

Louise Élisabeth writes to her mother. Having finished the letter, she rereads it, crumples it up, and eats the sealing wax.

The torments of his marriage are not all that the king must suffer; there are, in addition, affairs of state. The Spanish have not taken long to realize that their hopes for him were a utopian dream. It's true that Luis I was born in Spain, that as a small child he was nourished on Spanish chocolate, and that his first language is neither French nor German nor Italian. It's also true that he's a boy of great piety and totally without malice. But it has become equally obvious that his chief virtue is obedience, a characteristic hardly conducive to governing. At every turn, he asks Their Majesties for advice.

There are also his recurrent entreaties on a theme as agonizing as his wife's follies, namely Elisabeth Farnese's refusal to give him her hand to kiss. "I shall not be content until the Queen accords me the just favor that I have requested of her...which costs her nothing and which is at this moment the only thing I ardently desire."

On one of the mornings when his wife speaks to him, he's surprised to hear her ask him what his plans for the day are.

"Well, first we attend Mass together, then I have the Council of Messages, then dinner, and after dinner I shall go hunting." A faint smile appears on Luis's face: "Yesterday I killed a hare, a woodcock, a jay, two owls..."

Louise Élisabeth diligently bites her fingernails and says, "You are, Monsieur, *un as de la tuerie*, an ace at killing."

The king gives her a disconcerted look. Not only does she seem to be taking an interest in his life, but she's making a play on words besides.

"In fact," she adds, "what does 'Asturias' mean?"

"It is a region of the kingdom, Madame. In the north."

"Suppose we go there to see why it is that we're called the Prince and Princess of Asturias? Let's take a trip to Asturias—it would be educational!"

"We should have to get authorization from His Majesty my father."

"But aren't you the king, and am I not the queen?"

"Yes, I am the king and you are the queen, but the king my father is my master and yours as well."

The people have no need of overhearing this conversation to know that nothing has changed. All decisions continue to issue forth from Their Majesties; the young king is nothing but a puppet. A lampoon reads,

The king and the queen have retired to the mountains,
The king and the queen in the Court do sit;
The first, as before, are ruling the roost,
The second, as always, submit.

The project of a trip to Asturias is abandoned. A visit to San Ildefonso seems more judicious. Louise Élisabeth once again asks to go along. Her husband replies, "I am not certain that you would be welcome, and even less so your ladies. I have promised that you will conduct yourself decently; I am waiting for Their Majesties' consent."

A note more resigned than pleased invites Don Luis to come, accompanied by his wife, but without her throng of servants.

The way is long and winding. Louise Élisabeth contemplates the walls of rock. She bites her fingernails through her gloves, swallowing nails and leather indifferently. Once arrived, she's agitated and voluble. Philip V and Elisabeth Farnese ignore her. As always in his father's presence, Luis feels intimidated, and is moreover constantly on the lookout for a misstep from Louise Élisabeth. The courtiers who have agreed to follow Philip and Elisabeth into their religious retreat are, on the whole, elderly and devout. A sepulchral atmosphere reigns over all. Philip sniffs around everywhere, suspicious of the devil's sulfurous emanations.

"Sire, you should train some dogs," sniggers Louise Élisabeth. "They will track down the devil the way they flush hares."

She has removed her traveling clothes and taken a bath. She reappears wearing a chemise and a petticoat and then goes out into the garden.

Philip is sitting at one of his bedroom windows, staring out vacantly at the paths, the groves, the copper-colored statues. He fingers his rosary beads, and nostalgia, distraction, and his mystical inclinations combine to conjure up before his eyes a confused vision that mingles the Versailles of his youth, his intense affection for his brothers, their separate lives, and San Ildefonso, where he himself has chosen to lead a separate life. Against this background of reveries, in this fresh, green landscape, there suddenly appears, very close to him, Louise Élisabeth. She's barely dressed; her hair is still wet. For a second, Philip feels annoyance — and curiosity. There's something outlandish in the behavior of this young girl, who nevertheless — in contrast to her effect on Elisabeth Farnese — does not arouse his entire hatred.

First on one foot and then on the other, Louise Élisabeth jumps from square to square in an imaginary game of hopscotch. With each hop, her damp hair rises and falls. A gust of wind suddenly lifts up her light silk petticoat and exposes to the eyes of the "old king," a man imbued with prayer and sensuality, a man given to hallucinations and infernal visions, the little black triangle of the new queen's pubes.

Her legs have been burned golden by the sun, and what he should find hideous makes his mouth water more than a slice of gingerbread. "Mary, Mother of God, protect me from evil thoughts," the penitent murmurs.

In the midst of discussing various political matters, he decides to speak, in his languid voice, to his son about the hopscotch incident.

Now not only Philip but also the entire court is openmouthed with amazement.

Louise Élisabeth has sunk into vice so deeply as to go out barefoot. She has dared to expose that part of the body which a Spanish lady of high society is obligated to keep hidden. King/son leaves it up to king/father—whose eye is still troubled by his daughter-in-law's nakedness—to teach her a lesson. "But Sire, you need only say what you want me to do, and I shall do it without hesitation."

"What we desire, Madame, is that you comport yourself correctly. If you persist in your current behavior, we shall proceed from admonitions to punishment, *ex verba ad verbera*, from words to blows."

Louise Élisabeth listens, looking downright disconsolate.

At the end of the sojourn at La Granja, she is not allowed to bid Their Majesties farewell. Don Luis is authorized to do so, but only his father gives him his hand to kiss.

They're on the road back to Madrid. The girl's bare feet, even more than her uncovered sex, ought to encourage the king to follow his father's advice and impose a sanction. But he looks at her, at the locks of her hair falling over her eyes, at her silk petticoat and her chemise, an overly loose garment that permits him to glimpse the first swelling of her childish breasts. She has taken off her shoes. They drift around inside the carriage as the horses pull it through wrenching hairpin turns. When the vehicle is immobilized by a flock of sheep, Louise Élisabeth, who hasn't said a word since they left San Ildefonso, declares, "I thoroughly enjoyed myself, and you?"

She pops her head out of the carriage window and cries, "*¡Más rápido!*"

The coachman freezes with his whip in the air, caught between the sheep and a precipice. "Why faster?" he asks. "So that we can fall?"

"*Exacto.*"

Luis should detest her, but all at once he loves her, he adores her. He tortures himself in an effort to comprehend how this terrible misunderstanding could have come between them. He'd like it if she would try to ponder the question with him.

"A misunderstanding between whom and whom?"

A jolt more violent than the others sends them flying, striking their heads against the cloud- and cherub-painted ceiling of the coach.

King/son takes up some files to work on into the night. He makes the problems more of a muddle.

He goes to sleep later and later and gets up early, before she does.

He exhausts his small store of remaining strength in solitary hunts, in the worst of the summer heat.

Louise Élisabeth spends a great deal of time in her apartments. There she plays hopscotch, which is her frenzy of the moment. She drinks until she's no longer thirsty and then well beyond that point. She competes with her ladies-in-waiting to see who can eat the most radishes and drink the most wine. The competitions always come down to her and La Quadra, but in the end, of course, Louise Élisabeth emerges victorious. Together they drain the last bottle, and then the queen goes off to collapse onto her conjugal bed.

She spends a great deal of time in her apartments, or a great deal of time in the gardens, depending on her mood. One thing remains constant: she needs no pretext to remove most or all of her clothing. "We must keep an eye on the Queen, for yesterday she tried to go out onto the balcony in her chemise" (Buen Retiro, July 7, 1724). With the exception of the king, whom she never meets except when wearing a nightgown as alluring as a sack, many are those who, like the king/father, have got a look at her intimate parts. Gossip and complaints multiply. Santa Cruz, the chief majordomo, resigns. King/father orders king/son to crack down.

She goes out into the vegetable garden at nightfall, eats tomatoes and peppers, sits on the ground, chats with the gardeners. She takes off her chemise and stretches out on the grass. Her giggling fits perturb the nightingales.

One day in her library, she climbs to the top of a ladder and has an attack of vertigo. She calls for help. A French gentleman tries to assist her. He goes up the ladder and takes her in his arms. Her state of undress is so advanced that it leaves him incapable of making the least movement. He keeps his hold on her, at the top of the ladder. Louise Élisabeth calls for help again and cries rape. The accused is a French nobleman; the scandal is going to spread to Versailles. Elisabeth Farnese intervenes. She decides that things have gone far enough; Luis must put an end to the queen's extravagant behavior.

Louise Élisabeth grows tired of hopscotch, tired of competitions with her ladies, tired of the games they've invented together. She continues to eat and drink like a bottomless pit, but she often ends up alone and constantly gives herself over to the same activity: washing handkerchiefs. Leaning over a tub, naked from the waist up, sweating profusely, she scrubs her handkerchiefs. She leaves them to dry on her balcony, on her windows, on the corners of her mirrors, even on the floor.

When she abandons the handkerchiefs, she scrubs the windowpanes, the floor tiles.

The Duchess de Altamira is loath to enter the queen's rooms. Nervous spasms contort her mouth; she can no longer control her horror. But in fact, save for Louise Élisabeth's three favorites, no one willingly risks entering her apartments.

The expression "as for the rest"—that is, the problem of Louise Élisabeth—pervades the correspondence between king/father and king/son.

I am going to relate to Your Majesties that the Queen was in such an extraordinarily joyous state yesterday when I was going to supper that I believe she was drunk although I am not sure first she recounted to La Quadra everything that had happened to her and I verily believe that this woman whom she likes very much is quite pernicious to her this morning she went to San Pablo in her dressing gown to have a midday meal and wash some handkerchiefs...she was at high mass because I waited half an hour for her to get dressed and made her go and afterward she dined on a goodly number of vilenesses and after dinner she went out onto the big glass balcony in her chemise and she could be seen from all sides washing the tiles...I am desolate but do not know what is happening to me. (July 2, 1724)

King/father replies to "Your Majesty," his son:

I was extremely vexed by the report you gave me concerning the Queen your wife, and I pray that you will continue to inform me in detail of everything that happens in her regard, so that if she does not mend her ways I may be able to advise you as to what seems to me the most suitable course to take... (July 2, 1724)

King/son on the next day:

I am most obliged to Your Majesties for your support in my grief which only grows and thrives yesterday evening after supper The Queen ate some chicken and a salad of cucumbers and tomatoes with her ladies in waiting and afterward she put on a chemise and was there until I entered to go to bed. This morning she spent more than 2 hours washing handkerchiefs and after dinner she went to the Casón with La Quadra...and then she asked for a bathtub to be brought to her I do not yet know what she will use it for and she has not yet returned from her outing and she does nothing but scold all day long so that I can see no other remedy than to lock her away and that as soon as possible for the disturbances she causes are daily increasing...

King/father, more than alarmed, replies:

Your Majesty's situation as described in your last letter concerning your wife's conduct has caused me more pain than I can well express...but it seems to me that we must expect the chief remedy for all this to come from God, who alone can change hearts as He pleases, although we ought to bring to Him those who are dependent upon us, and indeed we are in duty bound to do so...You should have her shut up in her apartments inside the Retiro itself, forbidding her to leave and giving some wise and trusted officer of the Bodyguards the charge of preventing her from going out, unless it is too distressing for you to have her so near you in her present state and you therefore wish to move her to an apartment in the Royal Palace in Madrid. Do not see her at all, neither eat with her nor sleep with her...In this reclusion, let The Queen your wife be led to understand the extravagance of her behavior, which is an affront to God, to you, and to herself. I also think, as she is of the House of France, you will do well to inform M. de Tessé that you have been obliged to the making of this decision in order to correct her.

In Detention

Louise Élisabeth and her ladies are gathered in a pavilion of the royal palace of El Pardo for an afternoon snack and a concert. The young queen swallows a maximum number of pastries. Then, during the concert, she remarks with a laugh, "I can't hear a thing. I've got the sound of cakes in my ears." She puts a few pieces of tart in her pockets, rises, makes a sign that no one is to follow her, and disappears down a path. Her ladies, headed by the Duchess de Altamira, become alarmed. Following the queen's orders, they remain in their seats, but they can't listen to a single note. As soon as the concert is over, they rush off after the runaway. They find her playing in a fountain. She's removed her shoes and stockings and raised her dress to her thighs, and she wades back and forth though the spray, whirls around, lies down in the water, thrusts out her bare, suntanned legs, her bare feet. Her ladies are disgusted and afflicted with guilt for witnessing such a spectacle. The Duchess de Altamira forces herself to approach the fountain and snatch the girl from her frolics. After a consultation with the other ladies, she climbs into a carriage alone with the thoroughly drenched Louise Élisabeth.

"What have I done wrong now? I walked around in water, is that a sin? I shall ask Father de Laubrussel."

"You walked around! Excuse me while I laugh," coughs Mme de Altamira, who has long forgotten how one laughs. "The water and your…nakedness are not the king your husband's only grievances. There is also the matter of your table manners."

"I don't often eat at table. When I'm hungry, I nibble something."

"You 'nibble' against all good sense."

"Aha! There we are! You're like the king, you accuse me of eating too much salad, too many gherkins and tomatoes and radishes. I've had enough of your criticism. I like green vegetables with lots of vinegar — so what? I can also enjoy pastries, as you saw a little while ago. What I eat doesn't concern anyone but me, it's my business! My excesses, to use my husband's refrain, do no harm to anyone but me, as far as I know."

As she speaks the words "as far as I know," she hiccups and vomits her entire snack.

Because of her indisposition, she fails to notice that the vehicle transports her not to the Buen Retiro but to the Palace of Madrid, where she is immediately shut up in her room and has no servants left but a few appointed by Luis. The Duchess de Altamira receives orders not to leave her alone for a minute. Louise Élisabeth weeps, begs, shouts from the windows for people to come and rescue her. She writes to her husband that he must have pity on her. She swears to her parents-in-law to mend her ways, but in the same moment when she announces that she's prepared to beat her breast in penitence, she declares, so loudly and clearly that it's bound to be reported to Elisabeth Farnese, "I'm thirteen years old and I do foolish, childish things, what a surprise! She was twenty-two when she came to Spain, and she did worse things than I've done."

On a regular schedule, she's served hot meals she doesn't touch accompanied by water she spits out.

Don Luis finds it difficult to remain firm: "After having wept a great deal yesterday evening, the Queen wrote to me this morning and sent me by Father de Laubrussel the letter I am forwarding to Your Majesties" (Buen Retiro, July 5).

But king/father and his wife don't give up the fight: "We must wait for the future time when God, who sees our intentions and our suffering, touches her heart and makes you happier. To this end I shall, I assure you, most ardently offer up to Him my lowly prayers" (July 5).

From Elisabeth Farnese: "May God touch her heart, may He move her to everything that is for the best for her and for us as well. There is much talk of this state of affairs in Madrid, among other things it is said that it comes from here, and also that I myself have been the cause of it. I practice patience..." (July 7).

Louise Élisabeth is afraid. Suppose she were to be detained for months, for years, forever! She scribbles letter after letter. She gets no response. She's watched day and night to assess the strength of her desire to mend her ways. It's noticed that she has managed to spirit away a little pile of handkerchiefs and to find some water to wash them with. And she starts in again! At dawn, she's caught in flagrante delicto: scantily dressed, barefoot, scrubbing and rescrubbing the handkerchiefs and hanging them on a window, where they flutter like flags of neutrality.

But she's no more neutral than she is reconciled. She's made of the same stuff as the young witches who get burned alive without the mercy of prior strangulation.

Luis lives in obsessive fear of the little notes Louise Élisabeth writes. They distress him mightily. Through the incoherent, babbled sentences he hears her voice, the voice of an unloved child, and it's all he can do to keep himself from setting her free at once. He's ready to institute arrangements to this end, if the king/father will approve them. He writes: "The Queen begins to make good progress and mend her ways but I think we shall have to make la Quadra and the little Kilmalok [sic] girl leave the palace" (July 8); "Father Laubrussel has told me that he believes it necessary to dismiss the Duchess de Popoli la Quadra and all but six of the ladies-in-waiting the best-behaved of the lot who will remain with the Queen" (July 11); "The Queen makes good progress and does all that she is told" (July 12); "I continue to have the women's quarters searched" (July 15); "The Queen is better and better so much so that I think that once her women are sorted out I shall be able to let her come back if Your Majesties concur" (July 16); "This morning I gave the Camarera [the Duchess de Altamira] the order concerning all her women and as soon as they have gone, I can assure Your Majesties that I shall call The Queen back with great pleasure" (July 19).

King/father gives his approval: "It seems to me that after the execution of your orders there is nothing else that should keep her apart from you. I rejoice with you in the boar hunt and your excellent kill" (July 20). Luis recalls the queen. He doesn't hide his joy. With her "he lives through hell," but what would he be without her? On July 21, he has her released from the Palace of Madrid and waits for her in his carriage. Her suntan has faded, and she's covered with several layers of clothing: corset, chemise, underskirts, and frocks. Her feet are hidden. She's so pretty that Luis is touched at the sight of her, pale and submissive under her rigid coiffure.

> I begin my letter by announcing to Your Majesties that The Queen is already at the Retiro...having found her upon my return at the green bridge where I had left her. I kissed her and placed her in my carriage. It's late I have a great deal to do and I end by imploring Your Majesties to believe me your most obedient son. (July 20)

VERSAILLES, JULY 1724

Preparations

News of the queen's detention crosses the border, but it's relatively muffled. At Versailles, in a July not so torrid as to set anything ablaze but hot enough to keep the gossip pots boiling, the insiders, those close to M. le Duc are delighted by the punishment inflicted upon the daughter of Philip d'Orléans. *There's something rotten in the state of Spain*, more than one person thinks, but as Shakespeare is not M. le Duc's cup of tea, nobody risks this pretty allusion. There's general skepticism about the new beginning from the green bridge. "It passes understanding that this Luis I, who bangs away at anything that moves, seems incapable of banging his wife," jokes M. le Duc. The ensuing guffaws are so loud and long that he himself finds them excessive.

Louis XV and the infanta are kept in the dark about the embarrassing affair. The infanta gets her dolls ready for Fontainebleau. Louis XV finds himself bored at Versailles, which will nonetheless provide fertile ground for his future explorations.

In the months preceding the king's arrival, the Palace of Fontainebleau is the scene of feverish activity. An army of servants replaces the carpets, which were taken up in the absence of the court, as well as the curtains, the chairs, and even the chandeliers, previously stored to protect them from dust. The furniture, still fitted with slipcovers, has returned. The announcement of the royal sojourn triggers an enormous operation of slipcover removal. The uninhabited château rediscovers its paintings, its Gobelin tapestries, its sparkle, its colors. Cleaning and refurbishing Fontainebleau, dusting off, one by one, the panels of the Saint-Saturnin chapel and its carved wooden reliefs — all this leaves the servants exhausted and anxious at the thought of incurring even the mildest reproach.

During this same period, the courtiers at Versailles are also hard pressed, with the difference that for them the strain is not physical but mental. Everyone's fixed objective is to accompany the royal relocation to Fontainebleau; everyone is obsessed with getting on the list of those "named." The courtiers squander most of July on maneuvering to make sure they figure among the elect, and then, if those efforts are successful, to see to it that their lodgings are not too bad — and especially that their bad lodgings are not in the homes of the local inhabitants, that is, outside the palace. To have bad lodgings in the palace is still tolerable — unfortunate, of course, but the essential thing is to be in the same place as the king.

Among the novelties of his new profession, Louis XV takes great pleasure in giving the guards the password each evening, and — when stays away from Versailles are planned — in drawing up the list of those who have been "named." For the youngster who detests society when it's imposed on him, the act of "naming" amounts to eliminating the great majority of those courtiers he's normally forced to put up with. For sojourns at Marly, he can make huge reductions, he can provide lists that make people mad with envy. For Fontainebleau, he has to expand the selection. In any case, what sets the spiral of courtly life in motion and springs the passions that arise from that motion is the ever-present possibility that the circle of the elect may shrink and, even inside the circle, the regularly maintained consciousness of how arbitrary every position of favor is. Lack of experience, a taciturn disposition, and a profound lack of interest — which stems from his melancholy — make the young boy as hard to figure out as Louis XIV was, though the reasons for the old king's inscrutability were very different: concern for his sovereignty, well served by his megalomaniacal pride and strategic sense of stage-setting. M. le Duc advises the king. Like him, he wants the coming autumn to be especially sumptuous, utterly unforgettable.

MADRID, JULY–AUGUST 1724

Good and Obedient

The period of her detention has terrorized Louise Élisabeth. Now barely a quarter of her ladies-in-waiting remain to her, and the seven she's been allowed to keep—among them the noblewomen Taboada, Montehermoso, Marín, Brizuela, and Bernal, who hate her—are in the pay of Philip V and Elisabeth Farnese. The Kalmikov sisters have been forced into marriages; nobody has any news of La Quadra. Louise Élisabeth has asked about her, in vain, and has since given up. The way her three favorites have vanished exacerbates her fear and leaves her feeling lost. She's the object of close supervision, and messages exhorting Luis I to exercise severity arrive incessantly from San Ildefonso. But the Duchess de Altamira is sometimes absent, and as for the ladies who are Louise Élisabeth's other custodians, she can always buy them. So she sees her chance, takes off her clothes in a flash, and heads for the balcony. Since she's had access to sunshine again, her skin is lightly tanned. Wearing nothing but some necklaces and bracelets, she opens the curtains and exposes herself. The air of impudence radiating from her and the golden shimmer of her skin could make whoever chances to see her believe, in his distraction, that the queen of Spain has been replaced by a Gypsy, and that the royal person-age herself, incorrigible, unreconciled, has been defini-tively detained. But it's indeed her, and these fits of hers are quickly suppressed. The king has little difficulty ignoring them, first because he's exhausted, and second because, in his presence, Louise Élisabeth is completely docile — docile and glum. His letters to his father, therefore, are solely opti-mistic: "I am as contented with the Queen as Your Majes-ties can well believe for she does everything she is told this morning she asked my permission to go for a walk"; "The queen is getting along wonderfully"; "The Queen continues to do very well." All that remains is the increasingly urgent, all-consuming request that Elisabeth Farnese not refuse to let him kiss her hand.

"I implore Your Majesties to be so gracious as to allow me to kiss your hands whenever I have the honor of appearing before you" (July 29).

"I cannot too much complain that Your Majesties who so love me will not give me your hands to kiss, the which costs you nothing and would bring joy to my heart, but at least tell me yes or no so that I can cease to importune you, justified though I am in my pleading, today I was at Chamartin and there I killed seventy pigeons" (July 31).

He's practically certain that his father will grant his request; it's the absence of a response from Elisabeth Farnese that tortures him: "I await with impatience the

Queen's reply to my letter of yesterday" (August 4); "The queen says nothing about what I wrote to her the day before yesterday, no doubt because she will do what I have asked of her" (August 5).

The queen his wife will not give him her body to love.

The queen his stepmother will not give him her hand to kiss.

He walks on, clutching his hunting gun. In the night he follows bloody tracks, and at high noon he staggers, blinded by dust.

FONTAINEBLEAU,

AUGUST–NOVEMBER 1724

Pif! Paf! Poof!

The king's departure is accompanied by music and great pomp. The infanta's, on the following day, is not without style. Carmen-Doll is back in her hunting outfit. Dauphin-Doll has been "forgotten" under the bed. As for the chorus of dolls shut up in the trunk, it's conceivable that they will never again see the light of day, since after being removed from the infanta's apartments they've been stowed in the part of the attic known as the "trunk storeroom"—where dozens and dozens of trunks are lined up with no prospect of being reopened one day, no likelihood that their contents will ever be handled again and returned to the restorative circulation of things that go on trips. Their involuntary retirement resembles death. The prospect terrifies the wooden dolls so much that they've tensed up and, despite their robust constitutions, begun to split; they bear gaping wounds like stigmata on their legs and the middle of their foreheads. Their friends the cornhusk dolls have long since perished, and it's sad—and unhealthy—to remain shut up with their little greenish bodies, stuck to one another by the hair, gradually drying out. The dolls crammed into the trunk discover morbidity. Those that retain some sense of humor observe that their fate could be worse: they could have been thrown into a firewood chest, and then hello Joan of Arc!

Like the king, the infanta distributes, according to her mood, favor and disfavor, except that the beneficiaries of the former and the victims of the latter are her dolls. Which doesn't mean that the situation is any easier to handle. Whereas the king replies with silence, the infanta drowns problems in a flood of words. She's often to be found in agitated consultations with her dolls, which sit before her in several rows like her ladies on their stools, decked out in their finest attire but plainly unhappy. The cause of their unhappiness is their not being invited along on hunting excursions. At Versailles and even more often at Fontainebleau, where hunting is really the sole and exclusive occupation, the infanta and her favorites are regularly included in the party (which creates friction among the ladies of her retinue, because some places in her carriage must be reserved for her chosen dolls). The other dolls rant and rave. But what's to be done? "There will always be some of you who are disappointed," the infanta reasonably explains. "I shall convey your concerns to the king. He is generous, and he heeds my wishes." With these words, the infanta kisses the royal portrait in the medallion she wears. At Fontainebleau, her secret wish—to obtain a proof of her husband's love — grows more intense, for in a certain sense she's never separated from him, never excluded from a hunting party or a concert. But the royal presence is always surrounded by a multitude, always the center of a male entourage that is itself controlled by M. le Duc.

The infanta spends more and more time soothing her dolls' feelings. She asks them why, given the unending stream of musical events and festive gatherings they're invited to, they're never in a dancing mood and sometimes even fall ill. The sad dolls are impenetrable, like the Sphinxes on the Grand Parterre, half women, half beasts, lying in calm and mysterious repose above the Carp Pond and its delightful pavilion, to which the infanta will never go alone with the king.

One day, when the hunt passes near the town of Avon, she's taken to visit a quarry; gaunt, dust-covered workers, armed with chisels and hammers, are breaking up blocks of sandstone. The infanta covers her eyes with both hands and wails that the quarrymen are hideous. She doesn't listen when it's explained to her that their work is frightfully difficult, for sandstone can't be sawed but only smashed. Her good humor returns when she learns that the sound the hammer makes when it strikes the sandstone is classified, according to its sharpness, in one of three categories: excellent, good enough, and mediocre, or as they are called, *pif*, *paf*, and *poof*.

Pif! Paf! Poof! she repeats, echoing what she's told.

Pif, *paf*, and *poof* enchant her.

She uses them to conclude her three-part discourses.

Pif, *paf*, and *poof* are also the syllables she uses to assess the quality of her days and her joys, the degree of a person's charms, or the goodness of a dish.

On one particularly *pif* morning, when the infanta is in a boat headed for an encounter with a swan, a cry from the bank informs her that the king is on his way to her apartments.

He's dressed in purple and wearing a cap with no feather. His set features convey deep mourning. He bows and kisses the infanta's hand. Is he about to recite the *Madame, I am delighted that you have arrived in good health* refrain again? Before the little girl can get that maddening thought out of her head, the measured voice, the bated, bating voice, the voice that needs not express in words the order, *Stay where you are, come no closer*, announces, "Madame, it is my sad duty to inform you that your brother, His Majesty the king of Spain, Luis I, is deceased."

During the following days, the infanta is the object of the greatest consideration. At the funeral service held in honor of the poor young king, everyone's attention is focused on Mariana Victoria. She doesn't need to eavesdrop on hallway conversations to deduce for herself that the death of Luis I is going to bring Philip V back to power. She will be, once again, the daughter of the king of Spain. *Pif! Pifísimo!* Louis XV is touched by the suddenness of Luis I's death, by their proximity in age and situation, and by the fact that they shared a name and were the orphans of two equally astonishing sisters, a similarity that may have gone even further than he suspected. At his first interview with Don Luis, Count de Tessé, the French ambassador to Spain, observed in him the "same difficulty or timidity in speaking that takes the king by the throat..." Louis XV prays a great deal. They pray together, he and the infanta. She asks her late brother to intercede with the Lord, to take advantage of their new propinquity and whisper to Him, "My God, make the king of France, my cousin, love Mariana Victoria, my little sister, a good and kind girl. Make him love her as she loves him, with all her heart. Amen."

At the same time as the news of Luis I's death, reports circulate about the edifying behavior of his queen, "*la reina Luisa Isabel de Orléans.*"

MADRID, AUGUST 15–31, 1724

"This evening I shall be in Paradise" (Luís I)

On Assumption Day, while all the church bells in Madrid are ringing out and the *madrileños* are covering statues of the Virgin with cornflowers, calla lilies, and white roses, the king loses consciousness. He immediately reports the episode to his father: "This morning at the second Mass I suffered a little fainting spell, and this so frightened the Queen that she became ill and vomited, but now, thank God, I feel there is nothing amiss." A few days later, at yet another Mass, Luís faints again. Only briefly, but he takes to his bed. He feels bad, though he presents no alarming symptoms. "I am resting, I have a cold, this morning I suffered a little fainting spell, but I feel better since going to bed, and I end by begging Your Majesties to believe me your most obedient son." When headaches, fever, and copious sweats begin to take hold of him, he's bled at the ankle, and the bleeding leads to the discovery of several smallpox lesions. Children are removed from his vicinity. People are assigned to look after

Louise Élisabeth. As soon as she hears the word "smallpox," she scents danger. From the roughness of her treatment, she gathers that the elder king and his scheming wife have issued orders for a double burial.

Luis is going to succumb to his disease, but she won't escape either. She doesn't budge from her apartments. She'd like to be forgotten by everyone. Today she'd gladly consent to confinement in another château, in the royal palace of Aranjuez, for example, or in El Escorial, or in the Alcázar of Seville...but that's out of the question. Her presence is required in situ, in the Buen Retiro Palace, at her husband's bedside. The king/father's orders are perfectly clear; he himself has learned of his son's sickness while shut up in San Ildefonso. "Despite the King's exhortations, the Queen has desired to remain at the Buen Retiro, where she is almost always in the royal chamber," the *Gazette* reports. Louise Élisabeth is practically alone at her husband's side, and when his condition worsens, every time she steps into his room she has the impression that she's walking toward her own grave. The lesions now cover his entire body, with the exception of his eyes. The king is declared to be "without any hope except in a miracle," and while his long blond hair is being cut—its beauty strikes Louise Élisabeth as never before—he uses what remains of his breath to dictate a testament in which he returns all power to his father and implores him to take care of the young queen. Afterward he still has a few lucid moments, enough time to announce, "This evening I shall be in Paradise." From then on, Louise Élisabeth never leaves his room. People outside those four walls praise her exemplary conduct; she alone knows under what threats, equal to or worse than smallpox, she is condemned to the sacrifice. "There is nothing that has not been done to increase the likelihood of her contracting smallpox," Count de Tessé writes in a letter to France.

Count de Altamira, the lord chamberlain, decides to send for five physicians, who confer together for three hours before declaring themselves in favor of a supplementary bleeding. Not at the foot this time, but at the arm. The lancet slices into Luis's meager flesh, his blood flows, his heartbeat slows down. His fingers are curled tightly around a crucifix; his tormented eyes search out those of Louise Élisabeth. To Father de Laubrussel, a man as sensible as he is kind, the bleeding seems dangerous: there's a risk that the smallpox, which has reached the suppuration stage, will start its cycle anew. "We tremble for the King," he writes in a letter to Tessé dated August 29, "but we have no say in this matter, and our only recourse is to pray to God to let the remedy succeed, contrary to all our fears." The remedy does not succeed, and God refrains from intervening.

She's at the dying boy's bedside. A section of the bed curtains is open. The king, his head resting on sweat-drenched pillows, moans. His moan is soft and deep, a song of strangulation in the breathless dark. Louise Élisabeth bites her fingernails. All at once, it's too much for her. She bounds to her feet, shoves aside clerics and guards, overturns console tables and statuettes, and then begins to run; the carpets become elastic under her feet, she runs and runs, she's young and strong, her whole future lies ahead of her, she has nothing to do with that recumbent effigy, nothing in common with the ghostly husband who's pulling her into the grave; she runs. Her goal is to reach the stables, jump on a horse, and ride to Paris, to the Palais-Royal, she's almost at the entrance to the stables, she spots her own black horse, but two men block her passage, forcefully gather her up, and haul her into the antechamber of the royal apartments. "If you please, Madame, return to your place by His Majesty's side," the nearly dead boy's lord chamberlain tells her in an amiable tone. "This...foray of yours is due to nothing other than your generous sensitivity. Far be it from me to reproach you for that." Before she can utter a word in reply, her escorts give her several pairs of slaps, striking her with all their strength in front of the Count de Altamira, who distractedly arranges an orchid flower with the tips of his fingers. At a sign from him, the batterers desist and the Duchess de Altamira slips into the antechamber; then she brings the stunned, bruised Louise Élisabeth, who has one swollen eye and a bloody mouth, to the bed where Luis I lies, ready to depart for Paradise.

The King's illness having grown considerably worse during the night between the 28th and 29th days of last month, His Majesty made his confession on the 29th, and toward evening of the same day received the Viaticum from Cardinal Borgia's hands. Two hours later, he was given some potions as ordered by the Physicians who had been summoned for consultation, and prayers were ordered in all the churches: the Relics of St. James, those of St. Isidore, and the miraculous images of Our Lady of Atocha and Our Lady of Solitude were exposed to the veneration of the people, and extraordinary alms were distributed to the poor...The King died at half-past two in the morning of the 31st, in the eighth month of his reign, after having given all the signs of a perfect resignation to the will of God...On the first day of the present month, King Philip and his wife betook themselves from San Ildefonso to their Palace in this City, where the assembled Council of Castille implored His Majesty to put on the Crown again in order to console the Kingdom for the loss which it had just suffered. On the same day, the body of the late King was embalmed, after which it was exposed in his bedchamber until three o'clock in the afternoon, when it was borne with the customary ceremonies from the Buen Retiro to El Escorial, accompanied by the Grandees and the principal Officers and Lords of the Court. The Queen his widow, who hardly left his side during his illness, has repaired to an apartment separate from that of the late King her husband, where her grief is commensurate with the loss of the Prince who loved her so tenderly. (From the *Gazette*, Madrid, September 5)

Elisabeth Farnese will maintain that Louise Élisabeth shouted with joy when her virginal, tormented husband—the too-docile son, the seven-and-a-half-month king, the poor Luis—gave up his soul to God. The former queen, now once again the reigning queen, will further declare that her daughter-in-law had gone on to utter horrors that would not bear repeating. Could it be possible that scraps of abominable litanies rose to the young girl's lips at that moment, that she spat them out in all their filth, without any shame, indifferent to the aghast faces of those around her? But perhaps it was Elisabeth Farnese herself who couldn't refrain from such an explosion of outrageously inappropriate euphoria at the king/son's death, for it brought unhoped-for change to her life: king/father would return to the throne, and so would his queen.

Louise Élisabeth catches the disease and begins to show symptoms. Elisabeth Farnese doesn't hide her relief; should the girl survive as dowager queen of Spain, the new queen foresees new scandals. The depraved little baggage puts all manner of things into her mouth and will do the same with her sex. "It will be such joyful news both for France and for Spain," writes Elisabeth Farnese, "when someone comes to us one fine day and tells us that the Queen is with child, or that she has given birth." Despite the lack of care (maybe that's what saves her) and the violent hostility shown her—her ladies treat her quite nastily—Louise Élisabeth gets better.

As far as Philip V and Elisabeth Farnese are concerned, she's responsible for the death of Luis I. They long to be rid of her, to send her back to France, and not only because she's a source of scandal; they want to drive her out of their sight like a criminal whom they lack the power to eradicate from the surface of the earth.

Louise Élisabeth, Mlle de Montpensier, the Princess of Asturias, *Reina Luisa Isabel de Orléans* is fifteen years old. She's a widow, she's loathed by her in-laws, she bears the title of second dowager queen of Spain (because the first, Maria Anna of Neuburg, is still living in Bayonne), and she can expect no help from her own country, where, in the words of a diplomat of the time, she is as much desired as "a bundle of dirty linen."

FONTAINEBLEAU,
NOVEMBER 3, 1724

The Feast of Saint Hubert, Patron of Hunters

Hunting fever is at its peak. Incense burns on Diana's altars.
The Feast of Saint Hubert occasions an incredible deploy-
ment of colors and music. The king's hunt and those of M.
le Duc, the Count de Toulouse, the Count de Conti, and
other princes of the blood unite. This day's hunting mobi-
lizes about a hundred hunting-horn blowers, more than
nine hundred dogs, a thousand horses. *Le vin, la chasse et les
belles, voilà le refrain de Bourbon* (Wine, hunting, and beauties, that's the Bourbon refrain): the words of the House of
Condé's fanfare "La Bourbon" fill the air.

The infanta becomes infatuated with a hedgehog.

MADRID, NOVEMBER 3, 1724

Through the Eyes of a Courtier

M. de Tessé, after a visit to Louise Élisabeth, writes to M. de Morville:

> I had the honor of kissing her hand and found her much grown, and more slovenly and dirtier than a serving wench in a tavern. I remember the late dauphine used to say that princesses were so beautiful in all descriptions of them that anybody who approached one must find something else entirely. Between you and me, monsieur, if such a person were doing business in one of the third-floor establishments on rue Fromenteau or rue des Boucheries, I doubt that a crowd would gather there to bring her their pennies. (November 3)

A second dowager queen, but a whore of the first order. He has an unheated imagination, the old Count de Tessé, who deems Louise Élisabeth too dirty and slovenly to attract the patrons of a low-end brothel. As for attracting them, perhaps not; but as for satisfying them, she has the requirements.

FONTAINEBLEAU,
END OF NOVEMBER 1724

The Smoothness of the Pumpkin

Fontainebleau awakens in mist. A milky white blanket lies over the ponds, the gardens, the woods. The infanta is at her window. She adores this cloud-wrapped world and the way the sun soon fritters it away. She lets herself be dressed, babbling the while, and then, without interrupting her monologue, she begins her morning tour. The rooms are still in darkness, lit only by the flames flaring up in some unextinguished hearths. With some assistance, she clambers up on a wooden chest and there she sits, dangling her legs in the air. The wooden chests at Fontainebleau serve the function of her stepladder at Versailles. They put her at a good height for observing the courtiers' various movements and especially for spotting the specific form of agitation that precedes an appearance of the king. On such occasions, she gets down from her wooden chest and hurries to her apartments to be made up and more fetchingly arrayed.

She enjoys her life at Fontainebleau. Once again, she's the daughter of the king and queen of Spain. From them — through the intermediation of Maman Ventadour — she receives letters she's proud of. Moreover, the dimensions of the palace ensure that not a day passes without a chance either to receive a visit from the king or to cross his path. She has even discovered one of her young husband's secrets. Once she saw him stop in front of the statue called *Nature*, circle it, and look at it very closely. The creature's body comprises several rows of breasts. The king went away dreamily...And she feels certain that he, like her, was perplexed by that abundantly endowed female form, by that exuberant *Nature*. And on another occasion when he passed by *Nature*, not alone this time but with friends, she was particularly happy to notice that he had nothing to do with the pleasantries inspired in the other boys by the image of so formidable a nurse.

The happiness of early November, the pleasure of chestnuts, the rich aromas of roasting game and of the heady wines she's allowed to taste, barely wetting her lips, are all the more captivating in that she's also prone to uneasiness, to the premonition of a threat: she feels it very precisely when M. le Duc, while addressing Mme de Ventadour, pats her, Mariana Victoria, on the head. This absolutely infuriates the child. But when M. le Duc isn't there and she has managed to forget him, the infanta is content; she tends to her hedgehog, waddles like a duck behind the ducks waddling on the banks of the Carp Pond, jumps into piles of dead leaves, and crouches down to the level of the big gourds, obese things busily growing under their foliage, touching and mingling and piling up on top of one another in an excess that fascinates her.

Carmen-Doll is wearing an orange, crocheted cape with a hood. The infanta works over a pumpkin, carving a fairy nook for her favorite. She provides the little room with silver furniture from a dollhouse given her by the Duchess d'Orléans. After Carmen-Doll is settled in, she and Mariana Victoria drink chocolate with whipped cream together. The pumpkin walls are as smooth as silk.

The infanta has two preferred trees: in the forest, the magnificent century-old oak known as the King's Bouquet, which she venerates; and in the park, a younger and less robust oak, under which she has ordered the placement of a little bench. Every day she goes and sits on that bench. The day before she quits Fontainebleau, she refuses to leave the tree, she wraps her arms around it. Next, pointing at the rough trunk, she strokes the bulging bark and says, "The tree is crying," and then, touching the bump, "See how thick its tears are."

MADRID,

END OF NOVEMBER 1724

Petition

Father de Laubrussel is touched by Louise Élisabeth's situation and well aware of the fact that her return to France is not desired, not by the d'Orléans family and not—most assuredly not!—by the Duke de Bourbon. The priest writes a letter for her, addressed to the king and queen of Spain:

> I am much indebted to Your Majesties for Your attention to the assuaging of my troubles, which are more real than they may seem to those who do not know me. My trust in You leaves me in no doubt that You will deal with me in the way most conducive to my welfare. I shall therefore await from Your hands, as from God's, whatever arrangements You may be pleased to make regarding my future.

All Louise Élisabeth has to do is to copy the letter. Each time she tries, she blots it frightfully or writes a word wrong and has to begin again. She grows impatient and gives up. She decides to send Father de Laubrussel's original letter, after adding her signature in one of the lower corners, a crossed and twisted scratching from which the *l* of Élisabeth emerges like a piton with a weird eyehole.

VERSAILLES, WINTER 1724

The Die Is Cast

Having returned from Fontainebleau much taller and stronger, Louis XV keeps to a flexible schedule. He enjoys going
to bed late and puts back the hour of his rising to whatever
time he pleases. But how does he occupy himself during the
long winter evenings? Not with reading, or with listening to
music, or with going to the theater. He gambles. He has discovered games of chance. The necessity of relying on good
luck and accepting bad luck suits his melancholic convictions
and his religious fatalism: action serves no purpose. The die
is cast. From all eternity. As he has no notion whatsoever of
the value of money, Louis XV loses his louis d'or with great
unconcern. "Trifles, trifles!" he says. Under their makeup,
the other players go through all sorts of changes. They miss
the days, not so long ago, when the boy's preferred amusement was lead soldiers.

Although the infanta has, in accordance with custom,
followed close upon the king ("The Queen-Infanta left here

on the 27th of last month to return to the Château of Versailles, where she arrived the same day," the *Gazette* informs its readers on December 1, 1724), and although she has indeed returned to Versailles, the palace of Glory that she shares with him, she can't catch up with the way he lives. The older he gets, the more he escapes her. She doesn't participate in his daily life, she's cut off from all his pleasures and activities. If it weren't for the Mass, she would never see him. But there are *Masses*, plural, and plenty of them. The palace chapel is an extremely busy place. In the royal tribune, the infanta's armchair is always ready to receive her, and the king's, which faces the altar, faithfully performs its duty as well. Thus her husband almost never appears before her anymore except when he's in prayer, a vision so beautiful that it consoles her for all the hours when she lives the life of a foreigner. If Mariana Victoria's aura is starting to fade on the profane stage of the court, in the Lord's house the adorable infanta — the little girl-queen of France, the mystical bride — radiates. And all the more so now, when she's preparing for the momentous event of her first confession.

Her confessor is Father de Linières, who is also confessor to the king. When she talks to him, making an effort to concentrate on the spirit of confession, trying not to omit any sin, no matter how venial, digging for all her faults, for even the temptation to a temptation, she's entranced by images of the beloved, by individual features of his absolutely beautiful person, by subtle, ravishing details: the shadow of his eyelashes on his fair cheeks, his perfectly drawn lips, his dark, luminous eyes, his proud bearing, his muscular calves in bright red, apple green, daffodil yellow stockings. "His calves are flower beds," she whispers to her confessor, perhaps in the mad hope that he'll report her observation to the interested party. Father de Linières, who has been listening to her with folded hands and a smile of absolution on his lips, gives a start. He addresses the infanta with great firmness. He preaches to her of married love, emphasizing that it is above all a love in obedience to God and in conformity with dignity, with its ultimate purpose being the continuation of a lineage and therefore the perpetuation of the monarchy. It's not about calves, the priest concludes.

The Wolves

Snow blankets town and country. People hole up in their dwellings. To protect themselves from the cold, to escape the wolves. They've left the woods, they're causing terrible damage to the flocks and even attacking the sheepfolds. They advance as far as the fields that surround Madrid. At night they venture into the narrow, deserted streets and pounce upon solitary passersby.

Shut up in her room, Louise Élisabeth stares at the pallid horizon. Her fire's out. She rings. Nobody comes. It's been a long time since she last looked at herself in a mirror. She thinks, "If a servant brings me some firewood, I shall seize the opportunity to ask for a mirror." A little voice like a broken machine whispers, "You may as well look for your reflection in a stick of firewood, my dear girl…" It's also been a long time since anyone spoke to her, not even so much as a few words about the weather. Her only contacts with the world are the brief visits she gets from the royal family. Or rather, intrusions. The monarchs arrive unannounced: the spectral king, dragging his feet, his eyes inhabited by diabolical visions; and Elisabeth Farnese, her face and throat glistening with cream, her double chin heralding the heavy necklaces that hang down to her belly, the belly of a woman who's always pregnant; Elisabeth Farnese, with her too-long nose, her duplicitous smile, her vigorous health, which flourishes in perfect union with her meanness; Elisabeth Farnese, who delights in dropping in on the second dowager queen to hear her news. Louise Élisabeth would like to be able to ask, *What news could I have, as a prisoner in the Buen Retiro, completely at your mercy?* Instead she extracts herself from the sofa where she lay drowsing and makes her reverences to Their Majesties. Don Fernando, the Prince of Asturias, has also come, and he gives the girl a sign of greeting. He remains mute, determined in his desire for revenge. He too detests Elisabeth Farnese, but that hatred strengthens him, whereas Louise Élisabeth, anxious about her fate and stupefied by solitude, merely crumbles.

The little voice that commands her to wash handkerchiefs, always more and more handkerchiefs, and advises her to remove her clothes so that she'll be comfortable, swings between relative discretion and emphatic presence, and in the latter case bombards her with such exhortations as "Go on, leave this room, go get yourself laid, go to the kitchens, the stables, the chapel, surely there will be some monk, some scullion willing to put it in you, go on, my little hussy, my queen, why add chastity to the sum of your misfortunes?" And then the young girl rings and rings, tries to get someone to open her door, and sometimes, to her surprise, it so happens that a male servant heeds her call. He doesn't have time to inquire as to what service is wanted before she jumps on him, it's a furtive, violent thrill for her, a pleasure that saves her from the doldrums, it would be better if the first man were followed by another one, who would plunge into her like his predecessor, with the same voracity, the same blindness, the same murderous intensity. "If I may give you some advice, you poor thing," drones the voice, like a music box without music, "do not cling to the few sprigs of reason still growing in your head. Put your trust in the wild weeds that so abound in there."

Perhaps because the way they take to return from the hunt passes not far from the Buen Retiro, the king and queen stop there to pay her a visit. They've just come from a battue of wolves. Their clothes, their boots bear traces of blood. To Louise Élisabeth, they look curiously excited; their eyes are glittering.

VERSAILLES, DECEMBER 17, 1724

The Infanta's Confession

From the *Gazette*: "The Queen-Infanta made her first confession to Father de Linières, Confessor to the King, and on the following day went to the Parish church and heard Mass." The infanta confessed some plausible faults, trifling venial sins, including gluttony; a feeling of impatience with Maman Ventadour; a moment of distraction during her studies; two naughty pokes in her jester's ribs. She has stopped cutting up the exquisite paper figurine of the King of Absence, whose wife she is, into scraps like coats of arms. And in any case, she keeps him for herself. "His calves are flower beds, his earlobes are cherries, his hair sparkles in the sun, his cheeks are a pair of white Communion wafers."

MADRID, DECEMBER 1724

"Dear Majesties of Manure…"

Louise Élisabeth is sick and tired of jesuitical formulations. In her head, she begins a letter to the king and queen: *Dear Majesties of Manure, Your Most Filthy Excellencies, you Vultures, you killed Don Luis, my husband, you crushed him under the weight of the crown, it fell back on top of him as a gravestone.*

Louise Élisabeth rips up the letter and crushes the paper into a ball. Three kittens fight over it. In any case, she's drunk all the ink. Her words on the page are transparent. Just scratches.

VERSAILLES,

FEBRUARY 20–23, 1725

When the Veil Is Torn

Louis XV doesn't have time to say to himself, "I'm dead, I shall join Don Luis in Paradise," before he falls into a deep drowse accompanied by fever. He nearly falls off his horse. Practically carried to his bed, he sleeps like a person in a coma. Sometimes he groans, and his groans are repeated and amplified by M. le Duc. The latter passes a sleepless night. He bounces between his apartments and the king's bed-chamber. His long arms and legs generate a wind of panic. He cries out, "What will become of me? In all this, what about me, what's to become of me?" The king is bled at the foot, without much result. M. le Duc shakes the sick boy, imploring him to live. A second bleeding, again at the foot, is tried. M. le Duc propels himself out of the king's chamber like a whirlwind and shouts, "If he escapes alive, he must be married!" He assails the physicians, strikes dogs and servants, and comes within an inch of clouting the young Duke d'Orléans, who's waiting, petrified, to see what course his cousin's illness will take. After the second bleeding, the king's fever diminishes; in his sleep, however, he seems to be suffering still. But in the morning of February 21, the king wakes and "finds his head quite clear, his drowsiness gone, and his fever steadily declining." His progress continues into the afternoon. That evening, the king falls "into a calm, untroubled sleep that lasts nine hours without interruption." The next morning, February 22, joy is unconfined. M. le Duc, his nerves frazzled, knocks back a bottle of champagne. The infanta and Maman Ventadour, who have spent the past two nights between prayers and tears, likewise sleep the sleep of exhaustion, a calm, untroubled sleep.

The following day, at the first news that the king's health has returned and that he can receive visits, the infanta can no longer keep still. She *must* see the king. An effort is made to calm her, the convalescent's fatigue is offered as an excuse, but nothing affects her resolve. Tapping her foot, she repeats that her husband is waiting for her, that she *must* see the king. Mme de Ventadour herself takes the infanta to him. But the duchess doesn't cross the threshold of the king's chamber; she leaves the little girl alone with her beloved. So that she may all the better savor her happiness? It's more likely that the duchess has doubts about their welcome. The screen of deceitful words that have, from the beginning, run from letter to letter, nourishing her sentiments, arousing her emotions, and obstinately comforting her in the elaboration of her fiction—that screen suddenly shows its inadequacy. It doesn't work anymore. She's written and written, she's sent dozens, hundreds of letters in an effort to stymie the truth and outlast it; but the truth, reinforced by M. le Duc's explicit determination to see to the king's remarriage, can no longer be eluded. Such sophisms as "Your husband does not come to call upon you because he is entirely absorbed in very grave matters," or "your peace and quiet are sacrosanct to him; he does not speak to you, but his silence is in this case a special mark of his interest," reveal themselves for what they are: shabby camouflage meant to dissemble the young sovereign's total lack of feeling for the infanta and his strong desire to have done with this absurd charade. Mme de Ventadour capitulates; her feverish and overactive enterprise of self-delusion is at an end. She sees what's there: a little girl dazzled by love for a boy, a boy whose antipathy for the girl sets him on edge, a story of unrequited conjugal affection disguised as youthful romance to mask the cynicism of a political arrangement. *Barbarity with polite smiles*, the duchess says to herself, struck by a metaphor that springs into her mind as though someone has just whispered it to her; and in this brusque rending of every veil, this sudden collapse of all the illusions and lies she has used to build her daily refuge and the circumstances of her survival, she recalls a moment whose power to horrify her is undiminished: the moment when she, a radiant beauty with an idealistic temperament, recently wed to the deformed, perverted gnome who was the Duke de Ventadour, ought to have admitted, "My husband is a monster."

The infanta leaves the royal chamber almost immediately after entering it and rushes to Mme de Ventadour: "Maman, he will never love us." She clings to the duchess's skirts, sobs at the level of her knees, plunges her face into the folds of rough-weave silk.

At the end of the long short story of her love, she has come up against that realization. She has yielded to the evidence and pronounced the words that break her heart.

It has been decided that she will be sent back. It's only a matter of weeks. M. le Duc uses the king's illness to ensure that the decision goes into effect as soon as possible. The king has declared that he has no wish to marry again. No one gainsays him, but the search for a bride is launched.

M. le Duc attempts to place his sister, Mlle de Sens, but she's refused, allegedly because it would be unseemly for a king to marry one of his subjects. Mlle de Sens's candidacy is withdrawn, and research into the advantages and disadvantages of various other candidates begins. Religion? An heiress of what royal house? Fortune? Age? Princess Amélie, the Princess of England, the Princess of Lorraine, the Princess of Prussia? A big girl, that last one, ten and a half years old. "No, in truth," repeats the king. "I do not wish to marry so soon." Princess Stanislas, the infanta of Portugal, some German princess?

A letter is written in the name of the king, a document full of circumlocutions and diplomacy, wherein he describes the profound sorrow that the necessity of separating from the queen-infanta causes him. The king signs the letter. M. le Duc is triumphant. The chamber where the King's Council meets is abuzz with expressions of satisfaction. The king retains his absent air. He makes no response to the Duke d'Orléans, who bitterly observes, "Thus all that my father envisioned will be destroyed." Inside the four walls of his room, Saint-Simon sees things the same way. He who was the architect of two decisive matrimonial unions and dreamed of obtaining an important post in Versailles or Madrid is definitively dismissed, sent away to live only in preparing his *Memoirs*, in dancing with his ghosts.

MADRID,

BEGINNING OF MARCH 1725

It's late in the morning. The king and the queen are in bed. She's bending over her embroidery, he's saying his rosary. The infantes are being dressed to visit their parents. Somewhere in the palace, musicians are rehearsing for this evening's concert. The queen sings as she embroiders. They receive a letter and peruse it together. The king looks appalled, the queen mad with fury. They reread. The queen rushes to her cabinet, yanks out drawers, hurls the bundles of letters they've received from France since their daughter's departure to the floor. She jumps up and down on the letters, spurning them underfoot. Then she reads some passages at the top of her voice. She cries treason, insults France and the French. She says to Philip V, "Expel all the French who live in Spain. Expel them at once."

"But in that case, Madame, I should have to leave the kingdom first."

❦

VERSAILLES,
BEGINNING OF MARCH 1725

Mme de Ventadour's anguish is so vehement that she is willing to do anything to escape the infanta's questions. She's afraid her Mariannine will be able to guess what's in store for her from her governess's sorrowful face. The duchess offers pretexts: migraine headache, bad fever, gambling losses. In the cafés of Paris and the provinces, gossipmongers incapable of holding their tongues on the subject of the infanta's dismissal and its consequences are arrested. The law of silence that reigns over Versailles is extended to the whole country. The image of an adorable infanta cracks. It's replaced by caricatures formed—or rather deformed—in the minds of her enemies. The lawyer Mathieu Marais, who was in the beginning totally conquered by the infanta, now writes these lines:

> In truth, she is too young (turns seven on March 31); she is small and grows not an inch a year; she is knotted up in her

loins and unfit for bearing children, and neither her little graces nor her charming wit will serve for aught in that work.

MADRID, MID-MARCH 1725

The king of Spain attends to preparations for fighting a war against the country of his birth. He's contemplating yet another fratricidal war. In dread, in horror, in the most complete dejection.

VERSAILLES, MID-MARCH 1725

Torrential rain showers are inundating the Île-de-France. Louis XV attends Mass, leaves after hearing the sermon, and departs for Marly on horseback. As the king zigzags to avoid puddles, the valet holding the umbrella over his head has difficulty keeping up with him. The king seems to be running because of the rain, but in fact he's running away. He's running away from the infanta. He dreads a final interview with her. M. le Duc has taken the initiative of offering the king this sojourn at Marly so that he may avoid the chore of a farewell.

MADRID, END OF MARCH 1725

Philip V abandons the project of a war that would be, for his already sufficiently tortured soul, the equivalent of launching his own armies against himself. The queen must be satisfied with the expulsion of Louise Élisabeth. And it really does satisfy her. As her detested daughter-in-law's departure date, she selects the birthday of one of her sons. The young widow takes her leave, accompanied (according to the *Gazette*)

by the Duchess de Montellano, her Camarera Mayor, and by the Marquis de Valero, President of the Council of the Indies, Lord Chamberlain, and in his quality of Majordomo of the Royal Palace, Commander of the detachment of Officers of the Royal Household, which has been commanded to accompany the Princess to the frontier of the Kingdom. On the same day, the 15th, there was a celebration at the Palace in honor of the birth of the Infante Don Felipe, who entered that day upon his sixth year…On this occasion, the Ministers and the Grandees of the Kingdom had the honor of kissing the hands of the King and the Queen; after which the Bailiff Don Pedro de Ávila, Ambassador of the Knights of Malta to this Court, presented to His Majesty, on behalf of the Grand Master, several birds of prey…and to the Queen, a bouquet of gold and silver filigree, worked with all imaginable delicacy. (Madrid, March 20, 1725)

Elisabeth Farnese radiates satisfaction.

The "bundle of dirty linen" is packed off to the joyous sounds of a celebration. In fine weather and in the opposite direction, Louise Élisabeth retraces the disastrous winter journey that brought her to Spain. She'd been ill then, and she hadn't seen anything. Nor does she this time. She's not unwell in body, but a voice lodged inside her head, between her ears, makes suggestions she doesn't especially like, tormenting suggestions that nevertheless demand to be followed: "Look at that little stream on your left, look at how swift and clear it is, go on and dive in, it will refresh you, little sloven. Make them stop the carriage, take off your clothes, and jump in the water, go on, poor girl, poor dowager!"

Louise Élisabeth tucks up her dress and pulls at a garter. The Duchess de Montellano, assisted by a companion, subdues her.

VERSAILLES, END OF MARCH 1725

The infanta struggles through the suffocating atmosphere around her. Nobody dares to face her. Mme de Ventadour weeps incessantly and remains shut up in her apartment. She writes to Madrid:

> For my part, Madame, the death of my grandchildren would cost me a thousand times less grief than the separation from my Queen. That is what she will always be to me, and my God! Madame, since Louis XIV's death, how many revolutions have we not seen, and there will be more to come! God's hand is heavy upon us. It is a great upheaval for this realm, that for the present your dear child is to be removed from us. Madame, our King is in no state to recognize his loss, and there are a great many things which one cannot hold against him. As I have the honor to write to a royal couple of signal devotion, I need not say anything to you about submission to the will of God.

The infanta's ladies-in-waiting and other companions are afraid of letting the truth out in her presence. People avoid the infanta. Her apartments are deserted. For those desirous of the king's favor — and who isn't? — calling on the child to kiss her small hand has become a proscribed act. The courtiers try to stay out of the little girl's way, they no longer pet her little dogs, no longer flatter her dolls, no longer fight to play a game of blindman's buff or *la queue du loup* (the wolf's tail) with her; they no longer maneuver to determine who will have the honor of pushing her little swing or harnessing white mice to her silver coach. They tread on the paper figurines she so assiduously cuts out with her embroidery scissors. Carmen-Doll has stuck an organdy gag over her raspberry mouth. A lady-in-waiting gives her a tip: the gags being worn this spring are of felt, in dark colors.

The infanta doesn't grow, and she's getting thinner. She's lost her appetite for food as well as life. One day, Bébé IV, her sole remaining companion, shows her a plate of *crêmes frites* with an apricot coulis. They look good, he tells her, and they must be eaten hot—would Her Majesty like to try one?

"Oh!" she says, pointing to her mouth. "When you've had it up to here, you can't eat."

A Spaniard from the embassy attends one of the infanta's suppers. He tells her that her mother and father are saddened by the passage of so many years without their daughter and would love to see her again.

"How do you know?"

He takes out a sheet of paper and reads it by the firelight. It's news from Spain; it reports that the king and queen are going to visit their kingdom, that they will come very near Bayonne, and that, since they will be at the French border, they would love to kiss the infanta. "Will Your Majesty agree to go?" asks the Spaniard.

The infanta senses some confusion. Why is this man, whom she barely knows, the one proposing this journey? Why isn't it

Maman Ventadour? Maman Ventadour is not the same as she once was. It's as though she were in hiding, or hiding something...But of course Mariana Victoria accepts, she misses her parents and her brothers. Besides, from the way the matter is presented, it sounds like only a brief sojourn. She says, "Yes, it would be a great pleasure for me to see them, too," but she doesn't feel any pleasure. And having said those words, in which she's heard the click of the trap closing on her, she leaves the supper table. Carmen-Doll withdraws to work on the great gathering of dolls. At Versailles, even if the majority of the dolls normally live in the queen-infanta's apartments, that doesn't stop some of them from nosing around outside their territory. It's possible to come across one mixing with the riffraff in the kitchens of the Grand Commons or outside the Little Stables. Carmen-Doll works fast. She sends messengers to all the palaces where the infanta has stayed. At Fontainebleau, the forgotten dolls have already been put under covers. By bribing the official in charge of furniture storage, the infanta achieves their liberation.

Carmen-Doll is relentless in making sure that not a single one of the infanta's dolls remains on French soil. The dolls shut up in the trunk can't believe their good fortune. They exercise discretion. The important thing is to be included in the baggage.

❧

BURGOS, APRIL 1725

Louise Élisabeth is counting the days. The palace she's
been relegated to resembles a prison. Perhaps it's her last
accommodations. She's not authorized to go about in Burgos, and in any case the notion wouldn't occur to her. She
eats everything she can, becomes fat and soft. A perpetual
expression of alarm causes people to take her for an imbe-
cile. The dowager queen, her rare visitors say, "has no more
resolution than a seven-year-old child," whereas the infanta,
seven years old herself, continues to surprise those around
her with observations worthy of a young woman of eighteen
or twenty. Not that this plays to her advantage; it's inter-
preted as a slightly monstrous anomaly. Deficient or too
precocious, too fat or too thin, weak-willed or too decisive,
already worn out or too young, henceforth neither the one
nor the other can ever please.

When the order is finally given for her departure for
France, Louise Élisabeth is not reassured. How will things
be on the other side? How will she be treated? "Badly, very
badly," the atonal, metallic voice replies for her, the soft
and maniacal voice of her madness. "Do you really want to
know any more about it, piece of trash, putrid little tramp?
Well, suppose you start by washing a few handkerchiefs, and
then I shall see…" Lying abed in the middle of the day with
her head under a blanket, Louise Élisabeth escapes. It's not
that she doesn't have the strength to fight, it's that she has

no strength at all, neither to resist nor to obey. She has no energy for anything, not even her caprices.

During the trip, she keeps the curtains down and doesn't seem to recognize her entourage. She's a package easily forwarded.

VERSAILLES, APRIL 5, 1725

It's early in the morning. The Sun Palace is outlined against a cold light. The shutters are still closed on most of the apartments of the great château. Mme de Ventadour, desolated with sorrow, hardly shows herself. It's obvious that the infanta has her doubts about her parents' alleged request. It had been thought that drowsiness would help to soften the violence of the departure, but she's thoroughly alert, as is her habit. She considers what's around her attentively and precisely, as if while looking she were already beginning to remember. Her vivaciousness makes people ill at ease. The farewells and the plans for her near return ring false. She contains herself and pretends to believe. At the moment when she climbs up into the carriage, she doesn't even ask where the king is. Great infanta.

AT THE BORDER, MID-MAY 1725

Once again they meet, headed in opposite directions. When they cross over the border, they do not kiss. The original exchange is made in reverse. The dowager queen of Spain for the queen-infanta of France. A half-mad teenager for a deposed child.

AUTHOR'S NOTE

All the extracts from correspondence quoted in this book are authentic. The letters or excerpts from letters written by Elisabeth Farnese, Luis I, Louise Élisabeth d'Orléans, Mariana Victoria de Borbón, Philip V, and Madame de Ventadour are mainly to be found in the Historical Archive in Madrid and are, for the most part, unpublished.

Press extracts are drawn from the *Gazette*, which after 1762 was called the *Gazette de France*.

PRINCIPAL CHARACTERS

Mariana Victoria de Borbón, in French Marie Anne Victoire, infanta of Spain, known after her marriage to Louis XV as the queen-infanta of France. She was born on March 31, 1718. Eventually, in 1729, she married the Prince of Brazil, who later ascended the throne of Portugal as José I, and with whom she had four daughters. Her husband being ill, she assumed the regency of that country from 1776 until her death in 1781. She was Marie Antoinette's godmother.

Louis XV, king of France. Born at Versailles on February 15, 1710. After his marriage to Mariana Victoria was annulled, in September 1725 he married Marie Lesczynska (she was seven years older than Louis, the queen-infanta had been seven years younger, balance was restored!). Eleven children were born of this union. Louis XV died on May 10, 1774, at Versailles, after a reign of nearly sixty years.

Louise Élisabeth d'Orléans, Mlle de Montpensier, Princess of Asturias after her marriage in 1722 to Don Luis, Prince of Asturias, and then queen of Spain — *Reina Luisa Isabel de Orléans*. She was born at Versailles on December 11, 1709, and died in Paris on June 16, 1742, completely neglected. She became dowager queen of Spain at the age of fifteen and never remarried.

Don Luis, Prince of Asturias, then king of Spain as Luis I. His reign lasted seven and a half months. He was born on August 25, 1707, and died in Madrid on August 31, 1724, at the age of seventeen. His tomb is in El Escorial.

CHANTAL THOMAS is a noted philosopher and writer. She has taught at a number of American universities and is the author of twenty-five works, including novels, histories, short stories, plays, and essays. Her internationally acclaimed novel *Farewell, My Queen*, a fictional account of Marie Antoinette's final days in Versailles, won the Prix Femina in 2002 and was made into an award-winning film by Benoit Jacquot, and starred Diane Kruger. A film adaptation of *The Exchange of Princesses*, to be directed by Marc Dugain, is currently in the works.

JOHN CULLEN is the translator of many books from Spanish, French, German, and Italian, including Philippe Claudel's *Brodeck*, Juli Zeh's *Decompression*, Yasmina Reza's *Happy Are the Happy*, and Kamel Daoud's *The Meursault Investigation*. He lives in upstate New York.